Kelly Ormsby

FURTHER

~ THAN ~

PASSION

FURTHER
~ THAN ~
PASSION

Cheryl Holt

St. Martin's

FURTHER

~ THAN ~

PASSION

1

"A love potion?" Kate Duncan scoffed. "Tell me that you're joking. Please."

"I'm not."

"For what could you possibly hope to use it?"

Her distant cousin sixteen-year-old Lady Melanie Lewis was mutinous. "What would you suppose? I intend to make Lord Stamford fall in love with me."

Kate could barely keep from laughing aloud. "Lord Stamford? Fall in love?"

"Yes."

Struggling for calm, Kate took a deep breath. "Where did you obtain it?"

"From an apothecary." Melanie leaned in and whispered, "The man swears it's extremely potent, so I have to be careful that I administer it appropriately, lest I set off unforeseen consequences."

"What sort of *consequences* might those be?"

"Well, if I was careless, two unsuitable people could be brought together. It would be a disaster."

Kate rolled her eyes. "Melanie, you can't believe this tonic is real."

"Why would you say it isn't?"

"There's no such thing as a magic potion."

"Hah! That shows how little you know. I paid a fortune for it. It must be genuine."

Kate raised the vial and tipped it toward the lamp. It was filled with a dark liquid, and she'd bet her last penny that it was red wine. "What—precisely—am I to do with it?"

"You're to administer it, right before I'm scheduled to meet him. You'll slip it in his brandy or his soup. When he's not looking, of course."

"Oh, of course."

"Tomorrow evening might be best, when we're first introduced. I want him smitten from the start."

"Smitten?"

"Yes."

Kate sighed. Over the years, she'd served as Melanie's companion, tutor, governess, and chaperone. The girl had instituted a gaggle of nonsense, had developed numerous silly and bizarre ideas, but this was the most outrageous by far.

By all accounts, Marcus Pelham, the thirty-year-old Earl of Stamford, was a cold, dissolute, aloof scoundrel, and Melanie's yearning for him to be besotted was folly. Nay, beyond folly. It was lunacy. Was she off her rocker?

Marcus Pelham would never love Melanie. Despite what type of concoction she added to his supper entree, he wouldn't grow infatuated. Surely, Melanie understood the boundaries and ramifications of an aristocratic marriage! Her mother, Regina, had been tedious in expounding on the details. If Lord Stamford chose Melanie for his bride, it would be for the accepted reasons: money, property, familial alliances.

Affection would play no part.

"The timing is critical," Melanie continued. "You must talk with the staff, to learn when and where he'll be most likely to—"

"Melanie, listen to me." Kate grabbed her by the upper arms and shook her. "We're not going to do this. *I* am not going to do this."

"You are!"

"Stamford is an intelligent, shrewd, and clever gentleman. What if he caught me? How would I explain myself?"

"Honestly, Kate. You have no imagination." Melanie shoved her away. "You have to invent a story before you begin. That way, if you're discovered, you'll know in advance what your excuse should be. Now, when should we try it?"

Kate counted to ten, praying for patience. Melanie had always been intractable, and Kate was so weary of her moods. "Let me be more clear: I forbid you to attempt this. If you persist, I will speak to your mother and have her stop you."

Upon the mention of Melanie's mother, Regina Lewis, the Dowager Countess of Doncaster, Melanie's temper flared, her blond ringlets bouncing with fury. "If you dare," she threatened loudly, "I'll spend the rest of my life making you sorry."

"Be silent, before you waken the entire house," Kate answered, just as furiously. She'd lived with Melanie much too long, and had endured too many tantrums, to brook one with any grace. Especially in the middle of the night. She set the vial on the dresser, prepared to leave in a huff. "It's very late, and on the morrow, we have a busy day."

"Take the potion with you!" Melanie commanded, and she snatched up the vial, wielding it like a weapon.

"You can't order me about."

"If you won't take it, I'll do something drastic. I'll . . . I'll . . ."

Apparently, on the spur of the moment she couldn't devise a reprehensible behavior, but judging from her mottled countenance, she was on the verge of throwing a major fit.

"For pity's sake," Kate grumbled. "Give it to me."

She marched over and retrieved it, as Melanie glowered in triumph, having been confident that she could coerce Kate into whatever conduct she demanded.

Gnashing her teeth, Kate stomped out and closed the door. Their hostess, Lady Pamela—Lord Stamford's glamorous stepmother—was free with her coin, so a lamp burned next to the landing, illuminating Kate's route. She trudged toward the stairs, ready to climb to her bedchamber, but she was fatigued, exhausted from traveling to London, from dealing with Regina and Melanie. By the third step, she plopped down, her head in her hands.

There was no need to rush. Her room was tidy, clean, comfortably furnished, but it was sparse and quiet, at the end of a deserted corridor. The isolated location only underscored how alone she'd recently been feeling.

At least she hadn't been lodged in the attic with the servants! Since she'd been orphaned at age eight she'd suffered many slights, but her pride couldn't have borne that one.

It had been so many years since her father had reigned as Earl of Doncaster, since he'd passed away and Regina's son, Christopher, had been elevated from modest means and obscurity to assume the title. Kate could hardly remember that period of wealth and privilege.

Had she really been born the daughter of an earl? Had her mother really been the most beautiful female in England? Had she lived like a princess? Or was it all some odd, recurring dream?

Kate's mother had been wed too young. She'd been restless, unhappy in her marriage, and ultimately, she'd fled to Italy with a lover. The shame had been too much for Kate's father, and he committed suicide, leaving Kate unprotected, with no funds, no dowry, and no guardian designated to watch over her.

Before the shock of events had fully registered, the indomitable Regina had moved to Doncaster and seized the reins of power. For a few brief weeks, her ailing husband had inherited the earldom, but he'd conveniently died, so she was a widow, her baby son the new lord. Ever since, she'd ruled the property like a despotic queen, managing with an iron fist, and bullying everyone until they ceded to her mandates.

Regina never let Kate forget that she was an aging, irksome burden, that her selfish parents had declined to see to her welfare and had abandoned her to the vagaries of Fate. Regina constantly harangued as to how weak and crazed Kate's parents had been, how their tainted blood flowed through Kate's veins. She berated so vociferously and so often that Kate had taken the

criticisms to heart and, in case others learn of her ap-
palling lineage and judge her harshly, rarely told anyone her last name.

There was a mirror on the wall, and she studied her
reflection. In the dim light, she didn't look anywhere
near twenty-five, even though that was her age.

Her auburn hair was luxurious and rich, and not an
indicator of a hedonistic temperament as Regina regularly proclaimed. Regina maintained it was witch's
hair, that the color was an enticement to wild ways, and
had been the ruination of Kate's mother. For fear that
she be deemed loose of character, as her mother had
been, Kate kept it concealed under caps and hoods.

In the shadows, her green eyes were sparkling and
alive, her face pretty and appealing. Her thin figure was
feminine, her curves defined and alluring, and she
could detect no hint of the pathetic creature Regina had
dubbed her. It was as if she was staring at the woman
she yearned to be, rather than the woman she was.

Glancing down, she scrutinized the vial she still held.
"A love potion," she muttered. "What next?"

Early on, she'd ascertained the idiocy of succumb-
ing to ardor. As her parents had proven, an excess of
zeal led to misfortune and tragedy, and Kate wasn't
about to assist Melanie in any recklessness.

Kate pulled the cork from the vial, intending to
dump the liquid into the dirt of a potted plant, when a
strange impulse—puckishness? madness? boredom?—
forestalled her. Instead, she raised it and drank down
the contents.

The mixture didn't taste like wine as she'd anticipated. It was more earthy, more sweet and aromatic, as
if brewed from flowers and mint. She clucked her

tongue and licked her lips, wishing there'd been more to enjoy.

Suddenly there was a roaring in her ears, as though she could hear stormy ocean waves crashing on the beach. Overly warm, she slackened the belt on her robe, the lapels falling away, but she attained no relief. She was boiling, so she undid the buttons on her nightgown, and she tugged at the bodice, forcing air underneath. The fabric was hot, prickly, and she hated how it chafed her skin.

Though it was a pleasant June evening, the house was cold, yet it occurred to her that she was eager to shed her clothing, to run about with nothing on. As if she was drunk, she giggled at the notion.

Her hair was heavy, the lengthy braid burdensome and pinching her scalp. She yanked off the ribbon and riffled through the locks, freeing them, scandalously allowing them to hang unencumbered. The lack of restraint made her feel wanton, liberated, uninhibited.

She peered in the mirror again, and she seemed to be glowing with an unrealized attractiveness that mesmerized her. Her tresses curled around her hips, the red and gold highlights shimmering in a sort of halo. Her eyes were more emerald, and they shone mysteriously, like a cat's, and her cheeks were flushed. She appeared naughty, tempestuous, out of control, as if she'd just done something outrageous—or was about to.

Gaping around, she was surprised to discover that she wasn't sitting in the stairwell. Though she had no clue how she'd come to be there, she was in a long hallway, and she gazed down an expanse of doors that went on forever. Her vision had constricted and blurred, but her other senses were heightened. She could smell the wax on the wood trim, could distinguish the particles of dust under a decorative table, could perceive a mouse scampering inside the wall.

Where was she? She was certain she was inside Lady Pamela's mansion but confused as to her precise location.

Was this the corridor to her bedchamber? The doors were all the same. Which was hers?

Desperate to lie down, to quiet her dizziness, she started walking, the passage a never-ending gauntlet. Her limbs were like stone, her anatomy slow and listless, as if she were swimming through water.

She peeked down, and her fingers were on a doorknob, so she spun it and slipped inside, but this wasn't her room! What was she thinking?

She'd entered a grand suite—obviously a male's—complete with maroon drapes, plush rugs, and imposing mahogany furniture. The space was empty, but a second chamber adjoined at the rear, and she glided toward it, her feet not seeming to touch the floor.

It was larger than the first. There was an extravagant marble fireplace, and even though it was summer, cheery flames wastefully blazed in the grate.

In the middle, a magnificent bed was perched on a pedestal. With its sturdy frame, posh mattress, carved headboard and posts, it was the kind of bed in which a king or prince might sleep.

A man and woman were atop the blankets, sinfully naked, and Kate knew she should sneak out, but she was enthralled, and she couldn't quit watching. The man was on the bottom, the woman kneeling over him. She was blond, buxom, her golden mane flowing down her back. Her voluptuous breasts were thrust out, swaying to

and fro, her hips undulating as she rocked herself across
the man's loins. As if she were on a horse, she was riding him, her movements practiced, fluid, graceful.

Kate strove to identify her, deciding that she vaguely
resembled Lady Pamela, but she might have been anyone. In fact, when Kate narrowed her focus, she could
observe her own face where the woman's should have
been.

Was *she* the person on the bed? She was so befuddled!

Mute and agog, she spied on them, unconcerned as
to whether she might be noticed. She was invisible,
floating on air, an intangible phantom, and she shifted
farther into the shadows and concentrated on the man.

With his dark hair and eyes, he was the most handsome she'd ever seen, his features perfectly formed.
Slender, robust, muscled, he likely engaged in fencing
or pugilism as a method of keeping in shape.

Though she didn't recognize him, and had no idea
who he was, he seemed familiar, beloved, as if he were
a dear friend with whom she'd been reunited.

I've finally found you, she almost said, stopping herself before she spoke, but she suffered an exuberant
surge of joy at the knowledge.

He clasped the woman's nipples, massaging and
fondling them, and the woman shivered with ecstasy.

Kate's torso jerked in response. It was as if he were
caressing her *own* nipples, as if he were petting her
own breasts. Her womb spasmed and twinged. In the
secret area between her legs, she grew warm and moist.
Her body comprehended and welcomed the libidinous
conduct. She was blossoming, radiating a vigor and energy that caused her to pine and covet, and she vibrated

with a need and desire for things she couldn't begin to name.

The pair was involved in an incredible dance, a ballet of exquisite sensuality and finesse, with each having a role to perform. They stretched and strained, reached and rolled, their limbs in flawless coordination, and in some primal part of her, Kate grasped that they were making love. She was viewing the secret behavior of the marital bed. The act was so beautiful, so thrilling, and she could have hovered there into infinity, studying them and wondering about their relationship, their purpose.

You could be with him, a voice whispered. *You could love him. He could love you in return. Isn't that what you want? What you've wanted forever?*

The voice was so adamant, so firm, and so real. It rattled her, excited her, and she suspected that if she rushed over, she could become the female with him.

She was bewildered, not able to understand what had transpired, and she tried to leave, but she couldn't tear herself away.

The man glanced to the side and smiled at her, and she could see that his eyes were not brown, but a brilliant, sweltering shade of blue. They blazed with intensity, and she could discern his regard as tangibly as if he'd touched her.

Come to me, she heard him cajole. *Let me be the one.*

He kneaded his partner's breast again, then traced down her stomach, until he was stroking her crotch. Kate could feel the motion herself, could perceive the heat of his palm, could smell the exhilarating musk of his skin. He'd stimulated a sensitive spot she'd never noted before, and it throbbed and ached in a rhythm that matched the tempo of her pulse—and his. They were connected, joined to the very roots of their souls.

Inside of her, there was a strange pressure building. It was so potent, and so compelling, that she struggled toward it, positive she was about to explode with pleasure, about to burst into a thousand pieces.

She blinked, and he was directly in front of her, though she didn't know how or when he'd moved. He was tall, six feet at least, and he leaned in, his solid physique pushing into hers, forcing her back against the wall.

Every inch of him was crushed into her. He was flat where she was rounded, slim where she was curved, and she had the fleeting thought that they'd been specifically created to fit together.

I love you, she murmured silently.

You always have, he replied.

He raised his hand, and on it was a jeweled ring, studded with diamonds. They surrounded a sapphire stone in the center, which was the exact color of his eyes.

This is for you, he said. *Keep it so that you'll remember.*

I can't.

She was sufficiently cognizant to fathom that the ring was much too precious for him to relinquish and, more important, she was too insignificant to receive it. How could she explain her possession of it?

She shoved it away, but he slipped it onto her finger and curled her fist into a tight ball, sealing her grip so that she wouldn't drop it.

Do it for me.

His expression was so steady and true that she couldn't reject the gift.

All right.

He bent down, and she braced, certain he meant to kiss her, but at the last instant, he tugged at the bodice of her nightgown, baring her breast, the nipple puckering. He licked his tongue across it, rasping it, laving it, then sucking it into his mouth.

The action wrenched at something deep inside, prodding at the hidden place where her loneliness and desolation resided, and she clutched at him and urged him closer, wishing she could be subsumed until she was a part of him and no longer separate.

He nibbled at the taut nub, the agitation too painful to bear, and she lurched away, stunned to find that she was in her own room, in her own bed. There was ample evidence that she'd been tossing and turning. The blankets were mussed, the pillow on the floor.

She must have been dreaming. She must have been!

Staggering up, she winced as her head pounded with a violent headache, and her heart hammered so ferociously that her veins hurt. Between her legs, she was wet and sticky, her body weeping with an unfulfilled craving. She was drenched with sweat, and she shivered, needing to ward off her sudden chill.

She peeked down and was shocked to detect that her bodice was askew, that her breast was exposed. Trembling with unease, she rubbed her palm across the hardened nipple, moaning in agony at the flurry of sensation she unleashed, and she yanked at the fabric, concealing herself.

What had happened? What had she done?

Moonlight cast eerie shadows on the dresser, and she stared and stared, trying to deduce what she was seeing, when she realized it was the empty vial of the love potion she'd drunk on the stairs.

She jolted away, refusing to look at it, and as she retrieved her pillow, she noted an unusual weight on her hand. She lifted it and was alarmed to observe the ornate ring.

"Oh my Lord," she breathed. It was heavy, elaborate, the gold smooth and glossy, the jewels sharp and shapely.

Why did she have it? What did it indicate? If she was discovered with it, what would she say? She couldn't begin to guess.

She flopped down and squeezed her eyes shut, anxious to sleep for many hours. She hoped when she awoke the ring and the vial would both be gone.

2

"Who is the charming redhead visiting with the Lewis family?"

"The redhead?"

"Yes," Marcus said. "She's short, slender. Very pretty."

"I have no idea," Pamela replied. "As far as I'm aware, they're all blond."

Partially shielded by the drapes, Marcus peeked over the balustrade and stared down into the ballroom. A hundred people were mingling, Pamela's notion of an *intimate* supper party, and precisely the sort of society event he loathed.

The orchestra she'd hired struck the first chords of a gavotte, and couples rushed to take their places on the dance floor.

"Are you sure there's no one of that description with them?"

"Absolutely," Pamela insisted. "Lady Regina was tediously thorough at introducing her party. She's brought along her daughter, Melanie, and her son, Christopher."

"He's the earl?"

"And quite the sweet darling, I must say."

Marcus scrutinized her. At thirty, she was his own age, and a renowned beauty. Her ravishing blond hair was piled high, her expensive gown—for which he'd paid—accented her glorious figure, but her physical splendor couldn't hide the shark lurking within.

She was a shrew, a fortune hunter, and from her remark about the Earl of Doncaster it was clear she had designs on him.

Poor fellow.

"What is he? All of eighteen?"

"I suppose."

"Isn't that a tad young? Even by your low standards?"

At the insult, she bristled. "I didn't claim any heightened interest."

"You didn't have to."

They'd been acquainted since they were children. As an adolescent, he'd foolishly imagined that he loved her, that is, until she'd wed his widowed father. She'd been desperate to be a countess and had greedily grabbed for the distinction, which had certainly given Marcus a swift and decisive lesson in how the world worked.

He'd never trusted anyone again. Had never cared for anyone, either.

"I merely find him to be handsome," she contended. "And pleasant. He's a pleasant boy—unlike some peers of my acquaintance."

"He's rich, too."

"Well, of course he is."

Marcus rolled his eyes and watched the crowd, irked to realize that he'd have to befriend naive, innocent Christopher Lewis, so as to whisper a few words of caution. By all accounts, the lad was an unschooled country dolt. Pamela would eat him alive.

"You're positive there's no redhead with them?" Marcus hated to raise the subject again, hated to provide Pamela with an indication that the matter was of any importance, but he couldn't avoid it.

He was dying to learn more about the female who'd stumbled into his bedchamber the previous night. She'd looked drugged, or perhaps she'd been walking in her sleep, and he was intrigued. Pamela had begged him to tryst, and against his better judgment, he'd come by the mansion—which he rarely did. During their foray, he was convinced he'd locked the door to his seldom-used suite, so he still couldn't deduce how his enticing voyeur had gained entrance.

It had been such a strange encounter. When she'd been in the room, and he'd gazed into Pamela's face, he'd seen the other woman's face, instead, as if she was meant to have been in the bed with him, or as if he could have willed her there had he but concentrated hard enough.

Then, there was the dream he'd had later, of the two of them having sex. It had been so stirring, so realistic, that his trousers grew uncomfortable whenever he recalled it. He knew she had a small beauty mark on her left buttock, could describe the exact shade of her nipples. How could that be?

Their fantasy assignation had been rousing, thrilling, and when it had ended, he'd felt such joy and serenity. He was determined to meet her, to ascertain if the special qualities he'd detected would be evident, or if his sense of connection had simply been part of a bizarre reverie. But he could scarcely explain as much to Pamela.

She hadn't observed their visitor. She'd been too busy, trying to show him what a great lover she was, a pathetic ploy she'd hoped would render an increase in her allowance. She was a whore, and it was humorous to toy with her, to have her presuming she could rekindle his affection, but he was a smart man. He'd been bitten once, and wouldn't let the snake slither too near a second time.

"Why this sudden curiosity with redheads?" she asked.

Suspicious, she studied him, but he was a master at indifference, at remaining aloof and detached, so no hint of his intent was visible. She could stare to infinity and garner no clue as to his thoughts.

He changed the subject. "Have you seen my signet ring?"

"Why?"

"It wasn't there when I dressed this morning."

"Are you assuming this anonymous redhead stole it?"

"Actually, I suspected you."

Her mouth tightened into an unflattering pout. "You are such a brute! I don't know why I let you in the door!"

"Because it's my house?" He rented an apartment over the Stevens brothers' gambling hall, while permitting her to reside in the home he'd always despised.

"As you boorishly remind me, each and every occasion you stop by. If you detest me so, why don't you toss me out into the street and be done with it?"

"A marvelous notion. I'll take it under advisement."

"You are too cruel, Marcus. Too damned cruel." Her eyes flooded with tears, but in light of her thespian abilities, it was difficult to discern if the tears were genuine or faked. "Why persist with tormenting me?"

He shrugged. "It's so amusing."

"You trifle with me, you welcome me to your bed, but the next morn, you haven't a civil word to say."

"Don't blame *me* because you choose to act the harlot. If you're eager to spread your legs, I'll gladly crawl between them."

She glowered. "Ooh, I loathe you."

"Believe me, my dearest mama, the feeling is mutual."

"Don't refer to me as your mother!"

"Isn't that what you are?"

"Why not have the carriage brought round, and deliver us to the poorhouse right now? Put me out of my misery!"

She regularly harped on how soon he had to wed. His father had encumbered the estate, the dispersals tied to Marcus's marriage by age thirty-one, which was four months away, but Marcus could not care less.

He had stashed some cash, enough to sail off to India or Jamaica. He would start over, would abide as an ordinary man, without the burdens of the abhorred Stamford title dragging along behind. His father's decades of berating and disparagement, of duplicity and deception, had ground out any pride or fondness.

His distant cousin, Albert, could have it all, with Marcus's blessing, but then Pamela would be broke, too, a factor about which she never ceased to harangue. Marcus's father had bequeathed her no money of her own—a sign of their matrimonial bliss, no doubt!—so she was dependent on Marcus for everything.

If he didn't secure his assets, her fate was dire, and she suffered from a compulsion to speed his nuptials, which he didn't share. She was pushing every desperate, barely suitable girl in the kingdom at him, frantic for one of them to capture his fancy, but the harder she worked to finagle an engagement, the less inclined he was to consider any of them.

It occurred to him that he was lucky she'd declined to wed him all those years ago. With her whining and demands, she'd have driven him to an early grave.

"I'm not ready to abandon you just yet. It's much more fun to have you squirming."

"You impossible wretch!" She marched toward the stairs. "I'm weary of you. Let's go meet the Lewises. I want the ordeal concluded, so I can avoid you the rest of the evening."

"Until you need your midnight tumble."

"I'd rather eat hot coals than sleep with you again."

She was at the top step before she realized he hadn't followed. "Are you coming or aren't you?"

"What if I don't?"

Apparently, he'd goaded her beyond her limits, and she trembled with fury. "I swear to God, Marcus, if you don't accompany me, I shall walk into the ballroom and announce to all and sundry that you've decided to snub the Lewises, despite their being my special guests."

"Why would I mind if you make a scene?"

"Exactly. Why would you?" She waved at the throng below. "Do you suppose bridal candidates grow on trees? There are so few parents who've been willing to entertain a proposal from you. Of those who've been tempted, you've managed to insult and offend every one. Regina Lewis isn't aware of how despicable you are. Her daughter, Melanie, is our last hope. Now, what shall it be?"

Ladies Regina and Melanie could go hang, and he was unconcerned over what the assembled horde thought of his behavior. He'd contemplated not attending the gathering at all, but he was anxious to determine if his mysterious Peeping Tom was on the premises. She had to be an associate of the Lewises.

"Lead on, my beloved stepmother."

"Shut up."

Halfway down, she spun around. "I just remembered: There is a redhead with them. She's a chaperone or a maid or some such. Tell me the truth. Are you worried she's a thief? Should I lock up the silver?"

"No need. If anything else turns up missing, I'll search her room. Then, I'll search yours."

"Oooh, you . . . you . . ." Fuming, she stomped off, but as they reached the foyer, she reasserted her aplomb. When they were out in public, she pretended they were on amicable terms.

She latched on to his arm and escorted him into the ballroom. As expected, his appearance stirred a ripple, ensuring that speculation about Melanie Lewis would run rampant.

Pamela steered him to the back wall, where the Lewises were listening to the music and obviously impatient for his arrival. They were a dismal crew, attired in out-of-fashion clothes, an indicator of a lack of sophistication and preparedness for their London endeavor. A waltz was in progress, and they gawked as though they'd never viewed dancing before. They were so out of place that he almost felt sorry for them.

"Couldn't you have found a modiste for the girl," he whispered to Pamela, "before you set her loose among the vipers of High Society?"

"There wasn't time," Pamela hissed, her polite smile not slipping. "Besides, I'm not her mother. I'm not responsible for dressing her."

Obese, dour Regina was positioned in the middle. She exuded gloom, arrogance, and he shuddered from imagining her as his mother-in-law.

Melanie was awfully young, pretty and plump, with blond ringlets, big blue eyes, and rosy cheeks. Except for her permanent scowl, she looked like a porcelain doll.

Christopher was handsome and charming, and even though his suit was dated, he carried himself well and wasn't glaringly abnormal, as were his female relatives. He was tall, lanky, blond and blue-eyed like Melanie, but he had a twinkle and a friendly air about him that had to have been inherited from his father's side of the family.

Standing adjacent and slightly behind was Marcus's red-haired fantasy. Her fabulous auburn hair, the likes of which he'd never witnessed prior, was tucked under a silly cap, as if she was afraid to have anyone discover how striking it was.

She wore a drab gray gown that was buttoned to neck and wrist, revealing no hint of the creamy skin concealed beneath. Although she was outfitted to blend in with the wallpaper, she was so rare, so unique, and she shone like the brightest star. On seeing her again, his heart literally skipped a beat.

Would she recollect what had happened? He was dying to know.

They drew nigh, and Pamela was at her most fawning, her most ingratiating. "There you are!" she gushed to Regina. "We've been hunting everywhere. May I present my late husband's son, Marcus Pelham, Lord Stamford."

As Pamela babbled, his dream visitor glanced up, and when she espied him, she blanched with such shock and horror that he was surprised she didn't faint. He hoped she never gambled, for her expressions were far too revealing.

She was terrified, frantic to melt into the plaster and vanish, and in a vain attempt to separate herself, she sidled away from the Lewises. Regina had risen for the introductions, but Marcus snubbed her by walking past and advancing directly to the redhead.

He bowed. "Lady Melanie, you're much more beautiful than I had been led to believe. Thank you for coming. I'm so glad you're here."

It was outrageous conduct, but he couldn't help himself. He detested everything about the encounter, particularly Pamela's desire to have it transpire in such a public forum.

The redhead winced, wishing the floor would open and swallow her whole. Regina sputtered with affront, Christopher stifled a chuckle and winked at the redhead, and Melanie shrieked and fanned herself. The guests loitering nearby tittered with what they assumed was Marcus's delicious *faux pas*.

His gaze holding hers, he raised her hand to his lips, and had commenced to kiss it, when Pamela yanked him away. She was shooting visible daggers.

"Marcus," she scolded playfully, as if it were a joke they'd all enjoyed, "you're such a tease. This is Lady Melanie's chaperone. Miss . . . Miss . . . I apologize, but I can't recall your name. What is it?"

"Duncan," the redhead answered quietly. "Kate Duncan."

"Any relation to the Doncaster Duncans?" he inquired.

"Absolutely not."

She was appalled, horrified to have him questioning whether she had a connection to the previous earl. Why would any link need to be a secret? Had she a scandalous history? How marvelous if she did! "Well, pardon me then, Miss Duncan. I could have sworn you were a titled lady."

As if she'd been burned, she lurched away, flashing him an angry, reproachful frown, and amazing him with her bold nature. For some reason, he hadn't anticipated it. She wasn't simpering or timid, and his intrigue spiraled.

"Now, *here* is Lady Melanie," Pamela was saying, dragging him away, "and her mother and brother . . ."

Pamela went off, filling the awkward moment with idiotic chatter. Melanie and Regina curtsied, but their combined fury was so blatant that he had to wonder if they'd avenge the rebuff, if Miss Duncan would be punished. It had never occurred to him to think before he'd proceeded. In social situations, he cared so little for others' opinions that he never fretted over how he should comport himself.

He endured the Lewises long enough to smooth ruffled feathers, schedule a riding date with Christopher, and allow Pamela to coerce him into a supper party the following evening.

Out of the corner of his eye, he could detect the indomitable Miss Duncan plotting her escape, and the instant everyone had forgotten her, she faded into the crowd and sneaked out the closest exit, which led onto the verandah.

The second he could slip away, he did so, but he

couldn't rush after her. Too many people had witnessed his prank, so he had to stroll the ballroom before he could finagle himself outside.

He caught sight of her immediately, hiding under a tree by the rear fence. In a dither, she was pacing and assessing the house, waiting for the path to clear so she could creep in the servants' entrance without bumping into anyone.

She hadn't seen him leave the mansion, and presuming herself alone in the yard, she made a beeline for the door. He skulked in the shadows, watching her approach, and as she reached for the knob, he laid his hand atop hers. She jumped and bit down on a squeal of fright.

"Hello, Miss Duncan." He smiled like the cat that had eaten the canary. "Fancy meeting you here."

"You!" She reeled away.

"Is that any way to greet an earl?"

"I'd afford you the deference due an earl . . . if you acted like one."

"You wound me," he mocked.

"You contemptible oaf! Have you any notion of the trouble you've caused?"

"No. Why don't you tell me all about it?"

"You have the manners of a goat."

He chuckled. "This is not the first occasion where I've been so informed."

"I'm not surprised. You're a horse's ass, a certifiable maniac."

"As I've also been frequently apprised."

"You knew I wasn't Lady Melanie. What was the point of embarrassing her and her mother? And me?"

"Because I felt like it?"

"How old are you? Eight? Nine? You're naught but a child, and I'm certain a sound spanking could cure much of what ails you."

"I'm not a child, as you're well aware from your nocturnal adventure." He started backing her toward the balustrade. With each forward step, she retreated, until her legs were crushed against it. "I'm a man full grown."

"You're jabbering like a fool, and others may be required to tolerate your boorish behavior, but I'm not. Good-bye."

She tried to skirt around him, but he wasn't ready to let her go. He leaned into her, his body making contact, and he was jolted by sensation. Sparks ignited wherever they touched, and it was so thrilling to be near her. They shared a physical affinity, the type only the luckiest of lovers ever achieved. They were compatible, attuned, and should he be reckless enough to take her as a paramour, they would have fabulous, incredible sex.

Could she perceive it, too? Or was she an innocent? With her being so vibrant, so alluring, it was difficult to guess. She had to be twenty-five or so. How could she have lived so many years without some man claiming her?

"Why were you spying on me?"

"What?"

"I saw you last night. When you were in my room."

She tripped, her knees giving out, but she quickly regrouped. "I have no idea about what you're talking. I arrived in London yesterday, and up until a few minutes ago, when you obnoxiously thrust yourself in front of me, we were not acquainted. I haven't the faintest clue where your bedchamber is located or why you would assume I was in it."

She was the worst liar! It was evident she remembered every moment of the escapade, and he was delighted to learn that she hadn't been walking in her sleep, that she'd been conscious and intentionally studying him. Was her interest due to the fact that she was a mature virgin who was yearning to shed her chastity? Or was she a fallen woman, who hadn't had a man in her bed for ages?

Either way, he was tickled, and would be more than happy to oblige whatever whim was driving her.

He pressed himself closer and traced a finger across her ruby lips. They were moist, inviting, and he was tempted to kiss her. The experience would be novel and exciting, as amour had been at the outset, when he was still young and imprudent enough to let his heart become involved.

His world was filled with clinging, amenable trollops, who would do anything he requested, but he never garnered any pleasure from their company.

How refreshing it would be to spend time with her, to wallow in her glow, to soak in the elation he felt from being in her proximity. Perhaps he'd find a method of rekindling the elusive sense of wonder and contentment that had been absent for so long.

"I want us to be lovers," he told her. "I want to know what it's like to be with you."

The risqué suggestion had her gasping with offense. "My initial impression of you was that you were simply rude beyond measure, but I've changed my mind. I believe you're quite mad."

She attempted to push past him, and he gripped her wrist, jerking her to a halt. "Join me in my suite. At midnight."

"What suite? You don't reside here. This is Lady Pamela's home."

"I own this monstrosity. The master's chamber is mine—whenever I choose to use it." The prior evening, she'd appeared disoriented, so it was possible that she didn't recollect where it was, so he added, "It's in the south wing, at the end of the corridor on the fourth floor. Use the servants' stairs."

"I most definitely will not. I'm a respectable gentlewoman *and* Lady Melanie's chaperone. How dare you ask it of me!"

"I'm not asking."

"You're forcing me to agree?"

While his reputation was the most awful in London, he had *some* standards, and he never gadded about ruining chaste females. There were too many loose ones available, but with her, he couldn't seem to behave any better.

"If you don't come," he warned, "I'll accuse you of stealing my ring."

So . . . she had purloined it. He hadn't been sure, but now he had no doubt. She gaped at him, struggling to deduce the most appropriate response. Finally, she settled on, "What ring?"

"I can't say when or how you took it. Or why. You hardly have the look of a thief, so I can't begin to construe your purpose. I only want you to attend me at midnight, and if I must coerce you to command your presence, then I will."

"You're a brute."

"I don't deny it."

"A bully."

"Yes."

She stared up at him, her green eyes glimmering with tears of frustration and anger. "Don't do this to me. Please."

"I have to."

With a wail of rage, or maybe despair, she pulled away and ran inside.

~ 3 ~

Kate paced the floor of her room, the clock ticking its way to midnight and the moment Lord Stamford counted on her to arrive. She was so irate that she yearned to smash something.

How had she stumbled into such a mess? And how was she to get herself out of it?

Marcus Pelham! Of all the rotten luck!

He'd seen her when she was in his bedchamber! He knew who she was, and he was precisely the sort of scapegrace who would flaunt her embarrassing blunder at every turn. He would never let her live it down, would never let her forget it.

She plopped down on the bed, her head in her hands. How she'd hoped that it had all been a bad dream!

She had ten minutes to obey or ignore his dictate. If she ignored it, he would accuse her of theft, and then where would she be? Not even Christopher, an earl in his own right, would have the power to help her. With a ring of such value, she would be jailed, might even be transported to the penal colonies or—God forbid—executed.

If she went to him, she was well aware that his motives were far from innocent. With scant regard to her chastity, or any subsequent consequences, the blackguard would seduce her, and pitifully, she wasn't sure she'd mind. There'd be no force necessary.

Was it the love potion? How could it be? What had been in that blasted vial?

She'd be more than happy to succumb to his charms, which had her speculating as to whether the concoction hadn't driven her a bit mad.

Hadn't she learned any lessons from her mother's folly?

Though she'd been married and a countess, Kate's mother had run off with her Italian paramour. She'd been dissatisfied and miserable, had loathed Kate's stuffy, stodgy father, and she'd rushed to ruin, heedlessly leaving devastation in her wake. Kate's father had killed himself, she had been rendered a penniless orphan, and as a result of her reckless fling, Kate's mother went on to birth an illegitimate daughter.

The girl, Selena Bella, was sixteen, the same age as Melanie. She'd surfaced in England, unannounced, two years earlier, with a trust fund and Kate named as her guardian in their mother's will.

Kate had never met her, but with Regina's assistance, she'd worked with Selena's trustee—a London solicitor—to arrange her affairs. Kate had coordinated rental of a house, hiring of servants, installation of a companion, and she authorized payment of all expenditures, but that was as far as she'd allowed their connection to extend.

She couldn't bear the notion of having a scandalous

half sister, couldn't bear to recall their mother and her passionate nature. When Kate dared to examine her own life, she was horrified to note that, underneath her placid, amenable exterior, she was as despondent as her mother had ever been.

Was discontentment an inherited trait?

Kate was tired of her subservient existence, where she was disparaged as an unwanted obligation, where she was beholden to Regina for every little thing. She was suffocating, choking on the mundane, and she would leap at the opportunity to be rash and irresponsible, which scared her.

How closely did she resemble her beautiful, imprudent mother? If given the chance to revel, could Kate keep her riotous impulses tamped down?

The clock chimed the hour, and she peered at the dresser. The empty vial was still there, taunting her with how it had unlocked her hedonistic inclinations. She walked over, grabbed it, and tossed it out the window into the yard below.

Then she went to her bed and searched under the pillow. The ring was where she'd left it, folded inside a kerchief. She trudged to the fireplace, scrounged around in the hearth until she located a chink in the mortar, and hid the ring in the hole.

Stamford could accuse her of having his ring, but he'd have to find it first!

She retrieved her cloak and put it on, pulling the hood low so as to shield herself; then she crept to the door and peeked out. Seeing no one, she flitted to the stairwell, slipped inside, and climbed.

To her surprise, his suite was directly above her

room, naught but a quick jaunt to the next floor. The proximity could lend itself to easy assignations, if she were disposed to debauchery—which she wasn't!

She intended to set matters straight, to show him that she wouldn't tolerate misbehavior, and to convince him that she was a virtuous, honest individual. If nothing else, she'd use the appointment to study the design of the chamber so as to devise a method whereby she could return the ring without his being any the wiser as to how it had been restored.

His door was ajar, which meant he was expecting her—the rat!—but she tiptoed in anyway. Like a feral cat, poised to strike, he lounged on the sofa. He'd removed his coat and cravat, so his shirt was open at the neck, revealing a matting of dark hair across his chest, the sleeves rolled up to expose a dusting of the same hair across his forearms.

The prior evening, she'd observed him naked, but for some reason, his casual state of dishabille was more thrilling than viewing him in the nude.

"Shut the door," he said, his voice a soothing, sonorous baritone that tickled her innards.

Without argument, she complied, and she approached until they were toe-to-toe. He watched her with a fierce concentration that ignited a blaze in her belly, and the sensation alarmed her. She would not be affected!

He continued to stare, and the silence grew oppressive.

"I'm here, milord," she began. "What do you want?"

"Your name is Kate?"

"Yes. Kate Duncan."

"When we're alone, Kate, you're to call me Marcus."

She couldn't imagine being on such familiar terms with him, and she refused to fan his flames of fantasy that had him presuming they would meet privately a second time. "I won't, Lord Stamford. And you may not call me Kate. It's *Miss Duncan* to you."

With the grace of a leopard, he uncurled from the seat and stood, his body stretching out, and in the shadows, he seemed taller than she recollected. He was drinking a beverage, brandy or whiskey from the smell of it, and he downed the contents of the glass and set it on a nearby table.

Though he towered over her, she felt no air of menace, and she suspected that much of his bluster was a pretense. He might snipe and bark, might order and shout, but he would never hurt her. At the realization, she relaxed, much less anxious about any hazard to her virtue, or any deviousness as to his motives.

He pushed her cloak off her shoulders, and it fell to the floor and pooled around her feet.

"Have you any clothing that isn't gray?"

"I have a Sunday dress. It's black."

"I hate how you look in gray. It washes out your skin."

"Which is my biggest worry."

"You should be attired in a green that matches the color of your eyes."

"I'm sure I'd be lovely," she facetiously replied.

"I'll buy you some outfits, and I'll keep them here, in my room. You can wear them just for me."

"You most certainly will not."

"I will."

"I allowed you to coerce me this once, but if you assume I'll obey a subsequent command, you're an incredible optimist."

"I always get my way."

"Not with me."

He stepped in, his boots slipping under the hem of her gown, their legs tangling. She'd never been so close to an adult male, and her senses reeled. She could feel his heat, could smell the soap with which he'd bathed, and she was assailed by invigorating, masculine odors like tobacco and horses. There was another fragrance that was more subtle, more musky, and she thought it to be his very essence.

Her anatomy was electrified, and sparks shot between them. Suddenly, she was frantic to touch him, to smooth her hand across his shirt, or perhaps stroke her fingers down his muscled arm. She yearned to snuggle herself to him, positive she'd fit exactly right. The urge was primal, urgent, and she fought it with every fiber of her being.

He reached out and tugged at her heavy chignon, yanking at the multiple pins and combs that anchored it in place. They scattered across the floor, pinging and bouncing as they hit, and she winced, knowing she'd never find them, and wondering what the maids would think when they swept the next morning.

But then, his having a female guest in his private quarters was likely a regular event. His employees wouldn't blink over such a discovery, and she needed to remember that fact. He was an experienced, sophisticated libertine, while she was on the second day of her first trip to London.

"You have the most fabulous hair."

"And *you* are an unmitigated flatterer."

He riffled through the lengthy tresses, lifting and parting the strands, and her heart fluttered. She'd never had a man compliment her before, had never strolled with a beau in the moonlight, or been walked home from church.

With no dowry and no prospects, she was insignificant, invisible, a nonentity, who was not a servant and was barely a member of the family. No gentleman worth having would want her. His accolade pricked at her vanity, and she craved it to be true. It had been so long since another person had actually noticed her, and she was pitifully desperate for approval.

"Whenever you visit me," he proclaimed, "you're to have it down and brushed out."

The oaf was insufferable! Was he deaf? "I'm not coming again. Haven't you listened to a single word I've said?"

"No."

He clasped her wrist and reclined on the sofa, and he pulled her down so that she was sprawled on top of him. Squealing with affront, she tried to wiggle away, but he had her pinned to him. Escape was impossible.

They were molded together. Feet, thighs, loins, tummies, they were forged fast. Her breasts were squashed to his chest, and her nipples leapt to attention. When she shifted the slightest inch, they ached and throbbed.

She was embarrassed, and she increased her struggles, eager to create space between them, which he prevented by planting his hand on her rear.

He ground her crotch into his, and her torso recognized that this was what she'd been needing. Instinctively, her hips flexed, and he laughed! The swine!

"What a little hellcat you are."

"Release me."

"No."

He burrowed her even nearer, and *he* flexed into her, the action like nothing she'd ever felt before, like nothing she could have imagined.

"Why are you pressing into me like that?"

He ignored her question and asked his own. "How did you manage to sneak in here last night?"

"I've no idea to what you allude." She would deny it into infinity.

"Why have you taken my ring?"

"I haven't!"

He studied her, then cautioned, "You shouldn't lie to me, Kate. I can tell when you are." He was caressing her bottom, so it was difficult to concentrate, to maintain any distance. "So what will you do with it? Will you keep it as a memento? Or will you return it when I'm not on the premises to catch you? That way, we can pretend it was never missing."

She frowned at how he'd deduced her plan, and he smirked. "I see. You've decided to put it back when I'm not looking. Well then, why don't you advise me of when, so I can absent myself? It will make everything so much easier."

"I don't have your ring," she contended.

He rolled them, altering their positions so that she was underneath him. Instantly, she was trapped—and furious that she was. She'd intended to dominate the meeting, to briefly speak her piece, then be about her business, with her reputation and chastity intact.

How was she to proceed now? She was supposed to be convincing him of her high morals, but her body was rapidly conveying her to a spot where she didn't wish to be.

"Let me up."

"No."

She sighed. "Talking to you is like talking to the wallpaper."

"I'd heed you . . . if you ever said anything worthwhile."

He was fussing with her gown, trying to undo the buttons. "Are you about to ravish me?"

"Yes, but you'll like it."

"Stop it. At once."

"Sorry, but I can't oblige you."

"Lord Stamford!" The top button popped free. "Lord Stamford! Marcus!"

He grinned, never having doubted that he could wheedle her into calling him by his given name. And so quickly, too. "Yes, Kate. What is it?"

"I'm not about to simply relax, while you remove my clothes and . . . and . . ."

She wanted to inform him of all the things she would *not* do, but she had no terminology for discussing carnal subjects, and she wasn't about to start spewing such words as *naked* and *undressed*. In dealing with him she was so far out of her league that she never should have risked the encounter, despite how forcibly he'd commanded her presence.

She knew better. She really, really did.

". . . and?" he prompted.

"Never mind, you bounder. Just release me."

"Were you enjoying yourself, watching me trifle with Pamela?"

As she vividly recollected every erotic detail of the ribald scene, she blushed such a deep shade of red that she was amazed she didn't burst into flames. "You make the most outrageous allegations, and I haven't the foggiest—"

He kissed her. The deed was sudden, unanticipated, and she tensed, geared to push him away, to grapple and skirmish until he desisted, but before she could react, it dawned on her that the endeavor was so sweet, and so dear, that she couldn't fathom bringing it to a swift end.

His lips were soft, warm, and gently pressed to hers, and her eyes drifted shut. Having never been kissed before, she was overwhelmed by how precious it was. How could she be twenty-five and not have experienced this bliss?

Surprising her completely, he slipped his tongue inside her mouth, and he stroked it against her own, the gesture causing butterflies to cascade through her stomach. He tasted like the brandy he'd been drinking, and the tang was so splendid, and so naughty, that she moaned with delight.

Mesmerized, enthralled, at that moment, she would have done whatever he demanded, and it occurred to her that this was why females were chaperoned and counseled as to the wages of sin. Others comprehended the dangers of such reckless passion, and as she was a novice and entirely bowled over, the warnings by which she'd abided all her life held no significance whatsoever.

She craved more of this . . . this unbridled spiral, this rampant pandemonium, and whatever wild feat she need commit to have him continue she would gladly attempt.

She was so inundated that she wasn't aware of all that was transpiring, and it gradually registered that her bodice had been slackened, that he was tugging it down. In a few seconds, her bosom would be exposed, and she couldn't predict what might happen after that.

Alarm bells clanged inside her head.

Somehow, she'd jumped into a raging inferno that was beyond her control. She hadn't meant to land herself in such a jam! Was this her mother's tendencies leaping to the fore?

She'd striven so valiantly to be virtuous, to be upstanding and good, yet a handsome man had barely glanced in her direction and she was prepared to cast off her integrity and principles. Had she no pride? No dignity?

She wrenched away.

"Marcus, please."

He halted and frowned at her, so swept up, himself, that he didn't appear to recognize her, and her heart sank. He probably seduced every chambermaid who walked by his door. What woman was safe in such a den of iniquity? No doubt, she was but one in a long line who'd been kissed to high heaven on the comfortable sofa.

"What is it?" he inquired.

"I can't proceed." She felt humiliated, ashamed for not being the strumpet of base character he'd hoped she was.

"Why are you upset? We're only kissing. There's no harm in it."

"Yes, but you're expecting much more than a *kiss,* and I couldn't possibly." He slid to the side, granting her the chance to escape, and she squirmed away and sat with her back to him. "You believe I'm someone I'm not."

"You're hot-blooded, Kate, and you can't deny this aspect of yourself. Not to me."

"You have this crazed notion that I'm decadent, that I'm the sort who can blindly carry on as is your wont here in the city, but I'm a country girl. I have no capacity for debauchery, and I apologize if I've led you to presume otherwise."

Behind her, he rose and nestled himself to her, nuzzling at her nape. She hadn't known the spot was so sensitive, and she shivered, goose bumps billowing down her arms.

"Don't be sad," he whispered.

"I'm not; I just wish . . ."

"Wish what?" he prodded when she couldn't finish.

"I wish I *was* loose. I wish I could be the person you assume me to be. How pathetic is that?"

He chuckled. "You are so lusty, Kate. So ready for me and what I can give you."

"No, you're wrong."

She shifted, eager to persuade him that he'd misjudged her, but he was so close, his beautiful blue eyes inches away. He could tempt the Blessed Virgin, so how was Kate to resist him when she was a mere mortal?

Where he was concerned, she was so weak, so lacking in fortitude, and he could tear down any walls she might erect to keep him at bay. The realization terrified her.

"We'll be lovers, Kate, for the duration of your visit. It will be wonderful between us. I promise."

"We're not going to be any such a thing. I'm leaving and I shan't return. Don't ask me to; don't pressure me; don't order me. I won't relent."

As if she hadn't spoken, he announced, "We'll dally every evening. At midnight."

How typical that he'd disregard her! He was like a spoiled child.

"No, Marcus."

She stood and retrieved her cloak, draped it over her shoulders, and adjusted the hood. He observed, not moving to assist or intervene.

It was time to depart, but she couldn't force herself out. She stared at him, a thousand comments on the tip of her tongue.

What if she was never alone with him again? What would she yearn to have told him?

Nothing seemed appropriate, so she whirled around and rushed away, but before she could exit, he called to her.

"Tomorrow night, Kate. I'll be waiting."

"You will *wait* in vain," she insisted.

"I don't think so. You'll be here."

His confidence, his assurance that she'd yield, infuriated her. With a groan of frustration, she yanked open the door and sneaked into the hall.

~ 4 ~

"What is your opinion, Mother?"

"About what?"

Christopher Lewis sat in his mother's suite, watching her eat and eat and eat from an assortment of candies. He couldn't ever remember seeing her without food at the ready, and heaven help the servant who let Regina's plate fall empty. She obsessed over victuals as a banker might over his gold.

She was always wolfing down one tidbit or another. Because of this, she was extremely obese, and considering the tiny chair on which she was perched, he was surprised it could hold her.

Her hair was a dull gray, her features bloated and puffy. Supposedly, she'd once been pretty, but with how she currently appeared, it was difficult to discern if the stories were true.

"About the new seeds I wish to purchase for our tenants."

"A colossal waste of funds."

"But it's the latest scientific advance."

"Nonsense and folderol."

He sighed. She was so set in her ways, and she viewed any suggestion as suspect. He had so many plans for the estate, modifications he yearned to implement, if only he could wrest control from her. Her fingers were so tightly clamped around the purse strings that he probably wouldn't have the power to wrench them free after she was in the grave.

He was dying to assert himself as the earl, and he couldn't fathom from where he'd acquired his drive to improve Doncaster, but he guessed it was inherited from his father, who'd died when Christopher was a toddler. Without a doubt, he hadn't obtained it from Regina! A more cold-blooded, vindictive person he never hoped to meet.

At the next question, she'd scoff, as she did at everything, but he raised the topic anyway. "How about the chalkboards for the vicar's wife?"

Regina nearly choked on a bonbon. "Absolutely not."

"But it's such a grand idea. We could start a school so easily."

"What on God's green earth would possess you to presume that we must educate every waif who traipses past our door?"

"Our workers should know how to read and write. And to factor." He grinned, recognizing that she was more annoyed by the second. She loathed his novel concepts. "They'll be able to accurately count our money when they're making it for us."

"Never." Flushing beet red, she went back to gorging and scrutinizing her business papers.

Then and there, he decided he'd buy the blasted chalk-boards himself. Though she was a horrific miser, Regina gave him an allowance, of which he'd never spent a far-thing. He had a bundle stashed away, and he was deter-mined to establish a school, so he would forge ahead. It would be simple to hide the project from Regina. She never bothered with the routine lives of the people, so she wouldn't be cognizant of what was happening.

Melanie was over by the mirror, primping her curls, and she chirped up. "It's hilarious that you would waste your time and energy on such twaddle."

"You're correct, Melanie," he facetiously agreed. "I could exhaust myself at vital pursuits, like trying on clothes."

"Precisely," she concurred, too thick to realize that he'd been poking fun at her.

He sighed, again.

How had he wound up with Regina as his mother and Melanie as his sister? What twist of destiny had tethered them as a family? The country folks spread tales of changelings, and he often wondered if an elf hadn't snatched him at birth and deposited him in the wrong house.

If it hadn't been for Kate's calming presence over the years, he couldn't predict what might have become of him. She—and the male employees who'd befriended him—had guided him to discover the man he was meant to be.

Now that he was eighteen, that fellow was emerging more and more. He was anxious to extract his rightful place from his mother, but he wasn't sure how to ac-complish it.

He stood, needing fresh air, needing to be away from their stifling, insufferable company.

"Where are you going?" his mother asked.

"I'm riding with Stamford."

"You'll return for supper?"

"Yes, Mother."

"No carousing with him. There's no telling what sorts of trouble he might propose."

Christopher rolled his eyes. She still viewed him as such a child. If she ever learned of his sneaking out at night, of his reveling with the village boys, or his flirting with the tavern girls, she'd have an apoplexy.

"I'll fight his attempts to corrupt me."

She glanced up and scowled. "Don't be smart. I'm not in the mood for any sass."

"Yes, ma'am," he cajoled, not in the least repentant.

"Use the occasion wisely. Put in a few advantageous comments about your sister."

Melanie added, "You should inform him of how frequently it's mentioned that I'm beautiful."

Beautiful like a marble statue, he mused. On the outside, she was fetching, but on the inside, she was vain, petty, and malicious.

"I'll wax on till he's smitten," Chris lied.

Despite what the two females assumed, he had no intention of furthering their cause of bringing Stamford and Melanie together. Chris wouldn't deliver such a fate to his worst enemy. Native savages could tie him to a pole and threaten to cut out his tongue and he wouldn't utter a flattering word about Melanie. She had no redeeming characteristics, and he wouldn't join her and his mother in fooling Stamford.

He exited before they could issue any other frivolous orders he'd decline to follow.

Shifting her corpulent frame, Regina watched Christopher depart; then she perused the post that had been forwarded from home. Melanie was prowling about, and Regina considered hiding the top page, as she would once Kate arrived, but Melanie didn't read well enough to understand what was written, so there was no need for furtiveness.

Regina couldn't remember when she'd first decided to steal from Selena Bella's trust fund, but it was so easy to do. Others were too gullible, especially a person like Kate, who saw the good in everyone and never noticed the bad. It would never occur to her to double-check the bills the Bella girl sent.

Kate had never met her half sister, a circumstance Regina had striven strenuously to ensure, so she wasn't aware of how modestly Regina's thievery had forced Bella to live. Plus, Kate had never managed her own household, so she had no notion of what items cost, or how much was required for expenses. Regina altered Bella's invoices before passing them to Kate, so she was duped with the fakes, just as she'd been tricked into believing she'd had no legacy from her parents. It was simple to deceive Kate.

Of course, when her father had committed suicide, Kate had been very young, so she didn't know that she'd been manipulated. Regina had pilfered Kate's dowry, and by now, it had been missing for an eternity, so there was no trail that might lead to her as the culprit. She patted the satchel where she kept her records, smiling with how successful she'd been at duplicity.

Her nest egg was growing by leaps and bounds, and she almost wished she could brag about how shrewd she'd been, though she never would.

She couldn't rationalize her behavior to others. Usually, it was difficult to defend it to herself, but better than anybody, she grasped how rapidly fortunes could change. One minute, she'd been stewing in her home in Cornwall, her husband dying, their savings squandered on worthless medicines, and two mewling babies pulling at her skirts. The next, her husband was an earl. He'd perished straightaway, her son had inherited the title, and they'd moved into a mansion with two hundred rooms.

Christopher and Melanie didn't recall that embarrassing period when their father had been next in line to a great earldom, but they'd been snubbed by the local gentry because he worked to earn their living. They thought life was a celebration, filled with fashionable, wealthy people who frittered away at nothing, but Regina would never forget how it had been, and she would never return to that horrid condition of groveling before her neighbors.

She couldn't depend on Fate. If they could ascend so high, they could descend just as fast, and she declined to plummet to obscurity.

If disaster reigned, she would have Kate's and Selena Bella's assets to tide her over, and she felt no guilt about the situation. The two women didn't deserve the windfalls. They were both daughters of a whore. Let them suffer for the sins of the mother.

Regina gobbled the last petit four off the plate, irked she'd have to ring for another, that the staff hadn't supplied more without her requesting it. She liked to have food close by, liked to nibble whenever the urge caught her fancy. There had been a time when she hadn't had a French chef, when she'd often had to prepare her own desserts, and she'd never recovered from that dreadful experience.

"Where is Kate?" Melanie whined, tapping her foot in a show of petulance that annoyed Regina.

She'd struggled to provide a stable upbringing for her children, but with how they were surrounded by opulence, it had been challenging. Melanie presumed the world revolved around her, despite how Regina counseled to the contrary. The girl was shrill, spoiled, conceited, and Regina despaired for her. When reality slapped Melanie in the face, when tragedy crashed down, she would be incapable of coping, would crumble at the first signs of adversity.

Thank God, she'd birthed Christopher. He possessed Regina's intellect, her savvy and cleverness, and although on occasion he was overly compassionate, under Regina's tutelage he would go far.

"She'll be along directly."

"You said the same fifteen minutes ago."

"Then, quit harping. I'm always right."

She glared at Melanie, wondering when she'd evince an interest in something beyond her own self-centered objectives. Wasn't Regina's stake in any marriage as vital as Melanie's? For years, Regina had endured the rebuffs of the *ton,* and she'd seethed, while ignoring the whispers as to how there were questions regarding Christopher being the lawful heir, as to how they were interlopers into the circles of the Quality.

When Melanie wed Stamford, how Regina would revel in triumph!

"What are your plans for Lord Stamford?" she queried. "It's obvious you had no effect on him yesterday."

"Was that my fault?"

"As he mistook a servant to be you, whose *fault* would you imagine it to be?"

"Kate's. She was absolutely flaunting herself at him. You were there; you saw her. If she'd been more reticent, none of this would have happened. You'll speak to her, won't you?"

Regina definitely intended to *talk* to Kate about her forwardness. It was a topic about which she frequently chided. Kate was afflicted with many of her mother's worst traits—willfulness, pride, intractability—and was more striking than a woman ought to be.

Although Kate didn't perceive it, men were drawn to her, which was the main reason Regina had her conceal her hair. An unsuspecting gentleman could be lured to ruin, and Regina wasn't about to allow Kate to wreak the havoc her mother had instigated. Not when she was residing under Regina's roof and her conduct could reflect badly on Melanie or Christopher.

"Yes, I will admonish her, but in the interim, you must put your own house in order. Stamford is to visit this evening, so I ask you again: How will you impress him?"

"I won't." She stuck her snooty nose up in the air. "I hate him. He's a brute, and I shan't have him for a husband."

"You have no say in the matter. You'll wed whomever I select, and you'll wed him gladly."

"I will not. I'm marrying someone who loves me, and it won't be that cruel, vicious creature. He has a heart of stone."

"Be silent. I can't abide your romantic drivel."

Melanie appeared mutinously ready to expound, and luckily, they were saved from an argument by Kate's knock.

"You'll discipline her, won't you, Mother? For wrecking my debut?"

"You're worried about Kate when your own actions have been abominable. Go to your room, and don't emerge until you are prepared to specify the ways in which you will charm Lord Stamford."

"I won't do it, I tell you. I won't!"

Regina's temper sparked. She rose and walked over until they were toe-to-toe, and Regina towered over her.

"Not another word, you ungrateful wretch."

"Or what? Will you beat me? Send me to bed without supper?"

"Don't think you're too grown-up to be punished."

"You always suppose that you can force me into anything. But not this time. I don't care if we traveled so far. I don't care if I shame you. I won't accept a proposal from him."

Regina slapped her, and she stumbled and lurched to the side, catching herself before she fell to the floor.

"You will not disrespect me!" Regina bristled. "Not when I've worked so hard to garner this invitation to arrange your future." Kate knocked more quietly, an indication that she'd heard their quarrel, and Regina was even more furious. "Get out!" she hissed. "I'm sick of you."

Sniffling tears, and clutching her reddened cheek, she rushed out. Kate murmured about new dresses being delivered from the seamstress, but the information didn't slow her.

Looking distressed, Kate watched her race down the hall, but she wouldn't comment. Early on, she'd learned that what transpired between Regina and her children was none of Kate's affair.

She entered and shut the door, comprehending that she was in for a dressing-down, and Regina couldn't wait to dispense it. Kate had never come to grips with the fact that circumstances had laid her low. She carried on as though she were the Queen, as though her father still ruled at Doncaster, as though her veins didn't flow with the tainted blood of her crazed parents.

Lest she forget her insignificant status, Regina had to constantly remind her of it.

"Well," Regina began, "what have you to say for yourself?"

"I have no explanation for Lord Stamford's behavior."

At least she wouldn't pretend she was unaware of why they'd convened for the appointment. "I consistently warn you about making a spectacle of yourself. Are you eager to be deemed a whore like your mother?"

"You know I'm not."

Kate's lips thinned into a tight line. Though she'd never said as much, she abhorred Regina's disparaging of her parents, so Regina did it as often as possible. Kate resembled her mother, and Regina was positive that with the smallest push, she'd act like her, too. She had to be goaded into sticking to the straight and narrow.

"If you continue to flaunt yourself here in London, how long will it be before you're recognized? Before people realize who you are?"

"They won't."

"If the tiniest rumor circulates as to your ancestry, I will abandon you to your fate." It was an effective threat, and Regina had used it to pressure Kate on all manner of occasions. Her fear of being cast out of Doncaster was genuine, and a weapon Regina wielded repeatedly. "If I banish you, you have no skills, no funds, no contacts. Where will you go? How will you survive? Will you beg your bastard sister to take you in and support you?"

"Christopher would never let you expel me," she insisted, evincing a bit of backbone.

"How would he stop me? And if you could persuade him to countermand my edict, can you envision what your life would be like? I promise you, I would make it a living hell."

"I'm sure you would."

"I can't fathom why I permitted you to journey to London with us, but from this moment on, you will remain out of sight."

"Certainly."

"You will have no subsequent opportunity to embarrass Melanie or disgrace the family."

"All right."

"You will accompany Melanie on her outings, but you will not be present at any function where Lord Stamford might see you."

"As you wish."

"If you're unclear as to which events you may attend, and which you should avoid, ask me." She waved toward the hall. "Now, be off. I'm weary of you."

Without argument, Kate departed, and Regina went to the bellpull to muster a servant. Their discussion had left her famished. She hoped there were more petit fours in the kitchen.

Pamela dawdled at her dressing table and gazed in the mirror. Though she was thirty, she was still beautiful. She'd never been pregnant, so her body was curvaceous and lithe, her breasts firm and ample.

She was sexy, gorgeous, a woman in full bloom, who knew what she wanted and how to go about getting it. She leaned forward, checking her cleavage, and determining that the negligee she'd selected was perfect. The creamy swell of her bosom was visible, the outline of her nipples distinct and conspicuous through the sheer fabric.

Through the crack in the door, she had glimpses of Christopher Lewis lounging on the sofa in her boudoir. It had been simple to lure him to her. Though he was only eighteen, he was a man. Upon receiving her naughty invitation, he hadn't hesitated, and she was intrigued as to whether he grasped her intent.

Was he impatient and knowledgeable? Or was he an innocent?

Either scenario was enticing. If he'd been initiated in sexual intercourse, he would be a randy, enthusiastic lover—the younger fellows usually were—but if he was a virgin, she would be happy to indoctrinate him.

She paused to dab on a final whiff of perfume; then she sauntered out.

"Hello, Christopher." She sidled nearer, relishing how he admired her scanty attire. "May I call you Chris?"

"Yes."

"And you must call me Pamela. *Lady* Pamela is so dreary and formal."

With his big blue eyes, wavy blond hair, and lanky frame, he was too adorable for words. He was rich, too, a factor she'd always found alluring, and which became ever more interesting as Marcus frittered away the last of their money.

Christopher would eventually choose a countess, which she'd been for many years, but why should it be some simpering debutante? In light of his youth and naïveté, wouldn't he do well with an older wife? Who better than herself?

Her pulse pounded with excitement. "Would you like a brandy?"

"My mother doesn't care for me drinking. Especially not in the middle of the day."

"Well, Regina isn't here, is she?"

He chuckled. "No, she isn't."

"Will you join me?"

"What the hell?" he murmured; then, ever the little gentleman, he apologized. "Pardon me."

"There's no need to be sorry for what happens when we're alone." She walked behind the sofa and trailed a playful finger along his collar. "Feel free to be yourself."

She proceeded to the liquor cabinet, and she could sense him inspecting her. Her negligee was slinky, captivating, and she poured their beverages slowly so he could look his fill.

As she turned, a wave of understanding passed between them. He was no boy. He was aware of why she'd summoned him, and he was keen to dally.

She walked to the couch, as he observed her every move, and she snuggled next to him, offering him his glass. From the minimal contact a spark shot up her arm. She was so attracted to him, and had been from the first, though she couldn't figure out why.

They had nothing in common. Not background, or experience, or upbringing, or age, but she was enamored, so she wouldn't try to unravel the mystery. Physical appeal was often mystifying.

She sipped her libation, simmering under his blatant regard. "Tell me, Chris, have you a sweetheart at home?"

"There aren't many candidates around Doncaster who would be suitable for me."

"I don't suppose there would be. Will you hunt for a bride, while you're in London?"

"I'm not ready to wed. My mother says there's no rush."

"A wise woman." It would likely be the sole instance she'd ever agree with the unpleasant, provincial Regina. "So if you're not in the marriage market, you'll have to find other activities to keep you busy."

"I was thinking the very same."

He'd barely sampled his liquor, so she took his glass and set it on the table. She nestled closer, her breast crushed to his arm. Her nipple hardened, poking into him, and he grinned.

Perhaps he was more sophisticated than she suspected.

"Have you ever been kissed?" she asked.

"Many times."

She pouted. "But you said you didn't have a special girl."

"Can you keep a secret?"

"I can."

"I sneak out at night, to carouse at the village tavern."

In mock affront, she gasped. "Your mother would be scandalized."

"I'm sure she would be."

"I've heard it mentioned that tavern maids are strumpets."

He laughed. "Some of them definitely are."

"Why don't you show me what they've taught you? I'm dying to learn."

"I'll just bet you are."

For a fleeting moment, she had the impression that his tone was contemptuous, that he judged her to be a strumpet, too, but his expression was potent, his smile fixed. She must have imagined his disdain.

She stared at him, wondering if he'd initiate the encounter, but he was motionless, and the expectation was excruciating. She couldn't bear the suspense, so she progressed, her lips resting on his, and it was as if the gesture gave him permission. He assumed control of the embrace, enfolding her in his arms, and pulling her across his torso.

His fingers were in her hair, his tongue in her mouth, and she was ecstatic to discover that the harlots with whom he'd philandered had been excellent tutors. She was wild for him, and her craving wasn't generated by his fortune or his title.

He molded her breast until she was writhing in

agony, and desperate for him to clasp her nipple, but he never did, so she guided his hand to where she needed it to be.

Still, she wasn't receiving sufficient stimulation, and she dropped the strap of her negligee to expose her bosom.

"Touch me here." Breathless, aroused, she desired so much more than he was conveying. She directed him in how to squeeze and pinch, how to twist and tease.

He was an avid pupil, and he quickly grasped what was required.

"Like this?" he queried.

"Oh yes. Don't stop."

She was riveted, exhilarated, overwhelmed. Both during and after her marriage, she'd had many paramours, and the episodes had been so unsatisfactory. Always, she'd been left with the sense that she was missing out, that true passion would be forever denied her, and a glint of anticipation ignited.

Maybe Christopher would furnish her with what no other man ever had.

Inciting him, inflaming him, she massaged his crotch. His cockstand was rigid against the placard of his trousers, and she flicked at the buttons, loosening them and slipping her hand under the fabric.

"What are you doing?" he inquired.

"I mean to caress your private parts. It will feel marvelous."

His state of titillation matched her own. "Yes, yes."

His phallus surged up to greet her, and she wrapped her fist around it, and stroked him in a steady rhythm. He was so randy, so tenacious, flexing with a youthful exuberance that charmed her.

She was positive she was the only female who'd ever held him so intimately, so he wouldn't be able to endure for long. She wanted his initial voyage to be memorable, dramatic.

"I'm going to put my mouth on you," she clarified. "Has any woman attempted such a thing with you before?"

"No. Never."

"Do you know what I plan? Has it been explained to you?"

"I've listened to men talking."

Being renowned for her prowess at the lewd endeavor, she smirked. "My darling, allow me to demonstrate."

He reclined, and she slackened his pants, so that she had more space to maneuver. She scooted down and licked at the crown, lapping up his sexual juice. With scant foreplay, he was at the edge, and she took him inside, certain it would be a short race to the finish.

He thrust once, twice, thrice, and his seed gushed to the tip. With a moan of delight, he spilled himself, coming with great relish, pushing into her over and over, as if he couldn't reach the end.

Ultimately, the tempest subsided, his penetrations slowing, his erection waning. She enjoyed a last nibble across the sensitive head, savoring his taste, his smell; then she shifted away. Smug and pleased with her seduction, she cuddled herself to him, impatient for a compliment, or at least an upbeat comment, but he was silent.

"That was very spectacular," she ventured.

"Yes, it was," he concurred.

"I'm so glad you let me indulge."

She was a tad flustered by his reticence, but then, he was a virgin. Very likely, he couldn't decide on an appropriate remark.

"Shall we retire to my bed?" Anxious to continue, she cooed and stretched. "We can spend hours making love."

He glanced at the clock. "Actually, I have to meet with my mother in a few minutes."

"Your mother?" She loathed Regina and couldn't keep the derision out of her voice. "I thought you just spoke with her."

"I have to *speak* with her again."

"You're a grown man. And an earl. She can wait."

He shrugged. "When she's happy, it's easier for all concerned."

A spurt of temper flooded her. How dare he be so ungrateful! How dare he saunter out without so much as a fare-thee-well!

She almost disparaged him, but then, she remembered how new he was at carnal games. He didn't realize that it was uncouth to have his fun, then dash off. There was an etiquette attached to prurient enterprises, but he'd never been apprised. How could he be expected to follow the rules?

It was another aspect about which she would have to educate him during the leisurely, lazy trysts they would share.

"When will your appointment be concluded?"

"I can't say, but I'll be busy afterward. I have engagements scheduled from now till late."

"But I was so hoping you could sneak back upstairs."

"It won't be possible."

She bit down on a bitter retort. The foolish boy! Didn't he comprehend what he was passing up? Men begged for a chance to philander with her! She could have her pick, and she'd picked him, yet he was behaving as if the assignation hadn't meant anything, as if *she* hadn't meant anything.

She had her pride, though, and she wouldn't let him ascertain how furious she was. "Perhaps tonight, then. After everyone's abed."

"Perhaps," he equivocated, leaving her to conjecture whether he was interested or not, and she was stunned.

Lovers never spurned her, especially after they'd sampled her luscious fruits. His lack of enthusiasm was so shocking and so unusual that she was perplexed. For once, *she* was smitten and eager for a second rendezvous, while he could care less.

"I guess I'll see you at supper." She was determined to act as nonchalant as he.

"If not before."

Like a silly schoolgirl, she soared at the prospect that they might convene earlier.

"Have a grand afternoon."

"I will."

He stood and straightened his clothes, ran his fingers through his hair, and in the blink of an eye he was tidy and composed. He leaned down, bracing himself on either side of her.

"That was fabulous." He brushed a kiss across her lips. "Thank you."

Then, he turned and left.

She stared at the door, listening to his retreat. This couldn't be his sole visit! It had been too exceptional, too out of the ordinary, though in view of his inexperience, he probably didn't fathom how unique it had been. She would need to enlighten him.

The tang of his seed was strong, and the flavor had ceased to be pleasant. She reached for his glass and downed his brandy, washing away the remnants of their debauchery.

She didn't know why, but she was depressed, and she felt unclean. She poured herself some wine, drank it, too, then rang for a bath.

5

"Well," Melanie snapped, "if you hadn't spilled the first bottle of love potion, we wouldn't need to purchase a second. Is it my fault you're so clumsy?"

It was a sunny summer afternoon, but their carriage was dark, and Kate was glad for the shadows. They shielded her facial expressions so Melanie couldn't detect how she was gnashing her teeth.

That blasted potion! Hadn't it wreaked enough havoc?

Melanie had demanded to see the vial, and Kate couldn't explain its absence, so she'd fibbed about what had happened, when she should have avoided any fabrication. She was a horrid liar.

"I didn't drop it intentionally. It slipped out of my hand."

"I declare, Kate. With each passing day, you're less dependable. Mother says if you grow any more unreliable, she'll terminate you. What will become of you then?"

Kate was tempted to utter a few scathing retorts, but she resisted the urge. Regina frequently taunted her with termination, and when she'd been younger, the prospect had terrified. But anymore, she was so fed up that banishment would be a relief. She'd be compelled to make her own way, which she should have done years earlier, but habit and routine had kept her from forging a different path.

However, if she was to be fired, she was determined it be over a dramatic infraction. She wasn't about to lose everything due to an idiotic tincture, although she was nervous about condemning it as a fake.

Though she yearned to deny it, the elixir had mysterious qualities. Against her will, it had lured her into Stamford's bedchamber, and now she could concentrate on naught but him. Her mind had been so radically afflicted that she worried the concoction was dangerous, that it had altered her personality.

How long would the treacherous effect last? What if it never disappeared? Was she destined to be consumed forevermore by obsessive thoughts of Stamford?

A woman could go mad, languishing in such wicked reveries. Kate wished she could open up her head and bustle through with a stiff broom to sweep away all images and dreams of him.

"Can we forget about the potion?"

"No, we can't," Melanie griped. "Have I asked for the moon? I ordered you to put it into his wine, and you couldn't accomplish that simple feat."

"It's not as easy as you contend. What if I give it to him at the wrong moment? He might stumble upon a chambermaid. What would we do then?"

"Honestly, Kate," Melanie scoffed. "As if Stamford could be smitten by a servant. Even a magic tonic can't cause such an abnormal result."

"Will you listen to me? Please?"

"No. I'm quite resolved." The carriage rattled to a halt, and Melanie peeked out. "We've arrived. The apothecary's shop is down the block, tucked in the alley. I'll wait here."

Kate sighed, wondering how she could convince Melanie to heed her warnings. Stamford could drink a thousand gallons of the drug, without it producing any change in his behavior. He was despicable, would trifle with his own stepmother, with Kate, herself, so in what other debauchery might he engage? What female would willingly tie herself to such a dissolute villain?

She switched tactics. "Melanie, you've met Lord Stamford. You saw what he's like."

"So?"

"Your mission is fruitless."

"It is not. Mother claims he's very eager. Especially with his being aware of how pretty I am."

"She's *hoping,* Melanie." It was perilous to contradict Regina, so Kate was treading on hazardous ground. Regina often infuriated Melanie, but Melanie would never admit that her mother might be lying to her. "What if he proposes? He's so much older than you, so much more experienced and sophisticated."

"Are you implying that I'm not good enough for him?"

"No! I'm merely pointing out that he's not the man for you. You'll be miserable."

"I will not," she mutinously insisted.

"There are so many boys in town for the Season. They're closer in age, and they enjoy the same hobbies and diversions. Why don't you broaden your search? You needn't settle on him from the very beginning."

"Mother has decreed that it will be Stamford and no other, so I have no doubt he will be my husband." Bitterly, she added, "So shut up, and fetch me that potion!"

She yanked at the door and shoved Kate out, and a footman rushed up to steady her as she maneuvered the stairs.

They shared a wan smile, neither shocked by Melanie's temper. Her moods erupted frequently, and as Kate walked down the street, she pondered how intertwined her life was with Melanie's, how odd their association.

Kate had been born with everything and had had it snatched away. Melanie had been born with nothing but had had great wealth and position showered upon her, yet they were both unhappy.

Kate entered the shop, and as she glanced around, a bell jangled. It was a quaint place, filled with exotic odors and potted plants. The walls were lined with shelves containing peculiar bottles and jars.

The proprietor emerged from the rear, and Kate could barely keep from laughing aloud. Attired as he was in a flowing robe, he might have leapt from the pages of an ancient tale of dragons and knights. His hair was silvery, and he wore a pointy cap.

"May I help you?" he inquired.

"Yes," Kate answered. "A few days ago, an acquaintance of mine purchased a love potion from you, and I would like to buy another. For *her*. Not for me."

"Another?" he gasped. "The ingredients are very powerful. I wouldn't feel comfortable dispensing more."

She retrieved the wad of bills Melanie had provided and pushed them toward him, figuring cash on the counter would spur a different decision. Melanie could be insufferable, and Kate wouldn't climb into the carriage without a new vial.

"I dropped the first one. It broke."

Suspicious, he studied her. "You must guarantee that you haven't administered it to the gentleman of interest. I can't have you overwhelming him with a double dose, for there's no predicting what mischief you might render. If the poor chap grew too enamored, his heart could fail. I won't be responsible for . . . for murder."

"Oh for pity's sake." She rolled her eyes and raised her hand as if taking an oath. "I swear I dropped it."

"Well, then . . . I expect I could be *persuaded*—if the price is right."

"I'm not giving you a penny more, you charlatan. This is all the money I have."

"No need to get huffy." He traipsed to the adjacent room, and after a lengthy delay, he brought her another vial, which she tucked into her reticule.

She was about to leave, but at the last second, she paused. Since she was positive he was a fraud, she hated to quiz him, but she didn't know where else to turn.

"Might I ask you a hypothetical question?"

"Certainly."

"Supposing someone *had* ingested the tonic. For

example, what if an unsuspecting person drank it by accident? Is there an antidote?"

"An antidote?"

"Yes. If it was inadvertently swallowed, that individual could be a tad anxious. If so, there must be a . . . a remedy."

He was no fool, and he thoroughly assessed her. "You took it."

"I didn't mean to!" she blurted out.

He tutted and clucked. "Tell me this: Have you a piece of his property in your possession? It would be an object belonging only to him, and you can't account for your having it."

Her stomach plummeted, and she was dizzy. "His ring."

"Oh my . . ."

The tidings had him distraught, and his upset panicked her. "What? What is it?"

He went to a shelf and found a powder, which he poured into an envelope. "Consume this mixture in hot tea, three times today, and once tomorrow morning, then restore the ring to him. But if it resurfaces in your custody, there's no hope for it."

"Don't be so secretive. Speak to me in plain English."

"If the ring comes back to you, the antidote won't work. Some things are preordained. You can't alter your destiny."

His words terrified her. The elixir had impaired her logic and common sense, and it was obvious that she was incapable of fighting her fixation with Stamford on her own. She had to stop her obsession, but if the cure was ineffective, how was she to rectify the situation?

In a state, she grabbed the packet of powder and fled.

Marcus peered down the avenue and saw Kate Duncan flitting out of an alley. What was she up to?

She raced to a coach, which he identified as his. It was the one he allowed Pamela to utilize, so Kate must have borrowed it for a shopping excursion. But what had she bought? And what had her running as if the hounds of hell were on her heels? He was dying to know.

He was fascinated by her, though he couldn't figure out why. Many women had passed through his life, with very few tickling his fancy, but for some reason, she did.

She was so genuine, so unpretentious. In a world where he was surrounded by sycophants and hangers-on, she was so refreshing. Plus, she was so damned sexy.

How could he resist?

He dawdled out of sight until the coach lumbered away; then he walked to the alley from which she'd materialized. To his surprise, the sole establishment was occupied by an apothecary, and he stepped inside.

A strange elderly merchant was straightening bottles, and Marcus laid a gold sovereign on the counter. A wise fellow, the man snatched it up.

"I'm curious," Marcus began, "about the young lady who was just in here. What was she wanting?"

The merchant chuckled. "She acquired a love potion."

"A love potion?"

"Yes. Her friend—a snooty little blonde—initially sought a tincture for some rich bloke she's desirous of marrying, but *your* lady drank it when she shouldn't have. So she obtained another dosage for the blonde to mete out to her unwary fiancé."

"And for herself?"

"She was wondering if I had a remedy."

"Has the brew prompted her to fall madly in love?"

"*She* thinks it has."

At the ludicrous notion, Marcus chortled, but he was disconcerted. He couldn't have her believing she was smitten by another. Not for the immediate future, anyway. He had too many designs on her. "Are you claiming it's authentic?"

"With girls and their romances, who's to say? It's an ancient recipe, and the lady has attained an item of the man's, when she has no explanation for her having it. Purportedly, it's an indication that the magic is working."

"What item does she have?"

"A ring."

Marcus nearly choked. "You're joking."

"No. And she was quite distressed about it, too."

Tickled by this information, Marcus grinned. What fun he would have! "Have you provided a cure for what ails her?"

"Yes. I gave her a powder to take with her tea, and I advised her to return the ring to its owner, and to pray it doesn't wend its way back to her, but I doubt my prescription will be of benefit."

"Why?"

The man's eyes glazed over, and his voice sounded far away. "Once Fate has intervened, there's no changing the result."

With the pronouncement, Marcus could have sworn

a frigid wind blew out of nowhere, swirled around his legs, and slithered up his trousers. It was the eeriest sensation he'd ever felt, and he shivered.

"If she comes in again, contact me." He retrieved his card and set it on the counter, but the man seemed to be in a trance. Unsettled by their conversation, he rushed out without a good-bye.

Melanie fanned herself, eager to cool down. The crowd assembled in Lady Pamela's parlor was much smaller than the night before—just thirty people—and the chairs had been rearranged for dancing. A musical duo huddled in the corner, playing the pianoforte and violin, but she'd enjoyed so many trips around the floor that she'd had to catch her breath.

She adored dancing, and leapt in whenever she had the chance, which was rare. Regina didn't countenance such folderol, but she'd relaxed her rules. In London, everyone danced, so Melanie could, too, because if there was one thing Regina couldn't abide, it was sticking out, or behaving incorrectly.

Regina had never gotten over their humble origins and, to Melanie's perpetual chagrin, was forever trying to fit in but never succeeding.

She'd like to stroll in the yard, but with Kate banished from the festivities, Melanie was without a chaperone, and thus stuck in the house, which made her furious.

Kate was always showing off and drawing attention to herself. Melanie was weary of her undisciplined conduct, especially when there was so much riding on the assistance Melanie needed her to supply.

When Kate wasn't permitted in the same room with Stamford, how were they to administer the potion?

Beside her, a gentleman sidled closer. He was an individual of little consequence—the son of a dishonored, poverty-stricken baronet—so during supper he'd been seated far down the table. Regina had been incensed by his lowly presence, but everyone else was cordial to him.

He was much older than Melanie was, probably Stamford's age or greater, and he wasn't handsome, as were many of the male guests. His blond hair was balding, his face was ruddy and pockmarked, and he was very thin, as if he never ate when he should. But he was dressed fashionably, which was a sign of wealth, and that he wasn't the slacker her mother insisted.

All evening, he'd been watching her, and she reveled in his assessment. His regard was the exact sort she should be receiving from Stamford, the lout!

When would Stamford realize that she was not only pretty, but rich? Her dowry was fat and ripe, filled as it was with the money and property that should have been Kate's. Melanie wasn't meant to know from where the assets had derived, but occasionally she couldn't help overhearing.

She peeked to the side, meeting the man's gaze, and she was thrilled by his overt admiration. At least one fellow in the blasted mansion recognized a prize when he stared at it!

Anxious to look taller and more mature, she straightened. She wouldn't have him assuming she was a child, as Stamford seemed to do. With her shoulders back, her bosom thrust out, the bodice of her new gown accented her figure, and he relished the sight, though he attempted to shield his piqued interest.

He moved to her, bowed, and brazenly introduced himself. "Lady Melanie, Mr. Elliot Featherstone, at your service."

"Hello, Mr. Featherstone."

"Welcome to London." He leaned nearer. "You dance like an angel. You're so graceful."

She blushed. "Why, thank you."

"I'd ask you to partner with me, but I'm terrible at it."

"That's quite all right. I'm needing a rest myself. It's so hot in here."

"I was pondering the very same. I could use some fresh air." He glanced over at Regina, but she was boring some woman to tears, and hadn't noticed him. "I don't imagine your mother would allow you to stroll in the garden with me?"

"I'm sure she wouldn't."

"Pity."

He scrutinized her again, in a manner that had her feeling grown-up and able to make her own decisions, and she wished she had the temerity to simply walk out onto the verandah. Would the world end if she did?

"Perhaps we could have a glass of punch," she offered. The refreshments were in the next salon, and the door was open wide. It was innocent enough.

He smiled, liking how she'd resolved the situation, and he escorted her over. They sat, and a servant brought them beverages. When they were alone, he sneaked a flask from his jacket and added something to his.

"Scottish whiskey," he whispered when she raised a brow. "Would you like some?"

Seeing no eavesdroppers, she nodded, and he poured a generous amount into her cup. As she'd never had hard spirits before, she was elated to participate in the naughty misdeed.

She took a tentative sip, not caring for the taste, but she wasn't about to let him know. Though she followed the nip with several more, she had to shift away so he wouldn't detect how the sharp tang had watered her eyes.

The alcohol warmed her, and she was positive she appeared more sophisticated, more poised. "You're a horrid influence."

"I hope so." As though they were the dearest of companions, he chuckled. "May I confide in you, Lady Melanie?"

"Of course."

"You won't deem me rash, or too bold?"

"Never." It was the first conversation she'd had with an adult male, and she was ecstatic. She yearned to be flirtatious and engaging. Regina always scolded her to be more impressive but never rendered any hints as to how. "What is your secret, Mr. Featherstone?"

"I've noted how Stamford has been slighting you. Everyone's talking about it."

"They are?"

"Yes."

"He's acted abominably," she admitted, delighted to vent her frustration to someone who would listen.

"You poor babe," he soothed. "After you've traveled all this way. You're aware of what's transpiring, aren't you?"

She frowned. "Is there information of which I ought to be apprised?"

"I can't believe your mother didn't tell you."

She wasn't surprised that Regina would keep some vile detail to herself, and her blood was boiling. "What is it?"

"I shouldn't speak of it here, in the man's own house, when he's a friend. It's not fitting."

"You must reveal it to me!"

"You're such a sweet girl. I can't bear to have you hurt."

Just then, her mother saw them chatting. She scowled, which notified Melanie that she should immediately return to the dancing.

"I have to go," she said.

He peered over at Regina, grinning as if they were having a harmless exchange. "If I called on you, would she let us ride in the park?"

"No."

"Not even with a chaperone?"

"She's determined that I'm to wed Stamford. She'd never agree to our socializing."

His dismay was evident. "I don't dare suggest it. . . ."

"Say it!" She was panicked that Regina would drag her away before their discussion was concluded.

"I was thinking that we should meet." He paused so the gravity of his proposition would sink in. "No one could know."

Melanie studied him, then Regina, then him again. If Regina had discovered a dreadful tidbit about Stamford, she'd never divulge it, and Melanie had to learn what her mother was hiding.

Regina gestured to her, and she couldn't delay. She stood and murmured, "At midnight, out behind the mews."

He nodded his assent. "It was a pleasure to share my punch, Lady Melanie."

"The *pleasure* was all mine, Mr. Featherstone."

She spun away and went to sit beside Regina.

6

Marcus sneaked toward Kate's room, toting a bottle of wine and two goblets. He'd loitered at Pamela's soiree long enough to establish that Kate wasn't present, and when he ascertained her absence, there was no reason to linger.

Her door was shut, but candlelight emanated from underneath, and he tried the knob, elated when it turned. Had it been locked, he had a key and would have used it. He was that determined to be with her.

His heart pounding, he crept in so stealthily that he might have been invisible. She was on a settee by the window, her back to him, and staring out into the yard below.

She was wearing a green summer negligee, the thin straps revealing her slender shoulders and arms. It was slinky, likely made of silk, and the richness intrigued him. He'd assumed her to be a woman of extremely modest means, and he speculated as to whether it might be a cast-off from Melanie.

The elegant garment hugged her tiny waist, her curvaceous hips and thighs. There was a slit up the side, and he could see a shapely calf, a bare foot.

Her fabulous auburn hair was down and brushed out, the lush tresses loosely restrained by a green ribbon. The lengthy ends were deliciously curled and a striking contrast to the color of her gown.

She was engrossed in a cup of tea, a teapot on the dresser. An envelope was next to it, as well as a vial of red liquid, which he presumed to be the love potion and curative powder she'd obtained from the apothecary.

He grinned, tickled that she was so disconcerted by events. She seemed so pragmatic. Who would imagine she'd fall victim to such chicanery? And how could he manipulate her anxiety to achieve his own ends?

"Hello, Kate."

On hearing his voice, she whipped around, spilling her tea down her front. She screeched and leapt up, tugging at her bodice to keep the hot liquid from burning her. Her twisting and writhing provided several tempting glimpses of bosom and breast, and he was ecstatic to note that his dreams had been very realistic.

"Why are you here?" she hissed.

"It's after midnight. You never came to my room as I asked."

"You didn't *ask*. You commanded, and I told you I wouldn't obey."

"So I decided to stop by *your* room, instead." He gestured around. "Isn't this cozy? Just the two of us? Together?" He deposited the wine and glasses on the dresser.

"How did you slither in?"

"The door was unlocked"—he retrieved the key and jangled it—"and if it hadn't been, I was prepared."

"Get out! At once!"

"No."

"You can't barge in."

"I already have."

"I'll complain to Lady Pamela."

An idle threat. She couldn't risk others being apprised of his visit. "It's my house. Pamela resides in it at my discretion. I'm the king of this drafty castle, and I can do whatever I choose inside the walls."

"You are the most spoiled man I've ever met."

He laughed and went to the bed, sat on the edge, and bounced, testing the firmness of the mattress. "Are your accommodations acceptable?"

"Very. Thank you for inquiring. Now go!"

"Because I can have you moved, if you'd like."

"Don't you dare! The last thing I need is your taking an interest in me."

"That would create all sorts of trouble for you, wouldn't it?"

"Yes, and you've done enough."

"And I'm afraid I plan to do even more."

He assessed the furnishings. It was a small chamber, snug yet plain, and too ordinary for how unique he deemed her to be. With a nod to the housekeeper, he could have Kate transferred, but she was correct: A directive from him would be deadly for her.

Besides, there was an advantage to her current location. It was a simple jaunt from his room to hers, so trysting would be easy, the chance of detection nil.

She glared at him with no effect, so she stomped to the wardrobe. Desperate to cover herself, she grabbed a luxurious robe that matched her negligee. He wasn't about to have her donning more apparel, and he rushed over to prevent her before she could draw it on. The fabric was as exquisite as it looked, and he stroked it, the cool material gliding along his skin.

"Where did you get this?"

"I didn't steal it, if that's what you're thinking."

"It never crossed my mind that you might have."

Mutinously, she claimed, "It was my mother's."

Which meant she must have previously had a family of some affluence. What had happened to lay her low? It was a fascinating detail to probe later, but for the moment, he had more captivating aspects to unravel.

"She must have been very beautiful."

"She was."

He tossed the robe on the floor, and she didn't fight him. Scowling, she watched him as one might a dangerous predator, and she was wise to be wary. Where she was concerned, he felt capable of any nefarious conduct.

He leaned down to kiss her ruby lips. For the briefest second, she allowed the contact; then she turned away, and he grazed her cheek, her ear.

"Stop tormenting me," she whispered. "Please."

"You're so damned sweet. How can I resist?"

Shrugging, he was unable to further justify his mischief. Any coquette in London would gladly entertain him, so he couldn't explain why he persisted. A female of lesser morals would be so much more amenable to seduction.

At his refusal to go, she was so forlorn, and he couldn't bear that she was unhappy. She brought him an odd joy, and he was eager for her to experience the same contentment. They shared a special connection, which they needed to explore, and he intended to pursue her until he could comprehend it.

"What do you want from me?" she implored.

"Aside from terrific sexual relations?"

"Yes. Aside from that."

She blushed so furiously that he was certain she was a virgin. What if she was? Could he ruin her? Should he?

Though he had many faults, he wasn't that much of a cad. Yet he was convinced that being intimate with her would be a life-altering event. When something so marvelous could occur, what point was served by passing it up?

He yearned to have her smiling, but he wasn't sure how to cheer her. Her pot of tea was on the dresser, and he went to it.

"Is this tea?"

"Yes."

He lifted the lid and sniffed. "It smells peculiar. What have you put in it?"

"If you must know, I added a restorative. I've been under the weather."

"Since when?"

"Since I met you."

He picked up the envelope of powder, and she sprinted to him, determined to snatch it away, when he made an exaggerated fumbling motion and dropped it. The granules spilled and filtered into the weave of the rug.

"Oh no!" she keened. "Now see what you've done."

Falling to her knees, she tried to scoop it up, but the particles were impossible to salvage. She peered up at him, so distressed that he almost felt sorry for behaving like such an ass. Almost. He was too charmed by how each and every expression flitted across her pretty face.

"And what's this?" He grabbed the vial and held it toward the candle. The liquid appeared to be red wine, and he wondered if it was.

"It's for . . . for treating women's ailments."

"Really? Are you suffering?" He studied her bewitching figure, his gaze taking a leisurely journey across her breasts. "From feminine ailments, that is? You look fine to me."

She blushed another delicious shade of red, and he wedged out the cork, which panicked her. "Give it to me, Marcus! Don't joke about this."

He hoisted the bottle out of her reach, and she stretched and struggled, attempting to seize it. Their wrestling forced her to press herself to him, and he could discern every delectable inch of her torso. She was rounded yet slender, curved in all the right spots, and they fit together perfectly.

Sparks were flying, the air electrified by their proximity. He hugged her close, his naughty fingers creeping to her bottom, the gesture flattening her loins to his. His phallus reacted, growing rigid as stone, and he flexed into her.

She might be an innocent, but when his body moved with hers, she froze and gasped with surprise.

"You feel it, too, don't you?" he queried.

"No," she lied.

"It's meant to be, Kate." He was echoing the words of the apothecary, and she blanched. Had the man said the same to her?

He tipped the vial and swallowed down the contents,

and it wasn't wine as he'd supposed, but something more earthy, more sugary.

"Marcus, no!" She lunged, but he'd finished it off.

"I love it when you call me Marcus."

Immediately, his arms were heavy. They slumped to his sides, and she yanked the vial away.

"I can't believe you drank it!" she wailed. "Why would you? Are you insane?"

"Let's have some wine, shall we? There's nothing happening between us that a bit of intoxication can't solve."

"I don't need inebriation! I need privacy, and solitude, and . . . and . . . and . . ."

To his mortification, tears swarmed into her eyes. He couldn't stand to witness her dolor, so he walked over and poured the wine. His legs were sluggish, but his senses were more acute. Colors were brighter, odors stronger, sounds louder and more apparent. He actually thought he could hear a clock ticking on the floor below.

Perhaps the elixir was a narcotic, after all. He was no stranger to opiates and other soporifics. They were often distributed at the wild parties he was wont to attend, but while they induced pleasant stupors, none of them had ever so severely tuned his perception.

He turned toward her, and she was staring out the window. She was glowing, encompassed in a golden halo, her scarlet tresses radiating with a warm fire, and he experienced such a profound wave of joy that his chest ached. He felt as if his heart were enlarging, as if it no longer fit under his ribs. The ice in which it had been encased for so many years was melting, the droplets sweeping away in a refreshing flood.

Here she is! a voice blissfully proclaimed, and he was overwhelmed by a certainty that he'd been waiting for her forever, without his realizing he had been, and that his destiny had finally arrived. A rapid display of visions flashed, scenes from eras gone by, of the two of them together throughout many previous lifetimes.

Perturbed by the drug's powerful effects, he shook his head, trying to clear it. He had to keep his wits about him, for in his confused condition, there was no telling what he might say or do.

Needing to be with her, to touch her, he came up behind her, but she continued to gaze outside. He was so attuned to her that he could read her mind, and so many details were obvious.

She had always been solitary, isolated. She was pining to love and be loved, to find someone who cherished her. She was so lonely, so starved for companionship and affection.

As to himself, she was titillated by his interest in her, but afraid, too, worried that he would harm her, that her tender heart would never mend. Smiling, he gripped her waist and spun her so that she was facing him. She was silent, morose, and he snuggled her to him and kissed her forehead. "I won't hurt you. I swear it."

"I can't imagine you'll do anything else."

"I won't," he contended, desperate to reassure her. "I . . . I . . ."

Bewildered and unsettled, he stopped. He'd almost declared that he loved her, which couldn't be. He didn't love anyone. He never would. He knew better.

It was the potion talking, and he was amazed by its ability to muddle. No wonder Kate was disturbed enough to seek an antidote.

"Come," he coaxed. He linked their fingers and led her to the bed.

Resigned, she followed, and he reposed, then tugged her down on top of him. They'd traveled beyond the point where she could dissuade him. He jerked the ribbon from her hair, freeing it, and the auburn locks flowed over her shoulder like a crimson waterfall.

He eased her down, her breasts in contact with his chest, her nipples poking into him like shards of glass. The fabric of her negligee was so thin that it seemed as if she were naked. His phallus hardened further, pulsating with a renewed urgency.

"You're so intent on your pursuit of me," she ventured.

"Yes."

"To what end?"

"I don't know."

He rolled them so that she was beneath him, and he paused, recognizing that he'd dreamed this very moment. He could visualize everything that would transpire, how the encounter would progress, how it would conclude.

At least, he assumed he could. The fiendish concoction had him so befuddled that he couldn't attest to what was real and what wasn't.

"Have you lain with a man before, Kate?"

She snorted. "Dozens and dozens of them. Gentlemen beat a path to my door. I can't chase them away with a stick."

"Have you any idea what I desire from you?"

"No."

Except that she'd been in his room, had seen him with Pamela. So she had some notion.

Feeling like a virgin, learning his way, he kissed her. She was so unique, so fine, and he was so enamored. He was terrified that he'd proceed too fast, that he'd demand too much, that he would scare her with his burgeoning passion. He'd planned for every second to be extraordinary, and he had to show her how much he treasured her. But how?

His paramours never mattered to him. He wasn't concerned with their happiness, yet with her, he was like a lad with his first girl.

He deepened the embrace, his tongue flicking at her bottom lip. Asking. Asking again. She opened and welcomed him inside, and he toyed and played, teased and tormented. He caressed her everywhere, and tentatively her arms folded around him. She was eager to caress him in return, but hesitant as to whether she should.

"It's all right to touch me, Kate. I like it."

"You make me want to be so wicked."

"I've never considered a tad of *wickedness* to be a bad trait in a female."

"You wouldn't."

She joined in, her fervor exhilarating and enchanting. She dallied with the wantonness of a courtesan, but the naturalness and curiosity of a sheltered maid. The incongruity drove him wild.

Exploring, she sifted her fingers through his hair, ran them across his shoulders and back, but she wasn't brave enough to dip any further. The expectation, the yearning for what she might do, was careening him to a fevered ledge.

In no time at all, he was too aroused to be prudent, and he worried that he'd instigate something reckless, something irreversible. Was he bent on deflowering her? Could he steal her chastity, here and now, with scarcely an instant of deliberation or preparation? Was she ready? Was he?

He clasped the strap of her negligee and slid it down, baring the creamy swell of her bosom. Her breast was exposed, her erect nipple jutting out, and he pinched it, squeezing lightly.

"Oh, Marcus . . . we shouldn't . . . we can't . . . you don't . . ."

"We can do whatever we please, Kate. There's no one to tell us no."

"But it's wrong."

"It's not wrong."

"It's the tincture you drank."

"I thought you said it's used for treating womanly ailments."

Caught in a lie, she stammered, "Well . . . well . . . it is, but it's obviously causing you to behave irrationally."

"You regard making love to be *irrational*?"

"It is when you're so fixated on me as your partner!"

"Are you trying to persuade yourself that I need to imbibe of a potion before you'd captivate me?" He grinned. "You're so perfect, Kate. And all mine."

"I don't understand what you want from me," she protested miserably.

"Yes, you do."

Abandoning her mouth, he blazed a trail down her neck, her chest, to her nipple. He licked and laved it, then he suckled her, and he couldn't believe how the action calmed him, how it pacified and comforted.

"Oh, oh yes . . ." She sighed, and she seemed to add, "I dreamed of this. . . ."

He wasn't certain he'd heard her correctly. Had they experienced the same erotic reverie? Was it possible? Or was it merely another baffling consequence of the drug?

She drew him closer, urging him to feast. He bit and nibbled, until the extended tip was moist and inflamed; then he shifted to her other breast and gave it the same fierce attention.

Down below, he was pressing into her, letting her discern how hard he was, how desperately he desired her, and she adopted his tempo, her hips working with his in a furious rhythm. Her ardor was spiraling, and he was anxious to push her to the edge, to shove her over.

He started inching up her nightgown, and she was so overwhelmed that she didn't notice what he was about until he arrived at the vee of her thighs.

"Marcus, no!" She attempted to scoot away, but he locked his leg over hers and held her tight.

"Relax, Kate. Let me do this for you." He cupped her, slipping two fingers far inside. She was wet, primed for what was coming, and weeping into his hand.

She arched up and moaned. "Don't. It's too . . . too . . ."

"Naughty? Delicious?"

"Yes. I can't bear it."

With his thumb, he jabbed at her sexual center, and she yelped with surprise, her anatomy struggling toward the end, even as her mind wrenched her away.

"What's happening to me?" she managed to gasp.

"It's pleasure, darling."

"I don't want this from you."

"*You* may not, but your body is begging for it."

"I can't," she wailed. "I won't."

"For me, Kate. Do it for me."

He touched her once, again, as he sucked at her nipple, and she cried out and leapt over the precipice with a ferocity he hadn't encountered with any of his prior paramours. He was convinced it was her first orgasm, and he was ecstatic to have spurred her to such riotous turmoil.

The agitation went on and on, and finally, it peaked and waned. He moved over her, and kissed her, softly, tenderly, thrilled that she trusted him enough to spin out of control, to grasp that she could when she was with him.

Her eyes fluttered open, and he wasn't positive what he expected—perhaps a maidenly sigh, or one of her pithy remarks—but instead, she studied him, then burst into tears.

"What's this?" he inquired, his heart reeling, and he grabbed the quilt and swiped them away.

"Was that feminine passion?"

"A very dramatic example."

"I'm loose, aren't I?"

"Absolutely."

"Do you suppose it's in my blood?"

"I'm sure it is."

He was joking, but she was devastated, and a protracted bout of weeping ensued. Throughout the deluge, he cuddled with her, whispering soothing words, and he was amazed that he would.

He'd never before comforted a distraught woman, because he wouldn't have been inclined to remain through a display of histrionics. A female's emotional situation had no impact on his relationship with her, and thus, she wouldn't be welcome, in his presence, to vent her anger or hurt.

As he was special to no one, no one would dare impose on him, and it occurred to him that it was a sorry statement on the condition of his life. He was so isolated, and previously, his separateness hadn't bothered him. He'd liked his independent existence, but he was lonely, and there was a contentment in consoling Kate that he hadn't known he'd missed.

They were scarcely acquainted, yet she was rendering striking changes in how he carried on, in how he viewed himself. A flicker of excitement sparked within. Maybe he wasn't the cold, callous man others presumed him to be.

Eventually, her outburst diminished, her breathing slowed, and she dozed, which was another high spot for him. When he was philandering, he never dawdled after lusts were sated.

He lay very still, cataloging every detail of the precious moment. Her negligee was askew, and he tugged it down and covered her with the blankets. She was so exhausted that she didn't stir, and he brushed a kiss across her lips.

"Good night, my dear Kate," he murmured. "I'll see you on the morrow."

As if she'd heard and understood the comment, she smiled in her sleep.

He'd intended to rise and leave, but he couldn't bring himself to go, and he decided to rest for a few minutes. He napped, and when he woke, it was early morning. The mellow light of dawn crept in the window, and a bird chirped outside. He reached for her, but she wasn't there. Glancing around, he was astounded to find himself in his own bedchamber, in his own bed.

Stunned, he sat up, and his head pounded with such a sharp ache that he felt as if the top might blow off, as if he had the worst hangover in all eternity, when he shouldn't have been feeling poorly. He'd barely had anything to drink—except that blasted potion.

When had he left her room? How had he gotten to his own? Or had their rendezvous been a dream? He was disoriented, dizzy, his memory fuzzy. Were his recollections genuine, or simply another of the erotic fantasies his imagination kept conjuring?

Peering down at his hand, he was startled to note that the strip of green ribbon he'd untied from her hair was weaved through his fingers. A remark from the apothecary nagged at him, about possessing an object, about it being a sign that the mysterious elixir was working.

He shuddered. There was no magic in the world that could make him fall in love. Once before, he'd been bitten, and he'd nearly died from the viciousness of the wound, and he wouldn't be so foolish again.

The ribbon was merely evidence that the assignation had really transpired, that he'd been with her. It didn't mean more than that. It couldn't.

He wondered if she'd awakened yet, and he was curious as to what she'd think of the intimacies they'd shared. No doubt, she'd be embarrassed, and she'd try to hide from him, which he wouldn't allow. She was like a burr under his saddle, her proximity pricking at him, compelling him to talk to her, to be with her.

Ignoring the hammering in his head, he climbed out of bed, ready to dress and be about his business. With a renewed energy, he rang for breakfast, and as he waited for a servant to appear, he calculated all the ways he could guarantee that Miss Kate Duncan entertained him throughout the day and into the coming night.

The prospect was thrilling, and he realized that he hadn't been so enthused in a very, very long time.

7

"You're sweet to accompany me." Kate smiled at Christopher.

"How could I refuse?"

"You're sure you don't mind?"

"If I hadn't wanted to come, I'd have said so. Quit worrying."

"Well, wouldn't you rather be engaged in activities back at the house? Any of them would be more fun than traipsing across London with me."

"I've had my fill of the *activities* at Lady Pamela's." Relaxing against the squab, he stretched his feet, which was difficult in the cramped space. "Believe me, I was glad for the excuse to get away."

Was he as tired of the marital plotting as she was? Or was he weary of the sly looks from the mothers who sized him up, trying to determine if he might be a worthy husband for their rich, spoiled daughters?

He was always optimistic and eager, pleasant and courteous, and Kate cherished him for it.

"Promise me that you'll never apprise your mother of where we went today. And that you'll never inquire as to what I'm doing."

Exasperated, he rolled his eyes. "I gave you my word ten times already!"

"Make it eleven."

"On a stack of Bibles, I swear it!"

He clutched his hand to his heart, and she laughed. She had to visit Selena—not out of curiosity but out of duty—but hadn't had any coin to rent a cab, nor could she expect to utilize the family coach. She was in no position to impose on Lady Pamela, and the only other person she could have asked was Stamford, but she'd swallow a frog before she'd approach him.

The man was a wizard, a sorcerer, who preyed on unsuspecting females, and urged them to commit acts they'd never imagined. At least, that was how she'd convinced herself to view her behavior.

There was no way in the world she'd admit that she'd enjoyed their frolic, that she'd been complicit in her total fall from grace. If she'd protested, he wouldn't have proceeded. At any point, she could have stopped him, so her true colors were established. She was a strumpet, and it was all her own fault.

It was a relief, having a chore to drag her out of the mansion for the afternoon. She declined to mope in her room, speculating as to where he was, how he was occupying himself, and if—by chance—he might be thinking of her.

Christopher had been a lifesaver, happy to assist, and polite enough not to plague her with questions about her destination.

The carriage rumbled to a halt, and scowling, he peered out the curtain. "Are you certain you have the correct address?"

"Yes. Why?"

"It's not the best neighborhood. Perhaps I shouldn't let you out."

Hiding her dismay, she peeked out, too. The area was extremely seedy. Unsavory characters strolled past, and a pack of ragged children ran by. The building before them was dilapidated, the paint chipped, the fence in pieces.

She was confused. The structure seemed to hold many apartments, so it couldn't be the house she'd rented for Selena. Kate saw the bills her sister submitted, was aware of how much money was paid out every quarter. Such a large amount wouldn't buy so little. Would it?

But then, this was London, and Kate had no concept of what merchandise and services cost in the city. Still . . .

"Would you check with the driver, in case he misunderstood my directions?"

"Of course."

He exited to converse with the servants, and when he returned, he was disturbed.

"This is the place." He studied her, and must have noted her consternation. "Kate, you can confide in me. I won't tell a soul."

She couldn't guess how much Christopher knew about her parents' scandals. If she confessed the details, and advised him of Selena's ancestry, he might be shocked or revolted, and she couldn't bear to jeopardize their friendship.

"It's nothing awful, as I have you presuming," she lied. "I'm merely calling on an old acquaintance of my mother's."

Clearly, he recognized the remark to be an utter fabrication, but he let her maintain the ruse, and his obvious concern made her feel petty and small.

"Are you positive you should do this?" he probed.

"It will take but a few minutes. I'll be right back."

She hustled out before he could query her further, before he could compel her to spill the entire sordid story.

She marched through the broken gate, and up the walk, entering a decrepit, dirty foyer. A dank stairway led to the upper floors. A list of residents was tacked to the wall, with Selena's lodging shown to be at the end of the main hall, so Kate went to it and knocked.

Her half sister had no idea who was on her stoop, and Kate's pulse pounded with equal parts anticipation and dread. At the same instant, she was thrilled and terrified.

What would Selena be like? How would they interact? Suddenly, it dawned on Kate that Selena's opinion mattered very much. She yearned for a new dress or hat to have worn for the important occasion.

A maid answered and, on learning Kate's identity, was rude and curt, as if she detested Kate on sight. She was escorted into a cold, dismal parlor. Overhead, she could hear tenants banging about on the second floor.

As she waited for Selena to appear, she tabulated the threadbare furnishings, the frayed drapes and rugs, and her perplexity spiraled. She'd envisioned Selena in cozy surroundings. How could she have relegated the girl to this existence?

She had to rectify the situation, but she wasn't sure

how, and she couldn't decide who might provide guidance. Regina couldn't discuss the subject without venom and spite. Christopher was just eighteen and had had scant experience with adult issues.

Maybe she'd contact Master Thumberton, the solicitor who'd helped her when Selena had traveled to England. He couldn't be cognizant that they'd left Selena in this depressing condition.

"Kate! Kate!" Selena's merry greeting erupted from the rear of the apartment, her words lilting with an enchanting foreign accent. "You've come at last! I'm so glad!"

Kate braced, ready for anything, as Selena waltzed in. Slender, elegant, beautiful, she looked like Kate, but was more graceful and willowy, more exotic and mysterious. They both resembled their mother, with there being no doubt they were blood siblings, but Selena's hair and eyes were black, her skin a golden hue Kate had never seen before.

"Kate, my dearest sister!" Selena hurried forward and took Kate's hands, kissing her on both cheeks. "How I've longed for this marvelous day to arrive!"

Kate was disconcerted by the display of cordial emotion. Aside from Stamford's outrageous attentions, she couldn't remember when anyone had previously touched her. She was so isolated that she often felt as if she were living in a bubble.

Tears swamped her, and she swiped at them, as Selena clucked like a mother hen and ushered her to a nearby sofa.

"It's wonderful to finally meet you, too," Kate managed on a shaky breath.

Another woman joined them, an older matron, and Selena shimmered with unbridled delight. "Mrs. Fitzsimmons, Kate's here! Isn't it glorious?"

The woman had no comment, but she shot a glare at Kate that was critical, accusatory, filled with blame.

"Mrs. Fitzsimmons is the companion you hired for me," Selena clarified. "She's been such a blessing."

Kate nodded, trying to be sociable, which was difficult with how Fitzsimmons was frowning. "It's a pleasure, Mrs. Fitzsimmons."

When she offered no polite banter in reply, Selena's gay laughter smoothed over the awkward exchange. "Don't mind her; she's so protective of me. Edith," she said to Mrs. Fitzsimmons, "let's ring for tea. Or better yet, let's have some wine. This is a celebration!"

"There's no tea or wine remaining, Miss Selena," Fitzsimmons acidly explained, directing her hateful scowl at Kate, as if she had personally pilfered from the pantry. "Have you forgotten? We overspent our budget and couldn't afford any."

Fitzsimmons stomped out, and Kate watched her go, her confusion mounting. How could there be no beverages? She authorized so many expenditures, never refusing any of her sister's modest requests.

Selena blushed, but smiled through the hurled insult, and Kate was amazed by her maturity and comportment. She had a style and polish that were lacking in British girls, such as Melanie, but then Selena had suffered more than any of them. As Kate was well aware, tragedy aged one quickly.

"This is such a splendid surprise," Selena started, once they were alone. "Why are you in London?"

"Lady Melanie is making her debut."

"How *magnifico* for her." Selena sighed. "Wouldn't it be fun for us to be doing the same?"

"Well, I'm a tad old"—they both laughed, their voices sounding exactly alike—"but I wish you could have a season. The boys I've encountered would fall all over themselves to court you."

"Have you been to many grand balls and soirees?"

"A few," Kate lied, having gone to a single event and, due to Stamford's mischief, been banished from any others.

"Our mother adored parties."

At the affectionate statement, Kate's heart literally skipped a beat. She recollected little about her mother, so Selena's short sentence was electrifying. The snippet of information was like locating a rare gem in a pile of common stones.

She murmured, "No, I didn't know that about her."

"Oh yes. There was nothing she enjoyed more than dressing up in her most superb gown and her brightest jewels. My father, too. They were such a handsome couple, so happy and so much in love. Their life was like a fairy tale."

Dumbstruck, Kate stared at her. She'd gleaned few particulars about her mother's circumstances after she'd fled England, the vast majority having been culled through Regina's sarcastic observations.

On her learning a different version, the foundation of Kate's existence was rocked, and her world tipped off its axis. She couldn't find her balance.

"She was happy?"

"Very," Selena contended. "I have something for you." She walked to a desk and searched through the drawer, retrieving a narrow wooden box, and she passed it to Kate.

"This is for you."

"What is it?"

"One of Mother's fans. It was part of her wedding ensemble, so it was her favorite. She always took it with her when she attended the opera."

"She married your father?"

"Why, yes."

Kate was reeling. They'd wed? The fact meant Selena wasn't illegitimate. How could Kate not have known such a vital detail?

With trembling fingers, she opened the container. The fan was delicate, aged, and she spread it, scrutinizing the meticulously painted violets, the trimmed lace, and she was deluged by the strangest impression that she could smell her mother's perfume in the creases. Unsettled, she refolded it, returned it to the box, and closed the lid.

"It's much too dear. I couldn't possibly accept it."

"I insist." Selena pushed it at her. "She wanted you to have it."

"She did?" Kate felt dizzy, pummeled by unwonted emotion.

Selena nodded. "Besides, I have many mementoes of my own."

Just then, there was a knock at the door, and they both froze. Kate recognized, without being told, that it was Christopher, coming to check on her, and she kicked herself. She should have realized he would!

Momentarily, the maid showed him in, and they faced him like guilty schoolchildren who'd been caught doing what they oughtn't.

The servant was too bowled over to announce him, so Kate stepped forward. "My apologies, Christopher, for keeping you waiting."

"I wasn't growing impatient, Kate. I'm merely ensuring that you're all right."

"As you can see, I'm fine."

"Yes, you are." He shifted his admiring gaze to Selena. "Who is your lovely companion?"

"May I present Miss Selena Bella, recently moved to London from Venice, Italy."

"How do you do?" he courteously said, gallantly adding, *"Benvenuto in Gran Bretagna!"*

Kate gaped at him, having no idea where he might have picked up an Italian phrase. He'd been educated, but Regina had paid for the basics, and though his accent was atrocious, Selena was charmed.

"Grazie," Selena responded.

"Selena, this is the Earl of Doncaster, Christopher Lewis."

"Oh my!" Selena hadn't grasped his eminence, and she dropped into a perfect curtsy. He rushed over and begged her to rise.

"There's no need to stand on ceremony, Miss Bella," he asserted. "Deep down, I'm a farm boy, and I'm unaccustomed to all this formality."

He smiled at her, holding her hand when he should have released it, and Kate studied them, thinking what a striking couple they were. Chris had his blond, Adonis features; and Selena, her dark, lithe beauty. They were young and arresting, exuding a natural charisma, and it was a pleasure simply to view them together.

"I'm so thrilled that you've visited me," Selena exclaimed. "You've given me an opportunity to thank you for your many kindnesses to Kate over the years. She's often written of how considerate you've been. I appreciate it."

Kate had never done any such a thing, and she could barely prevent herself from gawking at her sister. In a letter or two, she'd mentioned Christopher, but she'd never waxed on about him. Selena had the regal bearing of a queen, and Kate was amazed anew by her decorum, her breeding.

Compared to her, Kate was such a country bumpkin, and not for the first time, she pondered what her life might have been like if her mother hadn't run away.

Chris was grinning. "Kate is my favorite person at Doncaster."

"I'm so glad to hear it. She's been an absolute angel to me. I don't know how I'd have survived if she hadn't assisted me in relocating."

Kate struggled to keep from glancing around the dreary parlor, mortified that Selena could be so effusive when Kate's aid had clearly been no help at all. Selena was entirely too generous.

"How *are* the two of you acquainted?" Chris queried.

He evaluated them in a fashion that was much too astute for Kate's liking. She was terrified by the recipes for disaster—images of an angry Regina lurched up to taunt her—and jumped in before Selena could clarify, but her tongue got rolling before she decided what she actually wanted to admit.

"She's my . . . my . . ."

She couldn't finish the sentence, for she had no notion of how to describe their relationship. Though she and Christopher were friends, she couldn't discuss such topics as illicit sexual affairs and scandalous offspring.

Selena was eager for her reply, and at Kate's lack of courage, her disappointment was palpable, but she covered it with her marvelous manners. "Her mother and mine," Selena fibbed, "were very close."

Chris assessed them again, his incredulity masked. "It's wonderful that you've connected."

"Yes, isn't it?"

Kate's cheeks reddened with humiliation. She was desperate to flee, to regroup and assimilate all that had been so rapidly thrust upon her. "Selena, I must be going. I'm embarrassed that I've delayed Lord Doncaster."

"You've been no trouble, Kate," Chris maintained.

"Nonsense," Selena interjected. "We've imposed on you horridly. But Kate, please promise you'll stop by, as soon as you're able."

"I can't fathom how I'll manage it," Kate revealed.

Chris offered, "I'll bring you whenever you ask."

"How very gracious you are," Selena intoned, her exquisite smile lighting the room.

Frantic to be away, Kate stumbled toward the door, and as she made her escape, Selena tucked under her arm the box containing her mother's opera fan. Kate was too distressed to remark or decline, and on the spur of the moment couldn't deduce what comment she could utter about it with Christopher listening.

She hurried out, Chris on her heels, and as she would have exited the apartment, Edith Fitzsimmons skulked out of the shadows, her disdain not having waned. "Take a good look around, Miss Duncan," she scathingly chided. "You should be ashamed of yourself."

At the insult, Kate blanched. Fitzsimmons blamed her for Selena's situation, though she couldn't figure out why, and she felt it necessary to defend herself. "I've approved every expenditure, Mrs. Fitzsimmons."

"A likely story."

"I have!" she insisted. "I'm not sure what's happening."

The woman snorted. "I realize what you're up to, missy, and you shan't succeed. Not if Edith Fitzsimmons has anything to say about it. I'll have you jailed. Just see if I don't!"

Kate gasped, but Christopher stepped in front of her, shooting Fitzsimmons a furious glare, which halted her tirade.

"Excuse us, madam." Curtly dismissing her, he ushered Kate outside. Pensive and dismayed, they contemplated the surroundings.

"Answer one question for me," he requested.

"If I can."

"How has such an enchanting young lady ended up residing in a place like this?"

"I don't know," Kate responded, "but I intend to find out."

8

Pamela reclined on Christopher's bed, listening as he walked down the hall. He entered his room, and she bit down on a spark of temper.

It had been three hours since she'd whispered that she'd like to tryst. Though she'd blatantly hinted, they hadn't since that initial glorious afternoon, and she didn't understand how he could resist her.

"Hello, darling," she cooed as he approached. She was naked, just a sheet concealing her, and for a second his smile appeared to slip, but she was positive it was a trick of the flickering candle.

"Pamela?" He seemed confused to see her. "What are you doing in here?"

"I waited in my boudoir"—she affected a credible pout—"but you never came. I was lonely."

Stretching, she let the covering fall so that her breasts were visible, and his attention perked up immediately. His randy phallus enlarged and pressed at his trousers.

"I was detained."

"By whom?"

She hated that she'd jumped to inquire—she sounded like a nagging fishwife—but she couldn't help herself. As she'd taken him under her wing, she couldn't have him cozying up to inappropriate people.

"Lord Stamford invited me to have a brandy. I didn't think I could refuse."

"No, you couldn't."

His gait was unsteady, so he'd had more than a single drink. They must have talked for hours, and the knowledge was bothersome. She wasn't keen on his being chummy with Marcus. There was no telling what the older man might advise the younger.

"What did he want?" she queried.

A shrewd gleam in his eye, he studied her. "He warned me about the perils of London."

"Were there many?"

"Mostly of the feminine variety."

"I should say so," she agreed. "You're not aware of how you've intrigued the ladies. You must watch the company you keep, or you could find yourself in trouble with the wrong girl."

"I certainly could."

She patted the bed, eager to have him join her. "Why don't you lie down and get comfortable?"

"What did you have in mind?"

"I thought we'd start up where we left off the other day." She stretched again, the sheet dropping to her abdomen, her privates barely shielded. "You look very tense. Would you like me to rub your back?"

For an eternity, he pondered the suggestion, and she

was disconcerted by his reticence. What was plaguing the immature fool? Considering how he was acting, he was lucky she didn't presume him to be a gay blade!

She shifted to her side, so he had an unimpeded view. "Have you ever had a massage before?"

"No."

"Why not let tonight be the first time?" She wet her bottom lip, taunting him with the memory of how she'd previously pleasured him. "You'll enjoy it very much."

His decision finally reached, he shrugged out of his jacket. "I'm sure I will."

She rose up on her knees, pulling him to her so that their torsos were melded, her nipples brushing his shirt. Without having to be instructed, he kissed her, and it was delicious, unrestrained ardor, his tongue in her mouth, his fingers on her breast. She'd spurred him past whatever restriction had held him in check.

She wanted him as naked as she, and she fumbled with his shirt, but she couldn't remove it fast enough, so she ripped at the fabric, tugging it down and off till his upper body was exposed. His chest was smooth, his skin silky, with no hair to mar it, and she stroked the velvety expanse, petting and caressing, plucking at his small nipples.

His cock surged, trying to burst from his pants, and she leaned back and dragged him with her so that, in a tangle of arms and legs, they tumbled onto the mattress.

He was limber, agile, and the embrace became more wild, his actions more confident. She rolled them so that she was on top, her hips straddling his, and she hovered over him with her palms braced on either side.

"I'm going to show you so many things," she murmured. "I'll make you plead. I'll make you beg. You
have no idea how much you'll come to love what I can
do for you."

Or how much you'll come to love me! she mused.
He would, too. He was so sweet, so naive, and she was
anxious to have him smitten. A wise woman could ac-
quire many boons from having such a charming boy
enamored of her, and no one had ever mistaken her for
being stupid. Christopher would forever celebrate that
he'd lost his virginity to her, and with her orchestrating
his future, his life would never be the same.

How could he fail to be captivated? And grateful?
Such a wealthy, powerful youngster might just be very,
very grateful.

"I'll tutor you so that you are a magnificent lover."
She dangled her nipple across his impatient lips.
"Would you like to learn?"

"Yes."

"You must focus on pleasing your partner."

"An excellent concept."

"A female can be aroused."

"Really?"

"She must be satisfied, more often than the man."

As if this was fabulous news, he chuckled.

"Suckle me," she directed. "As a babe would its
mother."

"Like this?" He latched onto the extended tip.

"Harder," she ordered. "Much harder. And play with
the other." She raised his hand to her other breast, il-
lustrating how he should mold and fondle.

He was an adept pupil, who implemented her every

command, and as he nursed, his gestures grew more assertive, more aggressive. He was a genius at reading her responses, at discovering how to make her squirm and writhe.

She'd meant to be in charge, to dictate the speed, but she was so stimulated that she could scarcely contain herself. He easily brought her to the edge, which surprised her. Normally, she had difficulty achieving an orgasm, and a man had to be extremely skilled to push her to climax.

The carnal endeavor was different with him, though she didn't understand why. She wanted the event to be special, for it to be more than the two of them groping around in the dark.

"Let's get your clothes off, darling."

She plucked at the buttons on his trousers, and he helped, shucking off his garments and shoes, and she gazed down the length of his athletic torso. He was flawless, virile and vibrant, his cock jutting out. She circled her fist around it, so he could thrust and parry.

His adolescent lusts were provoked, and he was ready to spill himself, but she wouldn't have him finishing in her hand. "Are you aware of how a man and woman copulate?"

"I've heard."

She guided his fingers between her legs, teaching him to investigate her shaved puss, her slippery sheath. "I'll take you inside my body. It will be wonderful for you. Like nothing you've ever felt before."

He had no reply, and if he was nervous, he didn't reveal it. Relaxing, she spread her thighs and drew him over her. She gripped his phallus and ushered him to her welcoming center, and he slid inside without impediment.

"Oh my!" His eyes widened with amazement.

"Yes, it's splendid."

She clasped his buttocks and moved her hips, demonstrating the rhythm, but the excess of sensation was overwhelming, and in the space of a heartbeat, he came, exploding with great relish. She hugged him until the agitation waned, and though his muscles had slackened, he was still implanted, his cock rigid and geared for another go-around. He looked sheepish, contrite, as if he'd done something wrong.

"I'm sorry it ended so fast," he said. "I couldn't stop myself."

"It was your first experience. A frenzied coupling is exactly what's expected."

"But it should be slower, shouldn't it? And more . . . romantic?"

What a dear boy! "With practice, you'll be able to control the spiral. That's half the fun, and the longer you delay, the more enjoyment you'll receive."

He grinned. "I think we should try it again."

"A marvelous notion."

Without so much as an intervening moment, he began to flex, instantly grasping what was required.

Kate sneaked into Marcus's room, determined to leave the ring and be shed of it—and him!—once and for all. She wasn't sure what she'd set in motion by drinking the potion, but she had to halt the whole bizarre business.

She couldn't be in love with Marcus Pelham! She absolutely would not be. She was too rational and pragmatic. Even though she scoffed at superstition, she was unnerved and desperate to break any connection she'd established with the licentious, influential noble-man. If parting with the ring would create peace of mind, and stability in her personal affairs, then return-ing it was worth any risk.

After her meeting with Selena, Kate was in a state, her emotions running at a fevered pitch. The slightest bump in the road would cause her to shatter, and should a catastrophe occur, she couldn't bear up.

The ring was a disaster waiting to happen. She had to discreetly dispose of it, and there was no better op-portunity than late afternoon.

Stamford lived in an apartment—over a gambling hall, of all places!—and he never showed his face in the town house unless he was bent on torturing herself or being rude to Melanie, so he was out. The servants were downstairs, having tea in the kitchen before they commenced with the elaborate preparations for supper. Kate could slip in and be gone in a thrice.

Her pulse galloping, she crept inside. She leaned against the cool wood of the door, listening, certain that if anyone jumped out, she would die of fright and morti-fication.

On a nearby dresser, there was a bowl where he'd thrown his jewelry. She tiptoed to it and deposited the ring; then she stirred the contents, making it appear as if the ring had been tossed in with the assorted clutter all along.

Oddly, as she relinquished it, she was deluged by a wave of sadness. It had represented excitement and drama, all the things she fantasized about in the dark of night but never had the courage to seek in the light of day. She was swamped by the impression that she was abandoning an important link to her real self.

A final time, she picked it up and clutched it to her heart. The gold was warm, and the stones seemed to glow and vibrate.

"Kate." Quietly, he called from behind her.

As if the ring had burned her, she dropped it and prayed. *Please, Lord, don't let it be Marcus. I'm so weak. I'm powerless to resist him or what he brings to my life.*

"Kate," he summoned again, "I'm so glad you're here."

As she spun toward him, her jumbled sentiments careened between dread and elation.

He was balanced against the doorjamb to the adjoining chamber, clad solely in a loose-fitting pair of white trousers that she imagined a sultan might wear when entertaining in his private harem. He'd been bathing, and his skin glistened with moisture. His hair was wet and swept off his forehead.

Never having viewed a male body before his, she was fascinated, enthralled, positive she was perusing a fine specimen. His shoulders were broad, his waist narrow, his legs lanky. His chest was covered with a matting of black hair. It was thick across the top; then it thinned in the center and descended to destinations she couldn't fathom.

He hadn't shaved, and his cheeks were shadowed, his eyes incredibly blue. He looked dangerous, tempting, seductive, and she was terrified about how she'd behave. If he but snapped his fingers, she would debase herself in any fashion he commanded.

Grinning, he asked, "Have you decided to filch more of my jewels?"

She couldn't speak, neither to deny his accusation nor to defend herself, and he pushed away from the threshold and approached until they were toe-to-toe. She was assailed by the smells of heated water and bathing salts.

Reaching around her, he tipped the bowl and detected the ring she'd hazarded limb and reputation to return.

"I see you've brought it back. Don't you want it anymore? Or has a gaudier trinket tickled your fancy?" Laughing, he held it up, studying it as if to ascertain whether the gems were still attached. "I'm afraid you can't have this one, but I'd be happy to have you choose another."

He offered her the collection, exhorting her to select a substitute, and the pile of priceless treasures glittered, impugning her, condemning her, for her commonness, her tediousness.

He sighed.

"You know, I really don't care if you steal from me"—he set the bowl on the dresser—"but I wish you wouldn't. I consider us to be friends. If you're in trouble, or you need my assistance, you can confide in me. I'll help you."

"I wasn't stealing," she blurted out. She was rigid as a board, her arms crushed to her sides, as she fought the overwhelming urge to stroke his chest. If she touched him, she couldn't predict what sin she might be spurred to commit.

He waited for her to explain herself or justify her actions, and when she didn't, his disappointment was clear. He'd expected more of her, or had presumed she'd trust him.

"Has something bad happened?"

She was startled by the question. "No, why?"

"You seem upset."

Gad, did she parade her problems on her sleeve, like some sort of banner?

"I'm not."

"You can tell me what it is, Kate. Despite what you've heard about me, I won't fail you."

He was so sincere, so earnest, and she yearned to divulge her woes. It was rare when people took an interest in her, when they evinced concern or bestowed their support. He had wide shoulders, the kind that could easily bear a woman's burdens, and it would be a relief to confess about her mother, about Selena, to probe his advice about the peculiarities with Selena's finances. He was rich, and likely dealt with money issues on a daily basis, but in the end, she couldn't proceed.

As Regina always counseled, Kate embarrassed herself when she talked about her parents. Their ignominies reflected poorly on her, made others speculate about her character, her integrity. Idiotic as it sounded, she was anxious for Stamford to like her and relish her company, which he appeared to do. Her meeting him was the only extraordinary event that had ever transpired to cheer her dull, dreary existence, and she wouldn't do anything to dampen his attention.

Besides, why would he immerse himself in her petty family dilemma? He boasted about his dearth of ties, and reveled in his seclusion and aloneness. He'd never understand why any of it mattered, and he'd deem her a fool for having imposed.

"I'm not distressed," she lied. "And I'm *not* a thief. I just . . . just stopped by because—"

"I missed you all day," he interrupted.

"Don't spew such ridiculous drivel."

"Why not?"

"Because I'm imprudent enough to want it to be true."

"Oh, Kate, do you think so little of me? That I would toy with you and lead you on with false flattery?" He mulled his words, then chuckled. "Don't answer that."

Without warning, he bent down and brushed a tender kiss across her lips. The move rattled her, flustered her. It was simply impossible to remain strong when he was so near. She was starved for affection, and she quickly lost the battle to contain her baser impulses. She pulled him close, the embrace growing into much more than it had started out to be.

They dawdled, kissing and caressing, and she couldn't have said how long they tarried, transfixed by the sweetness of the moment. Finally, he broke it off, and he clasped her hand.

"Come."

He escorted her into the adjacent room, which she knew from her previous misadventure was the location of his massive bed. It was the one fit for a king, where—she had no doubt!—he regularly consorted with all manner of decadent women.

If she went with him, what did it say about herself and her nature? What did it say about him and his attitude toward her?

Shockingly, she didn't care. He could suppose her to be promiscuous or rash, immoral or dissolute. She was eager for the pleasure and release he so masterfully gave her, and it dawned on her that, deep down, she'd been hoping he'd be at home. After her stressful visit to Selena, she'd needed to be with him. Even though she'd been sure he'd be off perpetrating whatever despicable deeds kept him occupied, a tiny part of her had wished he'd catch her.

How pathetic she was! Pining away and aching to be with him, even though it was folly! In such a short interval, he'd begun to mean too much to her, and though she was terrified by the prospects for heartbreak, she decided not to fight her attraction. There was something about him that called to her, that made her want to throw caution to the wind, to tempt fate and damn the consequences.

When she was around him, she felt alive and vital, not invisible but vibrant and appealing and worthy of his esteem.

She tightened their grip, signaling that she was complicit, a partner in debauchery, willing and disposed to misbehavior.

To her surprise, he ushered her past the bed, guiding her to the dressing room beyond. His ornate bathing tub was positioned in the center.

"What are we doing?" she queried.

"The water is still warm. I thought you might enjoy a bath."

A bath! It was such an extravagance, a normal occurrence during her childhood that had once been taken for granted but now was a delicious memory because it was hardly ever allowed.

"I believe I might," she tentatively assented, much more thrilled than she wanted to reveal.

"Just so you let me wash your back. Then, we'll make love all night."

A thousand wicked images careened through her

head, of the two of them wet, slippery, together in the basin. Did men and women perform such naughty antics? Was it common? How could she be twenty-five and never have heard of such dissipation? Dare she join him in his depravity? Was she ready to be corrupted?

With great deliberation, she pondered the questions, and the answer, when it arrived, was so easy, so exciting.

"Why not?" she responded.

Why not, indeed. After all, who was to tell her no?

9

Marcus unbuttoned her dress, taking his time, even though he yearned to rip off the drab garment. She was too exceptional, too spirited, to be relegated to a servant's dowdy attire, and it was a pity that she was consigned to such mediocrity.

The notion of her dreary prospects had him considering radical steps to alter her situation, but what would they be?

The only part she could play was that of mistress, and if he was reckless enough to ask her, he couldn't imagine her agreeing. What sane woman would have him? But if she said *yes,* was he prepared to follow through?

He didn't want her as his mistress. The label was demeaning and didn't express how he felt about her, yet he couldn't describe the role she should fill. He merely knew that he had to be with her, that he'd spent the entire day pondering her and devising furtive plans as to how they could philander more frequently without being detected.

How could such a massive mansion seem so accursedly small? There were too many inhabitants and not enough privacy. He'd like to whisk her away to his country home, just the two of them, flitting off in his carriage. They'd trifle and cavort until he'd sated himself, until he couldn't bear another second of her fascinating company, until he could concentrate on some topic besides her.

Was his obsession driving him mad? Or—perish the thought!—had that blasted potion impaired his mental capacities? If so, how should he neutralize the effects?

He tugged off her dress; then he eased her onto a chair. Her feet were so dainty, and he made a great show of removing her shoes, untying her garters, and rolling down her stockings. As with the negligee she donned when she was by herself, they were of a fine-quality lace, but worn to nothing, with many holes lovingly repaired, and he wondered again about her mother.

Blithely continuing, he stripped her, and she weathered it well, murmuring and blushing, and he suffered the strangest sense of unreality, as if he were outside himself, and observing as another man seduced her. While he had many faults, he never dabbled with innocents. They weren't worth the trouble, not when there were so many licentious strumpets available. It was out of character for him, but he couldn't desist.

She'd afflicted him like a terrible malady, an illness in his blood that he couldn't shake and for which there was no cure. He was pathetic, stricken, doomed.

Once he'd disrobed her to her chemise, he had her stand, and he slid the straps down her arms, watching as the tattered garment slithered down.

At the sudden nudity, he'd presumed she'd balk, but

she'd reached a conclusion about their relationship. She was anxious to transgress without being cajoled. What did her change of attitude portend? Was she growing fond? More than fond?

Oh, how he hoped she was! Throughout his life, he'd expended so much energy distancing himself from others that he could scarcely recall how to interact in a normal fashion. He wanted her to expect the best from him, to view him as a different man, a better man, from the one he actually was.

The chemise floated away, and confident and calm, she shucked out of it, as if her traipsing around so scandalously was a regular event.

"You're so beautiful, Kate." His appreciative gaze swept down her torso. She was perfectly formed, rounded where she should be, and flat where she should be, too. "Have I told you before?"

"No."

"Shame on me."

His body lurched to arousal, his cock heavy with the need to be pressed against her. With the pertness of her nipples, the auburn tuft between her legs, she taunted him to wickedness. He couldn't wait to touch her there, to taste her there.

Clutching her hand, he guided her into the tub, and she snuggled down, reveling in the heat.

"Ooh," she cooed, "what a luxury!"

"If I'd known I could get you to smile at me like that, over something as simple as a bath, I'd have offered it days ago."

"It's the sweetest gift you could have given me."

"Shall I scrub your hair?"

"It would take forever to dry."

"We can brush it out before the fire."

"You'd light a fire? In the middle of the afternoon? How very extravagant!" She laughed, the sultry sound of it billowing around the small room.

"I'm rich. If I want a fire in June, I'll have one."

"Have you any idea of how lucky you are?"

"Yes."

Pulling up a stool, he sat behind her, and she dipped under the water. He soaped her hair, then had her douse herself so he could rinse it. When he'd finished, he poured her a glass of brandy.

"Drink this."

"Hard spirits? I'll be useless the rest of the evening."

"We'll have more fun if you're a bit intoxicated."

"You're the worst influence."

"Good."

She relaxed against the edge, as he busied himself with combing her tresses, the lengthy strands dangling to the floor. She allowed him to pamper her, and he suspected she wasn't coddled very often. No doubt working for Regina Lewis made for a difficult existence.

Did anyone care for Kate? Did anyone love her? Or was she all alone in the world, as he was himself?

The water began to cool, and he quickly washed her, a few swipes with a cloth, but not indulging as he'd intended.

With each movement, he was teased with naughty glimpses, which were rousing him to recklessness, and he couldn't predict what he might do. He was close to climbing in with her, to relieving her of her chastity. Was she ready for such a consequence? Was he?

Earlier, when he'd realized it was she sneaking in his door, he'd had such nefarious designs on her, but now that the prurient episode had arrived, he wasn't sure how to proceed. He needed to rationalize and reflect, so he had to maneuver her away from the tub. It occurred to him that he should escort her to his bed, though why he imagined snuggling with her on the plush, wide mattress would be any safer was a question he didn't dare ponder.

He helped her out and wrapped her in his robe, cinching the belt around her tiny waist, and rolling the sleeves. She peered up at him, her green eyes unafraid and trusting him much more than she ought. She appeared impossibly young, out of her element, and his dormant conscience prickled to wakefulness.

What was he thinking, dallying with her? Was he bent on ruination? Was that his plan? Why was he so willing to endanger her welfare? If they were discovered, she could lose all, and he was undeserving of her assuming such a risk. He genuinely treasured her, and couldn't bear it if anything bad happened, so what was he about?

He led her to the outer chamber, but as they entered, she halted, staring at him, and seeming to see much more than he wanted her to discern. He shifted, uneasy with her perception.

"Is this where you entertain all your paramours?" she asked.

"No. Never."

"Marcus," she scolded, "I know that's not true."

Having temporarily forgotten that she'd observed him with Pamela, he flushed, surprised to find himself ashamed. What must her opinion be?

"It's very rare, Kate," he answered truthfully. Pamela was the only one, and those encounters were infrequent, instigated by her when she craved some boon to which he wouldn't agree. "I don't even live in this house."

"You're here constantly."

"Merely because *your* room is just down the stairs."

"You are so full of it."

"I am not! I'm crazy about you."

He grinned, wanting them to progress beyond the awkward moment, but she flashed a skeptical scowl. She didn't believe his pronouncement, and he was irked that she had so little confidence in his attraction to her. If she could read his mind, she'd be shocked by the level of his fascination.

"It will be all right, Kate," he said quietly, recognizing that the statement was inadequate but not certain how to reassure her.

He had no guarantees. He couldn't so much as swear to protect her from scandal or dishonor, but long after the Lewises had left town, and he never saw Kate again, he would remember how she'd looked lying on his bed.

Not a man prone to whimsy, he didn't comprehend why he was being overwhelmed by such romantic notions, but with each passing hour, his feelings were more outlandish. He was enamored, smitten, and he hadn't the faintest idea why. They were scarcely acquainted, yet he felt that he'd known her a thousand years.

He clambered up and stretched out, and though she was reluctant, she followed. He draped her across him, her breasts flattened to his chest, her thigh splayed across his own.

Out of the blue, she inquired, "Are you in love with Lady Pamela?"

"My lord, no. I loathe her."

"But you occasionally welcome her here, don't you?" It was an offhand way of admitting that Kate really had wandered in that strange night.

"She's visited," he blandly divulged, "but not at my invitation."

"Yet, you permit her to stay."

"I'm not so foolish that I'd decline what's freely offered."

"And you can engage in physical intimacies, even though you detest her? I don't understand how. I thought people had to be married."

While he gamboled through the seedy side of London, she was so inexperienced, and her naïveté underscored how low he'd fallen, how pure she was, and how defiled he was.

How could he presume to trifle with her? She was so fine, while he was so tainted.

"We're not married," he explained, "but we've been very intimate."

She blushed to the tips of her toes. "Is it common among adults?"

"What?"

"All this . . . this . . . touching and kissing?"

"Yes."

"So if I enjoy it, I'm not wanton?"

"You're very normal, Kate. Probably the most *normal* person I've ever met."

He conjectured about her history. Why was she always fretting about being too lustful? Over the course of their relationship, he hoped he'd alleviate her apprehension.

"Will you make me a promise?" she asked.

"Whatever is within my power to bestow."

"Swear to me that your days of cavorting with Lady Pamela are over. It's so wrong."

"Are you worried about my immortal soul?"

"Absolutely, you bounder. But I also can't tolerate the prospect of your doing the things to her that you do to me."

It was a possessive request, and typically, he'd have refused, just on general principles. He didn't like people telling him what to do, and he definitely never allowed others to order him about, but he was charmed that she was concerned, that she liked him enough to demand better behavior.

"It is an easy pledge to render," he declared, a cheerful tempest blossoming inside, "and will be a simple vow to keep."

"Thank you."

She kissed him, sealing their pact, and he felt so cherished, so extraordinary. Perhaps, in her company, he would be redeemed, after all.

He loosened the belt on her robe, then pushed at the lapels, baring her center so he could caress her breast. "I adore your body."

"Will you show me how you entertain the women you bring here? I want to know what it's like."

He considered reiterating that he never had guests, but she wouldn't believe him. Her estimation of his character was too miserable. Besides, they had limited opportunity for interaction, and he wouldn't spend it arguing about his flaws.

"I've already exposed you to some of it, and we can try more, but we can't fully make love."

"Why not? Don't you wish to?"

"More than anything, but it would involve my ridding you of your virginity."

"So?"

"Then, you could never marry."

"But if I later wed, how would my husband determine that I wasn't a maid?" She blushed again. "I'm sorry. I'm so ignorant in the ways of the world."

"Which isn't so bad." How marvelous it would be if *he* could return to that innocent era when there were still mysteries.

"I wouldn't agree. I'm always in the dark, wondering about information that other adults take for granted."

He let his hand slither down, to her tummy, to her crotch, and he cupped her. "This is a special spot on a female. It's for mating."

"How does it occur? I've been so curious."

"We're built differently. I have a sort of . . . of . . ." He hadn't realized it would be so difficult to clarify the details to someone who didn't know them. "A sort of rod between my legs, and if we were to proceed, I'd thrust it inside you."

"Inside me?"

"Yes, and then I would flex my hips. The friction is pleasant, and causes a liquid to spew out of the tip. It contains the seed that plants a babe."

"You're joking."

"No."

"But if we were to . . . to mate, I still don't understand how my future husband would detect it."

"You have a thin piece of skin, here, and at the initial joining, it's torn. There's a bit of pain, and you'd bleed."

"It won't grow back?"

"No."

"So if we would decide to progress, I would need to ponder the ramifications very carefully."

"Yes, and I can assure you that I'm not worth such a sacrifice."

"I wouldn't be too sure."

She smiled, and he hugged her close. "You are so good for me. You make me happy."

"Really?"

"Yes."

"I'm glad."

More bold than she'd been on any occasion previous, she rested her palm on his abdomen, directly over the area where his randy phallus was pressing at his pants.

"In these trousers, you resemble an Arabian sheik."

"They were a gift from a friend who'd traveled the Sahara."

"They suit you. Much more than your fashionable attire."

"Maybe I should scandalize London by wearing them when I'm out and about."

"Now that's a sight I'd pay to see." She laughed again, the sound trickling over him like a soothing waterfall.

"May I look at you?" she queried.

"I don't think you should."

She arched a brow. "Have you gone shy on me all of a sudden?"

"Never. A man can become too aroused, to where he can't curb his impulses. If we're both naked, I'm not positive I can control myself."

"You'd never hurt me," she insisted.

"Not intentionally, but there's a brute inside, waiting to leap out."

"I'm not afraid of what lurks inside you."

It was a comment on more than his sexual drives. She was saying she trusted him, but he was only a mortal human being, and she was so gorgeous and goading him beyond constraint.

For once, he'd meant to be firm, to let his buried chivalry save her from herself. She wasn't aware of how rapidly passion could spiral, how fiercely it could sizzle, or how much damage could be inflicted before cooler heads prevailed. But his body had disconnected from his mind, and he was pulling at the drawstring on his trousers, loosening the front so that she could begin her journey of discovery.

He guided her fingers under the fabric, folding them around his elongated staff, demonstrating how to squeeze and stroke. She was an eager pupil, and it was torture, trying to remain detached while she played and learned, while she murmured her maidenly oohs and aahs.

He steered her to his breast, instructing her on how to suckle his nipple, and she enthusiastically set herself to the task. She was adept at judging his reaction, and she quickly deduced how to make him squirm and writhe, how to garner the maximum response.

As he should have grasped, she wasn't satisfied with mere touching. She had to see him, and she abandoned his chest, and trailed down his stomach, till she was hovered over his loins.

"May I?" she repeated, her hands at his waistband.

"Yes," he ground out, unable to deny her any request. He was so provoked that he felt as if he were made of glass, that with her slightest caress, he would shatter into tiny pieces.

She moved the material and froze, studying him as if he were a curious scientific specimen, and he was delighted to note that she wasn't frightened or appalled.

"Oh my," she breathed, "it's so much larger than I imagined." She smoothed across the length, measuring the girth, flirting with the crown. "Are they the same on every man?"

"Nearly. Some are bigger; some are smaller."

"And yours?"

"Bigger than most."

"I can't fathom how it would fit into me. Will you show me?"

"Not today."

She pouted. "Why?"

"You're not ready."

"Why don't you let me be the judge?"

"No."

"Tyrant!"

"Always."

She was so beautiful, so rumpled and adorable. He yanked the robe off her shoulders so that it fell to her waist, so that he could stare at her bosom. He fondled her nipple, the sensation jolting his cock.

"Lick me with your tongue," he commanded.

Considering that this was her first encounter with male nudity, he was behaving badly, but he couldn't have the tryst conclude without somehow being inside her. He wouldn't forge on to ruination, so he'd settle for the alternative, though he didn't suppose he'd endure for two seconds.

He clasped her neck to direct her, but she went willingly, impatient to comply. She laved him with short bursts, lapping at the sexual juice oozing from the tip, driving him wild without even recognizing that she was.

"Is this your seed?"

"No. It's an indication that I'm very titillated, that I'm close to finishing."

"How will I know when you're through?"

"When I spill myself."

"So I'm doing everything correctly?"

"Oh yes." He clutched his phallus and brushed it across her lips. "Open for me. Take me inside."

"Into my mouth?"

"Yes."

But for an instant, she hesitated; then she eased over the blunt end. Not delving too deeply, he flexed, and she was so hot, so snug. He gazed at the ceiling, trying to clear his thoughts, to focus on nothing, so that the glorious moment would last, but he was too stimulated.

Jerking away, he drew her up his torso.

She didn't comprehend his abrupt rush. "What is it?"

"I need to come."

"I don't know what to do."

"Wrap your arms around me," he advised. "Hold me tight."

He hugged her to him, pressing against her belly, and he thrust, once, twice, thrice, and emptied himself. His seed surged out in a steamy wave, a sticky glue binding them together.

With a groan of elation, he careened across the universe, the spiral so intense that he couldn't believe his level of gratification. If his cock had been buried in her sheath, his heart might have quit beating.

Gradually, the bliss waned, and he floated to earth, Kate snuggled to him, and he was chagrined, wondering how she'd weathered the ordeal. He shifted away, and peered into her exquisite face. She was so lovely, so exceptional, so much more than he deserved.

"I'm sorry," he started.

"For what?"

"I'd planned to go slower." Embarrassed by his display, he shrugged. "You arouse me beyond my limits."

"How fabulous."

"You vixen." He swatted her on the rear.

Looking shy and demure, she mentioned, "I liked it."

"Good. Because there will be many more such frolics in our future."

"You're insatiable."

"Only with you. I can't get enough."

Charmed by his statement, she sighed. "I'll pretend you mean it."

"Oh, I do, my darling Kate. I definitely do." He kissed her, then scooted away, walking to the dressing room and returning with a wet cloth and a towel. He washed away all traces of his iniquity; then he cuddled himself to her, once more.

"When you have a release like that," she inquired, "how does it feel?"

"I expect very much how it feels when it happens to you."

"Ooh, you lucky dog."

"I am, aren't I?"

She reached down and stroked him, and though he'd just come to high heaven, his phallus leapt to attention. "I didn't realize it could occur without your being inside me."

"I can proceed at the drop of a hat," he boasted, "and I'll teach you all the ways to make it transpire."

"May we commence right now?"

"Absolutely."

He rolled her onto her back, excited and eager to begin anew.

∾ 10 ∾

Elliot Featherstone dawdled at the rear of the ballroom, hoping to bump into Lady Melanie. Though he'd
finagled a prior rendezvous, he'd grown too foxed, tot-
ted off to gamble, and forgotten that he'd planned to
meet with the blasted girl.

She was so naive, so ripe for the plucking, and he
couldn't believe how he'd messed up. As evidenced by
her letting him spike her punch with whiskey, she was a
weak child, who would be susceptible to all manner of
bad influence, and thus, precisely the sort with whom
he was desperate to associate.

He was out of funds, out of luck, and ready to alter
his circumstances. Whenever Regina extolled Melanie's
fat dowry, he listened carefully, taking special note of
the cash that would be unloaded on her fiancé, immediately upon signing the marital contracts. While
members of the *ton* smirked, writing off the family as
provincial and coarse, he recognized a golden opportunity.

At age thirty-five, and the fourth son of an impoverished, scandal-ridden baronet, he was dead broke. His
meager inheritance was spent, and his markers due.
Among the Quality, penury was not a cardinal sin, so
he was still welcomed in the finest homes, but he flitted
from engagement to engagement so that his creditors
wouldn't catch up with him.

Pamela was diligently working for a match between
Marcus and Melanie. Should a union be arranged, Elliot
would fade into the background, but he couldn't imagine
Stamford proposing. When it became clear that matrimony was out of the question, what would happen to
Lady Melanie's money? When the fortune could be
showered on himself, it was a shame to have it wasted.

The crowd on the dance floor parted, and she espied
him. For once, she was away from her mother, her chaperone absent, and he nodded toward the verandah, indicating that he was going outside and she should follow.

Would she?

Probably, she was furious that he'd stood her up,
and he had a dozen good excuses as to why he had.
There was no way in hell he'd have her suspecting that
he'd been too intoxicated to recollect the assignation,
too bent on winning a few pounds at the faro tables to
worry about her delicate sensibilities.

However, if there was one thing at which he ex-
celled, it was talking. He could charm himself out of
any embarrassing situation, and she was so inexperienced, it would never occur to her that he was lying.

He slipped out and hurried down into the massive
garden, desirous of being shielded by the trees and
shrubs. Guests were strolling the lanterned paths, and it

wouldn't do to have anyone see them together. Not yet anyway.

When he was *discovered* with Lady Melanie, it would be orchestrated to produce the maximum consequence, and he was determined that she be safely snared in his net before he made a rash move.

In a matter of seconds, she flitted out behind him, and she wandered into the garden, too.

"I'm here," he murmured as she went by his hiding spot.

She crept off the walk, and he motioned for quiet, then guided her to the gardener's shed at the back of the yard. It was isolated and a perfect location for privacy.

Moonlight flowed in a small window, enough for him to observe that she was nervous, but excited, about the clandestine tryst.

Foolish tart! His scheme to lead her astray would be so easy to implement.

Shocking him, she commenced with, "I'm sorry I couldn't sneak to the mews the other night. Can you forgive me?"

There is a God! he thought to himself, and he changed tactics and feigned affront. "I waited for over an hour! Where were you?"

"My mother insisted on chatting. I couldn't escape till after two."

"She treats you abominably." It was the best direction to wend the conversation. They would be allies in their dislike of her mother. "What did she want?"

"She was ranting on about Stamford and his intentions toward me—when I'm convinced he has none."

She shook with fervor. "I'm sick to death of hearing about him!"

"I'll bet you are, you poor dear."

A veritable reservoir of compassion, he patted her shoulder, as he retrieved his flask, had a hefty swallow, then offered it to her. She imbibed, and when she tried to return it, he urged her to indulge. Hastily, she swilled much more than was wise, and he was tickled by her lack of restraint.

"I've been so anxious to speak with you," she confessed.

"Have you now?"

She gripped his wrist, her cheeks rosy with the alcohol's effect. "Tell me what you've learned about Stamford."

He pretended to consider, when he wouldn't dream of keeping her in suspense. "I'm not positive if I should, Melanie. May I call you Melanie?"

"You may when we're alone," the little snob stated. "In public, I can't have others realizing we're friendly."

The petty upstart! Who did she think she was? Centuries before her family had dug its first vein of coal out of the mines in Cornwall, *his* family had been one of the most prominent in England!

He forced down his anger. "Melanie, it might be too distressing for you to be apprised of Stamford's motives."

"What do you mean?" She leaned nearer. "Divulge your secrets. I'm begging you!"

"You're the innocent in this." He sighed. "I suppose I must."

"Don't omit a single detail!"

"Stamford needs to marry for money."

"But he seems so rich."

"For the moment. But if he's not wed by his thirty-first birthday, he will lose it all. It's detestable that your mother hasn't enlightened you."

"I'm not sure she knows."

"Trust me," he said. "I'm cognizant of the facts that Lady Pamela imparted in garnering your mother's decision to sacrifice you." He let the implication smolder that Regina and Pamela were plotting against her.

"If he's so disinterested, why has he agreed to my being invited to London?"

"Because no one else will have him, darling."

"I was his last choice?"

He acted pained, and she blanched and swayed. To steady her, he hugged her to him. "My apologies. I shouldn't have been so blunt."

"No . . . no . . . it's all right."

She was distracted, and he used her perplexity to touch her as he oughtn't, resting his hands on her waist, stroking her arm. Down the bodice of her gown he had a stellar view of her cleavage. With her plump, curvaceous breasts, she was a sweet morsel who would entice him sufficiently when the time came.

"Why have others refused him?" she asked.

"He's a cad and a scoundrel. He drinks and gambles and cavorts with wild women." He paused. "Dare I mention it?"

"Yes, yes!"

"He supports three mistresses." A nasty lie, but she could never investigate whether it was true.

"Three!"

"The city is agog with stories of his low character,

and there's not a father in town who'd allow him in the door."

"Mother is aware of this situation?"

Having no idea of what Regina knew or didn't, he shrugged, affecting an air of possessing much confidential information.

"Are they all gossiping and laughing at me behind my back?"

"Don't take it to heart, Melanie," he soothed. "They're a vicious bunch."

Fuming, she stared at the floor, and finally, she muttered, "I have to return to the ballroom."

"You can't leave. Not when you're so upset."

"Regina will be searching for me."

"But there's so much more I need to reveal, so much I want us to share." He brushed his thumb across her bottom lip, studying her carefully, having her sense his manly appreciation. Though she was a maiden, she'd have to be a dunce not to deduce his intent.

"I have to go."

"You deserve a husband who loves you," he declared. "A husband who cherishes you for who you are, who understands and reveres you. Not some selfish, immature knave who will bring you naught but misery."

"I'm so confused." As if she had a dreadful headache, she rubbed her temples. "I'm not certain what's best."

"If you wed him, he'll continue to philander with every strumpet in town. He'll flaunt his paramours in your face. Could you bear it?"

"No . . . no . . ."

"Let me help you, Melanie. Let me rescue you from your mother's folly."

"I have to go," she repeated. Visibly disturbed, she stumbled out of the shed, and he permitted her to escape.

Smiling, he watched her race away. He'd planted fertile seeds, and he'd water them and wait for them to grow.

"Selena!" Agitated and out of breath, Edith Fitzsimmons rushed into the parlor. "The Earl of Doncaster is here."

"You're joking."

"No."

"Dio mio!"

Selena couldn't believe it. During his prior, abbreviated visit, she'd experienced a stunning connection with him, but she hadn't anticipated that he felt the same. In the past few years, she'd suffered too many disappointments to be optimistic.

Her first gentleman caller! And an earl! After she had spent so many poverty-stricken, lonely months in the dreary, gray city, it was too much to absorb.

Pulse pounding with excitement, she leapt to her feet, patting her hair and smoothing her dress. How she wished she'd had some warning, that she had a new gown or exotic jewels to wear for the marvelous occasion.

"How do I look?"

"Fabulous, as always." Edith linked their fingers and squeezed tight. "He seems like a fine young man. He could change your life."

"I'm hoping."

"At a minimum, he could find out what your sister's done with your money."

"Let's not discuss it now, Edith. Please."

Convinced that Kate was a thief, Edith constantly blamed her, but Selena wouldn't listen to any accusations. Edith had been a godsend, had mothered and guided Selena through her assimilation to England. Selena trusted her and valued her advice, but Kate was Selena's only living relative, and she wouldn't tolerate a bad word being uttered about her.

"You should broach the subject," Edith chided. "He might assist you."

"Edith"—Selena was determined to be happy—"all of a sudden, it's a grand day. The earl is here, when we least expected it. We can't have him dawdling on the stoop! Show him in; show him in."

With a smile, Edith recognized that she couldn't win the argument. Selena might be sixteen, but she was strong willed. Adversity had been an excellent tutor, and she knew her own mind, was definite in her decisions, mature beyond her age.

"Shall I remain while the two of you chat?"

"Don't you dare!"

"But I've never actually acted as your chaperone before. I ought to earn my keep."

"What are you supposing he'll do? Make mad, passionate love to me—with you loitering in the hall?"

"He's a handsome lad," Edith acknowledged. "If he gets frisky, it wouldn't be a catastrophe."

"No," Selena giggled, "it wouldn't be. Go let him in!"

Posing herself on the tattered sofa, she tarried, as Edith greeted him, as they started toward the parlor. At the last second, Selena tugged at the bodice of her dress, lowering it to display more cleavage.

She didn't imagine Lord Doncaster had arrived to converse about the weather!

Edith maintained that British girls were very prim and proper, that they were strictly raised, and their interaction with boys severely controlled. Selena had been reared in Venice, and her father's Italian blood flowed through her veins. She was on her own, and forced by circumstances to forge her own path.

The Fates had brought Christopher Lewis to her home, and there had to be a reason. She would seize whatever joy she could from the astonishing opportunity.

As he entered, her heart literally skipped a beat. He was so attractive, so tall and sure of himself.

"Lord Doncaster," she welcomed, "how wonderful to see you again."

"Call me Christopher."

"I will. And you must call me Selena."

She rose and tried to curtsy, but he wouldn't permit it. For an eternity, they stood, not talking, but staring at each other like a pair of enamored half-wits.

"I had to come to you," he admitted.

"I'm so glad you have."

He was so close that the toes of his boots dipped under the hem of her gown. Their bodies were almost touching, and sparks of exhilaration shot between them.

"You're Kate's sister, aren't you?"

She couldn't predict how Kate might wish her to answer the question, but as for herself, she wouldn't lie. "She's my half sister."

"Ah . . . that explains the resemblance. You have the same mother?"

"Yes. Are you familiar with the details of her torrid *amore*?"

"Not very. My mother rails about it whenever she's

in a mood, or when she's being horrid to Kate, but at Doncaster, it's mostly been swept under the rug."

"*My* mother would have been devastated to hear that!" Remembering her flamboyant mother, Selena laughed. "She liked to make a stir, and she'd have hated to think her antics had been forgotten."

"She must have been quite a character to have braved such a scandal."

"She was in love, and she didn't feel she had any option but to run away."

"Yet she left Kate."

"Not intentionally." It hurt to have him assuming the worst. "She sent for Kate, after she was settled in Italy."

"Really? That information was certainly kept quiet."

"There were legal proceedings, but she was deemed an unfit mother, so her custody requests were denied. She went to her grave regretting her loss of Kate."

"How did you end up in London?"

"I traveled here after my parents died. Mother arranged for it in her will. She'd planned for Kate and me to be a family, but it never occurred to her that it would be so difficult for us to be together. Or that I would have to reside in London."

"Why don't you move nearer to Doncaster?"

Blushing, she was saddened that he'd mention the painful topic. "You know why I can't."

"No, I don't."

She assessed him, speculating as to whether he was a very proficient liar or he simply didn't recollect. "Your mother told Kate that she'd discussed it with you, and that you'd said no."

He sputtered and fumbled for a comment. "Regina claimed that she'd discussed it with *me*?"

"Yes." Ashamed to dredge it up, she looked down at the rug. "You thought my presence would be harmful, that I might rouse animosity among the neighbors or the servants."

He was silent for such a lengthy period that she was in agony. It was ruined before it had begun! Oh, when would she learn to curb her tongue!

"Selena," he murmured, and his voice was so sweet and so gentle that she hazarded a peek at him. "This is the sole reference I've received as to any of this. Until I met you the other day, I had no idea you existed. I swear it."

"Why would your mother spew such a vile tale?"

"It's her way, but it's not mine. She can be very vicious."

"Why don't you stop her?"

"I've only recently grown old enough to where I can stand up to her. She makes many decisions without consulting me, which was necessary when I was younger, but I'm gradually wresting control. She doesn't want to relinquish it, so it's challenging."

"Kate says you'll be a fine earl."

"Kate is right." He glanced toward the hall. "Will Mrs. Fitzsimmons be joining us?"

"I believe it's her nap time"—she winked—"and she's a very heavy sleeper."

"Marvelous."

He led her to the sofa and sat down. When she would have seated herself next to him, he tugged her onto his lap, her bottom balanced on his thigh, and he tipped her forward so that her breasts fell onto his chest.

She wondered what he had in mind, and was already deliberating as to how much she'd allow, and she was sure she'd *allow* quite a bit. She was no simpering miss. From her mother's experiences, she was aware of the trouble in which men and women could entangle themselves, but she wasn't about to forego the naughty behaviors he'd attempt—although she wouldn't let him go too far.

A female had to keep some of her secrets, had to give him a reason to visit again.

"How long can you stay?" she asked.

"Till Mrs. Fitzsimmons arrives and chases me out." He grinned. "If I'm lucky, she won't awaken till tomorrow morning."

She grinned, too. "Why don't I lock the door so we're not disturbed?"

"Why don't you?"

She probably should have been worried or afraid about being sequestered with him, but she wasn't. If they spent a few hours together, who was to protest? There was no one to catch them, so there would be no damage to her reputation, and as to what Christopher might instigate, he would never hurt her.

He helped her to her feet, and she raced across the floor, spun the key, and hurried back. With open arms, he was waiting for her, and he pulled her close and kissed her, his lips resting lightly upon hers.

Her first kiss! Bestowed by the most handsome, most dashing man she'd known since her gallant father. It was heaven, it was bliss, and, reveling in every second of the embrace, she shut her eyes and let him sweep her away.

Regina lounged on Lady Pamela's verandah, fanning herself and nibbling on a plate of candies that Pamela's slothful servants had finally been trained to keep filled. With how lazy some of them were, it was amazing they retained their employment. At Doncaster, she'd have had them flogged, then discharged.

Out in the garden, Melanie was walking with Kate. It was clear that they were arguing, and Regina was curious as to what had them in such a dither, although with Melanie it could be any frivolity.

Regina had tried to rear her appropriately, to inspire good manners and a pleasant disposition, but a mother could only do so much. Despite her efforts to the contrary, Melanie was spoiled, and she didn't comprehend how privileged she was to be so pampered and about to marry Stamford.

At the moment, he was playing hard to get, which was pointless. Regina had concluded that the marriage would transpire—if for no other purpose than to show Stamford that she would have her way.

She had unlimited perseverance and stamina, and if Stamford had any notion of her resolve, he'd speed matters along by making an appointment with his tailor to be fitted for his wedding suit.

Just then, both girls turned toward the verandah and frowned. It was obvious they'd been gossiping about her, and Regina scrutinized them. They were acting oddly, having furtive conversations and hurling barbed remarks. Melanie, in particular, had something eating at her, but she was too timid to voice it aloud.

She was surly, defiant, eager to quarrel, and Regina was weary of her attitude. Melanie was about to be Stamford's wife, and the sooner she came to terms with the idea, the smoother the nuptials would be.

The pair strolled down another path, and it was Kate

who held Regina's attention. She hadn't seen Kate in days and was shocked to note that her appearance was greatly altered.

Her eyes were brighter, her skin more radiant, her hair more lustrous. Even though she was attired in the most drab gown, she was glowing, and as she stood next to Melanie there was no question who was more attractive.

Unfortunately, Kate's mother's reckless beauty was surging to the fore, which bothered Regina enormously. The prospect of Kate's exuding some of the harlot's winsomeness and elegance had always terrified Regina, and her worst fears were being realized.

There was an aura of . . . of *joy* about Kate, too. She emanated a happiness and contentment that hadn't been there previously.

When had this happened? And what had caused it?

Regina was disturbed. If she'd been pressed to describe the transformation, she'd have said Kate looked as if she'd fallen in love, which was ludicrous.

What man with any sense would be interested? She was the impoverished daughter of a whore, and blood would tell.

Still, Regina was concerned by the peculiar metamorphosis. She had the immediate future arranged, and she didn't want any surprises.

As they advanced toward her again, Regina waved them to the verandah, and they marched slowly, trudging on as though facing the gallows. They approached and Melanie snidely queried, "What is it?"

"You've been out in the sun too long."

"So?"

Her insolence had to end! Regina wouldn't have the

servants tittering that she couldn't garner respect from
her own child. "Head to your room and have your maid
lay out the clothes you're wearing for tonight's soiree.
I'll be up shortly to check them."

"I don't wish to go to my room."

Regina counted to ten, calming herself before she
behaved rashly where everyone could view her ill hu-
mor. When her temper was under control, she rose.
Melanie stood her ground, though she was trembling.

"Leave at once," Regina ordered very quietly, "before
you get yourself into even more trouble." She grabbed
Melanie's forearm. Anyone watching from a distance
would have noticed nothing untoward, but Regina was
pinching the skin so tightly that Melanie would be
bruised.

Melanie's eyes flooded with tears, from pain but
also rage. "You think you can make me do anything."

"Yes, I do."

Melanie yanked away and flounced off, slamming
the door as she stormed into the house, and not caring
what the servants might say about her tantrum. A whipping would settle her down, and Regina would administer it as soon as she'd finished with Kate.

Kate was hovering, embarrassed at having witnessed the squabble, but over the years she'd observed
many, and she would keep her comments to herself.

Regina returned to her chair, feigning boredom, as if
she hadn't just been humiliated by her impertinent offspring, and gestured for Kate to follow.

"My post was delivered from Doncaster, and I have
correspondence for you."

"From Selena?"

"Yes. She's remitted a stack of outrageous bills, and

you'll need to sign the authorizations so I can send them to Mr. Thumberton for disbursement."

As a female, Kate couldn't function as Selena's trustee, so her mother had named the attorney Thumberton. But for some reason, she'd dictated that Kate review and approve the payments before they went to the solicitor. Regina figured the deceased woman had wanted to force her two daughters to interact, which had resulted in a huge boon. For Regina!

Selena's communications were conveyed to Doncaster; Regina examined them, and proceeded accordingly.

How was naive, gullible Kate ever to learn that the receipts weren't genuine?

Kate seated herself, pouring through the *faux* invoices, and she scowled, for once, perplexed by the lengthy columns of numbers. On a page of household expenditures, she traced her finger over and over the line where Regina had added several cases of expensive wine to the list. She stared at the sum as if it were written in a foreign language.

"It's such a large amount of money, isn't it?" she murmured. "It seems so excessive for one young girl."

"Your sister is a terrible spendthrift. But then, so was your mother. She must take after her."

Kate glanced up, and there was an anger about her that had Regina unnerved. While usually Kate didn't listen when Regina deprecated her mother, suddenly the remark had her steaming.

"Why would you presume to be an expert on my mother's fiscal habits?"

In the nearly two decades Regina had been acquainted with Kate, she had never dared sass on a single occasion. No matter how Regina belittled or goaded, Kate swallowed down the insults and innuendoes, accepting that her parents' shame was her own to bear.

"Why would you suppose?" Regina sneered. "When we originally moved to Doncaster, I analyzed the books. She was a spoiled, wasteful nuisance, who almost bankrupted the estate with her selfish acquisitions."

"I don't believe you," Regina was stunned to hear her retort. It was the only truly rude, discourteous statement Kate had ever uttered in her presence, and Regina was even more disconcerted. What had come over her?

"Your mother raised Miss Bella in the same lavish fashion, giving her everything, coddling her by making her assume she could have whatever she wanted. Bella can't practice restraint, because she's never had limits."

"You don't know about what you're talking."

Regina bristled. "If I needed your opinion, Kate, I'd ask for it, and I suggest you be silent. I've had enough disrespect from Melanie lately, and I'm not about to brook any from you."

Not cowed in the least, Kate boldly met her livid gaze. "Something's not right about these debts, and I should like to discuss them with Mr. Thumberton. It would be very convenient to speak with him while we're in London. How would I contact him for an appointment?"

"Write him a note." She pushed pen and ink across the table. "I'll have it dispatched to him, although why you'd imagine that such an important gentleman would allow you to bother him is beyond me."

"I'll inquire politely," she said, oozing sarcasm.

Regina watched as Kate drafted her request, and she smirked to herself.

Poor Kate. It was like stealing candy from a baby. She was so trusting, so unsuspecting.

Thumberton would never receive her letter, and if she foolishly grew impatient and conferred with him behind Regina's back, she would be in for a surprise. With the false costs Regina had concocted to hide her embezzlement, there was a clear trail as to the thief, and it led directly to Kate.

What a pity it would be to lose her! Of all the people at Doncaster, she was the easiest to mold, the simplest to manipulate. Their relationship had been so fruitful, so rewarding, but Regina hadn't expected it to last forever.

As Kate sanded the ink and folded the message, Regina speculated as to whether she shouldn't parlay with Thumberton, herself, and set the conclusion in motion. From the very start, she was anxious to shape the ending, but there was no hurry.

She had all the time in the world, while Kate's destiny had speeded up and was hurling toward her like a runaway carriage.

~ 11 ~

"Are you going to marry Melanie?"

"Do you think I should?"

Kate studied Marcus, trying to decipher his thoughts. He was across the room, naked, fussing with the fire, and grinning as if she'd just told a humorous joke.

She was sprawled on his bed, naked, too, which was her normal condition when she was with him. They never crossed paths during the day, but by night they philandered as if each rendezvous would be their last, and Kate was astonished by how quickly she'd become a fallen woman.

With Marcus urging her to transgress, the plunge had been effortless, and she hadn't found any reason to stop. Why deny herself such pleasure and joy?

When her magical trip to London was concluded— which would be soon—and she returned to Doncaster, she wanted to have as many perfect memories as possible. There was such a short time remaining, and she was convinced that this would be the only enchanted, special thing that would ever happen to her, which certainly put her mother's predicament into perspective.

Kate had always judged her mother harshly, had viewed her abandonment through the narrow scope of childhood, her opinions colored by Regina. But had her mother's feelings for Selena's father been akin to Kate's for Marcus? Had her mother been consumed, obsessed, addicted to him and what he brought to her life?

For once, Kate was examining her mother's affair from a different angle, from that of a female hopelessly in love with the wrong man. If their situations were at all similar, the poor woman hadn't stood a chance.

Kate never revealed her sentiments to Marcus. The mood of their furtive romance was light and gay. They trifled and flirted, they engaged in forbidden conduct, but their conversations never delved into any crucial topic, or focused on their lives away from his bedchamber.

They were sealed in a cocoon, where they were separate and detached from their real selves, and the outside world had no impact. If they ran into each other belowstairs, how would she react? If she was walking down the hall, or sitting at supper, and he suddenly appeared, what on earth would she say to him?

He finished with the fire and approached, climbing onto the mattress, and stretching out, both of them on their sides and facing each other.

"Will you?" she asked again.

He'd already forgotten her question. "Will I what?"

"Marry Melanie?"

His answer was nagging at her. While she was sequestered with him, it was easy to pretend that external concerns didn't signify, but more and more, she was troubled over his probable response.

As was typical of their association, he never mentioned the purpose for Kate's being in London, never talked about Melanie, or squired her about town. His matrimonial plans were a mystery, and Kate was frantic to determine what they were.

She'd assumed she could have a frivolous *amore,* that she could frolic without regard to the consequences, but she'd miscalculated. She couldn't be impassive and uninvolved. In the end, he'd break her heart, and she had to buck up so that the pain wouldn't be too terrible.

If he chose Melanie, Kate would have to flee Doncaster. She couldn't reside in the same house with him, especially with what she'd learned about marital intimacy. She couldn't bear to lie awake at night visualizing how he was fornicating with Melanie just down the hall.

So what would she do? Where would she go?

She'd toyed with the idea of moving in with Selena. Her sister was sweet enough to consent, but considering her impoverished state, it wouldn't be fair to impose. Kate's other option was to press Christopher for a settlement so that she could support herself, but Regina would never agree, and Kate couldn't predict if Chris would stand up to her or not.

Recently, Kate was bothered that no aid had been extended to her. She'd never doubted Regina's contention that she wasn't entitled to any financial assistance, but why shouldn't she be? She was the daughter of an earl, and she'd lost her position simply because her father had died. Why should the tragedy have negated her right to subsistence?

They were scheduled to be in London two more weeks, and she had to have some clue as to what would transpire when she left. What was in store?

"Sure, I'll marry Melanie," Marcus said, as if he'd given the subject no more thought than he would what shirt to wear.

"Don't be flip," she scolded. "I'm serious."

"But how can my reply matter to you one way or the other?"

He was wiser than she, and he fathomed—as she could not—that they couldn't have a civil dialogue about anything vital. There were no suitable answers he could provide to any of the issues that were eating at her.

Still, she was resolved to hash it out. If he slew her with his words, so be it. It was better to die now than to perish later from anguish and sorrow for which she hadn't been prepared.

"Do you think you could wed Melanie, but it would have no effect on me?"

"No, but why wallow in debate? Why torture yourself?"

Why, indeed? "With a bit of *torture,* maybe I'll figure out why I put up with you."

Cocky and smug, he laughed. "You do it because you're crazy about me."

He was correct, but she hated being so weak! She rolled onto her back and stared at the ceiling, glad she had somewhere to look besides into his apathetic eyes. How could he be so important in her life when it was clear she was so insignificant in his?

She forged on. She'd started the discussion, and

she'd see it through, despite how excruciating it was. "Why are you cavorting with me?"

"Because it's pleasurable. Because I enjoy your company."

She wasn't positive what she'd been expecting, but his justification wasn't anywhere close. It sounded as if she were his pet lapdog. "If you wed Melanie, what association have you envisioned for us?"

"What do you mean?"

"Will we keep on as we have been?"

"Certainly."

His insolence made it apparent that he hadn't reflected on their circumstances, that when he dreamed about his future, he didn't picture her in it. "So you'll be sneaking in and out my door, causing the servants to gossip, and risking discovery by your bride at every turn?"

"How I carry on won't be any of my wife's business."

"Not even if you're sleeping with your paramour under her roof?"

She'd finally managed to exasperate him, and he blew out a heavy breath. "Why would you fret about it, Kate? You can't tell me you have any loyalty to Melanie."

Had she any allegiance? While she'd never been keen about Melanie, she'd never wish Melanie undue harm. Melanie was young and immature, cantankerous and infuriating, but after being raised by Regina, who wouldn't be?

"Has it ever occurred to you that I couldn't trifle with a married man? Even if Melanie and I aren't friendly, she's eager to have a loving rapport with her husband, and if you believe I could betray her, then you don't know me, at all."

He scoffed. "If she presumes she can have a *loving* relationship with me, then she's a fool."

"If you marry her, I can't continue to reside at Doncaster."

"Don't be ridiculous."

"Would you help me to relocate? To find a new situation? Could you do at least that much for me?"

"You're painting all these calamitous scenarios, and I don't understand why you are. Let it go, Kate. Stop worrying."

He'd avoided supplying any guarantees, which told her that if the worst came to pass, and he joined the family, she'd be on her own and couldn't count on him. She shouldn't be wounded by the notion—after all, she'd always been alone—but she'd so hoped that he cared enough to, at a minimum, have her safely settled elsewhere.

"Why are you contemplating marriage to her? It's obvious you're not interested. Why not bluntly advise her that she has no chance? Put her out of her misery and send her home."

"I have to wed by my thirty-first birthday," he explained, "and I don't want to, so it's all the same to me."

"One girl's the same as the next?"

"Yes."

"Oh, Marcus . . ." She yearned to shake him! How could he be so cavalier about such a fundamental decision? "If you don't propose to her, we'll be gone in two weeks."

"I'm aware of that." His tone was cool, noncommittal.

"You'll never see me again."

"No, I won't."

A wave of melancholy billowed over her. Would it kill him to give a small hint that he was fond of her? Was she truly so irrelevant? An image flashed, of the dozens of women who'd lain with him before she had, and the dozens who would after she left, and she was so despondent.

"Doesn't my imminent departure bother you?" she humiliated herself by asking.

"Kate," he soothed, "what would you have me say? Should I profess my undying devotion and claim that I'll be devastated, that I won't be able to persevere without you?"

"Maybe it's what I need to hear."

"I'm sure it is, but where would it leave us?"

"I don't know."

"Should I beg you to remain in London?" He was growing angry, and she was glad to have him evince an emotion, even if it wasn't what she'd been longing to detect. "Fine. Will you stay and be my mistress? Is that the existence you visualize for yourself?"

"No."

"Come now!" he sarcastically cajoled. "I'll establish you in an expensive house, and buy you a fashionable wardrobe. I'll pop in twice a week, so that you can earn your keep, flat on your back. The neighbors will remark on the odd hours my carriage is parked out front, and they'll titter about who you are, and how you support yourself. We'll persist till I'm weary of you, and when the allure has faded, and another tickles my fancy, I'll pay you a stipend and toss you over. It will all be so congenial, so tidy."

She glanced away and peered at the wall. "There's no need to be cruel."

"I'm not being *cruel,* my darling Kate. I'm being brutally frank." He cradled her cheek in his palm, forcing her to look at him. "Can you conceive of what your life would be like if you hooked up with me? You're very special, and you should be cherished and adored, but I'm not the man to love you. I have no idea how."

"I think you are."

"It's a waste of energy to weep and lament over what can never be."

"But I wish for more than this . . . this sneaking around, and these fast gropings in the dark, where we're constantly fretting that we'll be caught."

"Of course you do."

"Why can't there be more than this?"

"Because you deserve someone better than me." He kissed her on the nose, on the mouth. "We have such limited time together. Let's not squander it. Let's be happy for what *is,* and not grieve over what might have been."

She tried to salvage some consolation in having wrangled his admission that she was *special,* which was a tepid compliment, but she'd hold it dear. What was to be gained by mourning reality, by pining for more?

She hugged him tight and whispered, "After I go, I will miss you every minute of every day."

Stupidly, she waited for a similar comment, but he replied with, "I know you will."

She groaned and punched him on the shoulder. "You are such a vain beast!"

"I've never denied it." Turning serious and pensive,

he stared at her, a thousand sentiments streaming across his beautiful face, but he didn't voice any of them. "Don't be sad, Kate. I can't bear it when you are."

How could she rue and regret? Particularly when he was gazing at her like that, as if she was unique and exceptional, and every bit as extraordinary as he'd contended.

"I won't be."

He kissed her again, and it quickly altered into a profound embrace that seemed to embody all he couldn't speak aloud. Men weren't the most astute creatures, and it occurred to her that perhaps he liked her, but couldn't confess it. Or perhaps he hadn't realized the depth of his affection.

She relaxed, relishing their bond, and she was ecstatic that she'd had the opportunity to discover what it was like to be so close to another human being.

Lately, she'd been anxious, feeling as if she was laboring under a sinister cloud, that they didn't have the two full weeks she anticipated she'd be in London. What if this was their last rendezvous? If something happened, and they never subsequently dallied, she'd never forgive herself for not forging ahead to the ultimate conclusion. He'd explained it to her, in graphic detail, and she was so curious, so eager.

Their passions heated, and he blazed a trail down her neck, her bosom, to her breast, and he suckled until she was writhing and straining. He journeyed on, down her stomach, her abdomen, until he was rooting across her womanly hair.

"Open your legs for me, Kate," he ordered.

"Why?"

"I'll show you."

"Show me what?"

"Kate," he scolded, "just do as I say."

"Not until you tell me what you intend."

"You trust me, don't you?"

"No, I absolutely don't."

The bounder chuckled, and she glared at him, unsure if she should acquiesce, but he was grinning at her, like the devil personified, and she couldn't refuse. She widened her thighs, furnishing him the access he'd demanded, and he dipped down, his tongue laving her, jabbing at her.

"Oh, oh my," she panted. "What are you doing?"

"I can make you come this way."

"We shouldn't . . . we can't . . ." She couldn't put into words all the reasons they shouldn't do such a wicked thing. It felt too good to be allowed. "It's too . . . too . . ."

"Too what?" He paused in his torment. "Too marvelous? Too naughty?"

"Yes."

"Precisely why I knew you'd love it. You have the heart of a strumpet."

"No, I don't!" she was compelled to insist, but he started in again, and any further protest was pointless.

He worked his arms under her legs and reached for her breasts, so that he could fondle her nipples, and after he'd grabbed hold of them, it was easy to hurl her over the precipice. With scarcely any effort on his part, she shattered into tiny pieces.

She was soaring, out of control, and she thought she screamed her delight, but she wasn't positive. Waves of pleasure deluged her, and they took forever to crest. As they waned, he was meandering up her torso, nibbling at her navel, nuzzling at her cleavage, and she was irked that it had ended so soon. When they philandered, he was always able to resist the onslaught, to contain the spiral, but *she* never could.

He was right! She did have the heart of a strumpet!

He moved to her nape, to her mouth, and he kissed her slowly, letting her taste her sex on his tongue, and she wallowed in the dissipation.

Oh, what a wanton she was!

"Make love to me, Marcus."

"Kate . . ."

"Please."

He regularly claimed that he couldn't deny her any request, and she studied him, having him see how much she wanted it to transpire, how fervently she wanted him to be the one.

"Quit looking at me like that."

"Like what?"

"Like you can coerce me into it."

"I want it to be you."

"I don't."

"Liar."

She caressed his phallus, and he was rigid, throbbing. He'd taught her how to tease him with her mouth, how to satisfy him with her hand, but tonight, she yearned for a different conclusion. She couldn't go to Doncaster without it.

With a tad more titillation, perhaps he'd be beyond refusal. She rolled him so that he was on his back, so that she could goad him to the brink.

He was so hard, so impatient, and she traveled down his stomach, to his cock. She licked across the tip, over and over, driving him to distraction. Then, she sucked him inside, letting him thrust, letting him revel, until he was set to explode.

When he couldn't stand any more, she pulled away, and straddled his loins, her privates in direct contact with his own. She flexed across him, his phallus gliding along her sheath, and he trembled with anticipation and frustration. He was desperate to progress, but fighting his primal instincts, declining to relent, declining to harm her.

Blasted oaf! She was an adult, and she knew her own mind.

"Take me, Marcus!" she commanded. "Now."

Gripping her thighs, he manipulated her across his erection, each touch like a lightning bolt striking both of them.

"You're so ready for me."

"Yes. For you, Marcus. Only for you."

"It would be so simple," he muttered, more to himself than to her, and he urged her down, her breast dangling before him, and he nursed at her nipple.

"Show me how it can be, Marcus. I'm begging you."

He rotated them, so that she was on the bottom, and he was hovered over her. He appeared sinful, decadent, and inclined to commit any nefarious deed.

"I'm not a saint, Kate."

"No, you're not."

"I can't say no to you. I want this too much."

"Yes, you do." Maybe this was how he could demonstrate that he cared for her. He could attest to his affection with his actions, rather than his words.

"It will hurt—the first time. It can't be helped."

"You've told me."

"Promise me one thing."

"Anything, my dear man. Anything, at all."

"Promise that you'll never regret asking me."

As if she could ever *regret* the experience! She felt as if her entire life had merely been a journey to this place, where she would become a woman in his arms.

"I will always celebrate that it was you. I swear it."

"Oh, Kate . . ."

With their mutual decision to proceed, his intensity heightened; his lust increased. Rapt, engrossed, bent on achieving his goal, he was focused as he'd never been before.

His hands were everywhere, as he propelled her up and up, his desire escalating in proportion to her own. She was on the verge of unraveling, her ardor at a fevered pitch, when he centered his cock and stroked the blunt crown across her; then he prodded in, the slightest bit. Suddenly not as confident as she had been, she tensed and arched up.

"Relax."

"I'm afraid."

"Don't be."

"I can't stop myself."

"It will be over soon."

He was too big! Like the innocent ninny she was, she struggled against his invasion.

"Marcus!" She wasn't certain what she was seeking. She was about to receive that for which she'd pleaded. It was too late to demur.

"You are so perfect for me."

"Marcus!"

"Hush!" he barked.

He was riveted on his task, so her entreaties were for naught. He clutched her thighs and splayed them even wider.

"I'm scared. I . . . I . . ."

"No regrets, Kate. Remember?"

She fought in earnest, but he wasn't about to desist. He lunged forward, his rod insistent and determined, and he broke through her maidenhead, plunging to her womb. Stunned by strange sensations, she cried out, and he kissed her, swallowing her wail of agony and surprise. He held himself very still, as her virginal body acclimated, as her mind came to grips with what they'd done.

He'd warned her what it would be like, but she hadn't listened, and she supposed that the process was very much like dying. A person could have it described, but until she actually went through it herself, it was impossible to comprehend the enormity of what would transpire.

"That's the worst of it," he murmured.

"And I survived." She tried to chuckle over her display of feminine histrionics.

"You did fine."

He smiled, which made it all right, and gradually, she adapted, her anatomy welcoming him.

"You fit inside me!"

"Told you I would."

"I didn't believe you."

"You never do, you scamp!" He was contented, merry, and incredibly aroused. "Let's finish it."

He flexed, and the feeling of him, planted deep, was like nothing she'd encountered prior, and as the initial pain passed, she was eager to join in. She met him thrust for thrust, her hips working with his in a precise rhythm. He was more agitated, more frantic, his motions crisp and exact.

Waves of excitement built, and with him embedded inside her, the surge was much more powerful. Another orgasm resonated through her, and as her inner muscles clamped around him, the pressure brought on his own release. He pushed into her once, again, again, and his seed rushed out. But at the last instant, he drew away, denying her the final and definitive knowledge of the culmination.

He spilled himself onto her stomach, and she sighed—with bliss but also a touch of melancholy. She should have known he wouldn't risk siring a babe. While she recognized that it was his way of being gallant, of protecting her, she mourned that he couldn't grant her this piece of himself.

As their ardor waned, it was terribly quiet, and now that it was over, she was curious as to what they'd talk about. She was much more overwhelmed than she'd imagined she'd be, and a sprinkling of tears dribbled down her cheeks. He was disconcerted, and he took the sheet and swiped them away.

"Why are you sad?"

"I'm not," she claimed, which was true. "I'm very, very happy."

"They're tears of joy?" He was extremely dubious.

"Yes."

"You're no longer a maid."

"A situation I heartily embrace."

"My little beauty. How glad I am that you are mine!" For a few minutes, he nestled with her; then he retrieved a towel and washing cloth and cleansed away the evidence of their reckless behavior.

"Are you sore?"

"I'll mend."

He snuggled next to her. "Let's nap awhile; then I'll ring for a bath. You won't ache quite so much if you soak a bit."

"That sounds splendid," she agreed, though she'd never let him order up a bath. He was so spoiled! It hadn't occurred to him that it was two in the morning and she'd never permit him to rouse a servant with such a frivolous request. "Afterward, can we do it again?"

He laughed. "I'll die in your arms!"

He covered them with a blanket, and she rested, taking note of every detail, and thinking how easy he made everything. Her deflowering could have been awkward and embarrassing, but he was so sweet, so blithe and nonchalant, which induced her to cherish him all the more.

Within seconds, he dozed, which gave her the chance to study him without his being aware, without his being able to hide his thoughts, or conceal his vulnerabilities and emotions.

In sleep, he looked so young, so carefree and untroubled, and she pondered what his childhood had been like. He never spoke of it. She'd heard gossip that his mother had died when he was born, that he'd been raised by his distant, aloof father. He never mentioned the man, never waxed on about youthful pranks, kindly governesses, or doting aunties, and she suspected that he'd been a lonely boy, that much of the detachment and arrogance he exhibited as an adult was a reaction to those earlier trials.

The air had cooled, and she tugged another blanket over them. She was as weary as he, but she daren't fall asleep. Her worst nightmare would be to wake up at dawn to see a maid reviving the fire, or his valet laying out his jacket and trousers.

She absolutely could not be caught with him!

His slumber deepened, and he snored lightly, and she leaned in and kissed his cheek. He smiled, though he didn't stir.

"I love you," she whispered, and she sneaked off the mattress, hurriedly donned her clothes, and tiptoed out.

The corridor was dark, the stairwell even darker, and she stumbled to her room and crept in undetected. It was so silent, so forlorn, and she was inundated by the impression that this dismal, dreary world was how it would be after she'd gone back to Doncaster.

Would he ever reminisce about her?

The answer was surely *no,* which was too depressing, and she lit a candle to ward off her sense of isolation. The flame sputtered and strengthened, and she stripped, then shrugged into her negligee. As she turned to fetch her brush and braid her hair, she was startled.

There, on the center of her dresser, was his signet ring. The sight was too spooky for words, and she picked it up, praying it wasn't real, but it was.

As usual, it seemed to glow and pulse, as if it were alive, as if it were trying to import some message she didn't understand. He'd drunk the potion, too, and he'd subsequently grown so enamored of her, and she wondered whether he possessed something of hers.

The moment the possibility popped into her head, she shook it away. Was she now relying on witches' remedies and ancient superstitions to guide her path?

Maybe she should visit the apothecary and purchase some eye-of-newt and bats' wings!

She groaned. How was she to be shed of the accursed bauble?

She slipped it onto her finger, and clutched her fist around it; then she crawled into her bed and ducked under the quilt, hoping—once more!—that the ring would have vanished by morning.

⊷ 12 ⊷

Pamela stood at the rear of the ballroom, cooling her face with her fan. As it was a masquerade, the attendees' identities were supposed to be a secret, but Pamela knew all of them too well for them to have any anonymity.

Melanie had attired herself as a medieval maiden, and was dancing up a storm with anyone who asked. Her chaperone was absent, so no one was advising her as to appropriate associates, and her mother was too stupid to realize that someone should be screening Melanie's choices.

Regina sat in the opposite corner, dressed as Good Queen Bess, but she was too fat and dour to pull it off with any aplomb. As gluttony was her sole entertainment, she was eating—no surprise there!—and Pamela was counting the days till the grim harridan departed.

Pamela looked out across the crowd, trying to keep an eye on Christopher, while wondering how she could persuade him to stay on after his mother left. Since

Pamela had an image to maintain, she pretended not to be focused on anyone in particular. It wouldn't do to have stories spreading as to her enamoration. Rumors might be disseminated that she was aging and growing desperate, that she was robbing the cradle, and she refused to have gossip circulating.

Across the way, she espied him escorting his partner down the row. The girl giggled with delight, as others enviously observed them. He was now the male belle of every ball, his charm and attractiveness having won over the fickle members of High Society, which had Pamela jealously gnashing her teeth.

His dancing instructor had been an idiot, so Christopher wasn't very adept at the trickier tunes, and the debutantes had taken him under their collective wings. They garnered significant amusement from showing him the various steps, which, of course, he picked up immediately. As she'd learned of him in her bedchamber, he had a natural athletic grace that lent itself to physical endeavor, so he had the little ninnies fawning and cooing as he whirled them in circles.

Elliot approached, sipping his whiskey and not nearly as foxed as he generally was. Before she could divert her concentration, he recognized at whom she stared.

"You've had quite a trio of houseguests visiting," he commented. "How are you holding up?"

They'd been friends for years, and he was one of the few people with whom she could be frank. "Less than two weeks remaining. There will either be an engagement very shortly or they'll go home."

With his glass, he gestured toward Christopher. "He seems to be a fine boy."

"Yes, he is, and I'm pleased to announce that he doesn't resemble his mother in the slightest."

"Praise the Lord!" Elliot sarcastically chimed as she smiled.

Regina was the talk of London, with everyone palavering over her. Bets were being waged as to whether she could dupe Stamford into wedding Melanie and, if she could, how long Marcus would last before banishing both females to some godforsaken locale.

"You've developed a certain *interest* in the lad. . . ."

He let the sentence trail off, let the innuendo hang between them, and she was anxious to cut off any speculation. "I'm merely worried about him. In this sea of fortune hunters, any calamity could befall him."

"Too true."

"I wish Stamford would make up his bloody mind."

"What have you heard on that front?" His gaze settled on Melanie. "I'm told he's barely conversed with her."

"With Marcus, I can't begin to predict what his decision will be."

"I've discussed the entire sordid business with Lady Melanie," he shocked her by admitting. "In great detail."

"Really?"

"Yes."

She was amazed that he'd had the opportunity, but then, his cozying up to Melanie was a blatant example of Regina's apathetic parenting. Any sane mother would have chased him off with a stick.

"What does she say?"

"Her mother has convinced her that the match will occur."

"How can she believe it? Stamford's given no hint as to his intentions."

"Melanie's so sure that she's purchased a love potion."

Pamela sputtered with astonishment. "To use on Stamford? You have to be joking."

"She's bound and determined that he be in love with her before their wedding night, and she has a servant prepared to slip it into his brandy the moment his back is turned."

"Oh for pity's sake. What next!" She rolled her eyes. "Where did she find such a thing?"

"Some apothecary. His shop is in the alley behind that milliner where you buy your hats."

She chortled. Maybe Melanie would accidentally poison Stamford, and put them all out of their misery. It would serve him right for being such an impossible beast!

"Lady Melanie is crazy."

"Very likely," Elliot concurred. "So . . . what is your estimate as to Stamford's feelings where she's concerned?"

"I haven't a clue, Elliot. This very instant, he could walk in and propose."

"If he's not brought to heel, what would you calculate she'll do?"

"She'll *do* whatever her mother orders. She doesn't have much spine."

He evaluated Melanie, his scrutiny visible and transparent. "Has Regina selected a second choice?"

"God, Elliot, don't tell me—" The notion was so ludicrous that she guffawed.

"Who can foresee what Melanie might be influenced to want for herself?"

"You'd presume it to be you?"

"You just never know, Pamela." He shrugged. "Anything could happen."

Especially if she's not cautious, and her mother isn't watching too closely.

The statement rang between them. The social whirl of London was beyond the ability of Melanie or her mother to manipulate with any finesse, and Regina wouldn't take advice, even when it was warranted and politely offered.

Well, Elliot had always been a steadfast companion, and Pamela had no loyalty to the snotty, unrefined brat. If he could wrangle himself a marriage and get his hands on her dowry, more power to him. No one could benefit from the money more than he, and Pamela wasn't about to interfere.

With being so involved in their conversation, she'd lost sight of Christopher, and she rose up on tiptoe to peek through the milling throng. Finally, she spotted him. He was still dancing with the same partner. Pamela didn't recognize her, but although her face was masked, it was obvious she was a girl of excellent breeding. She moved with a fluid, remarkable grace that equaled Christopher's own. They were poised, elegant, captivating, and as they promenaded down the line, others stopped to stare approvingly.

Christopher was focused on her, gazing at her as if *he* knew who she was. He was transfixed, riveted by her hidden beauty and her lithe, willowy style, and Pamela shifted uneasily. It almost looked as if he was in . . . in love!

How could such a terrible event have unfolded? Without Pamela being aware of the situation? She kept tabs on him at all hours.

This won't do! she thought, and she excused herself to Elliot and marched toward Regina. Though Pamela avoided Regina as much as she could, it was time the two of them had a blunt talk.

Pamela desired Christopher, and Regina was eager to snag Stamford. If they could strike a satisfactory deal, they could both attain exactly what they wanted.

Much like Cinderella, Selena raced down the stairs of the grand mansion, and she curled her toes in her fancy slippers, to ensure they stayed on her feet.

As she departed, she'd heard the whispers of the guests, endured their curious analysis, even sensed occasional hostility. Everyone was conjecturing as to her identity, but in this crowd, none would ever guess it. There wasn't a member of the *ton* who had an imagination vivid enough.

Her carriage awaited, the footmen Christopher had hired treating her as if she were a princess, and that's precisely how she felt. As she approached, they leapt into action, lowering the step, and opening the door.

She paused to admire the imposing house where she'd attended her first ball. It was so splendid, the windows lit, the orchestra music drifting across the yard. There were couples strolling on the lawn, the women's diamonds glittering under the lanterns.

Before coming to England, she'd assumed her life would be filled with such parties, that she'd fraternize with rich, dazzling people, that she would build the sort of existence upon which her parents had thrived in Italy. But society in London was more restricted, moral tenets more rigorously enforced, and acceptance as an outsider more difficult to finagle. Unfortunately, there was also her financial disaster, which prevented her from procuring the clothes and accessories she needed for an entree.

None of her dreams had become reality, and she'd been upset, but not anymore.

Now that she'd met Kate and Christopher, Selena couldn't be sorry. Destiny had a peculiar way of having everything work out as it should. Her recent trials were mere bumps in the road, brief delays on the path to where she was supposed to be.

She sighed with delight. It was all so fantastic, and she would love Christopher forever for giving her such a magical gift. He'd sent a dress; he'd sent jewelry; he'd sent combs for her hair, and gloves, and a fan, and a lace shawl, and a beaded reticule—items the most exquisite lady required for an evening on the town.

Edith had wanted to be scandalized by his generosity, but neither of them could think of a reason for Selena to decline. Of late, her affairs had been so dreary, expectations dashed, hopes shattered. Christopher was the lone ray of sunshine she'd encountered, and if Edith had counseled against allowing his largesse, Selena would have ignored her. What was to be gained by refusal?

He'd brought food, wine, and tea. Coal had been delivered and, without his informing Selena, he'd dispensed an envelope of cash to Edith. Their small cadre of servants had been paid, accounts with merchants balanced. It was a magnificent night to be alive!

A footman lifted her in, and she settled herself, being extra careful with the skirt of her new gown. Momentarily, the horses started down the lane, but before rounding the curve, the driver pulled up. There was a cordial salute, male laughter. The door was flung wide, and Christopher was there, as he'd promised he would be.

"Ah, the most beautiful woman at the ball!" he teased. "And she's sitting in my carriage! How lucky I am!"

"Get in here—before someone sees you!"

As the coach lurched away, she tugged at his jacket, and he tumbled into her. In a tangle of arms and legs, he wound up on the seat, with her on his lap, and he drew off their masks.

"Did you enjoy yourself?" he queried. Moonlight shone in, illuminating his bright smile. His golden hair shimmered like a halo, and he was so radiant that she felt as if she were traveling with an angel.

"Yes, yes, yes!" She kissed him, chuckling at how enthusiastically he joined in. "It was fabulous."

"Good, because I plan to bestow many more entertainments just like it."

Her heart fluttered with excitement, but she didn't dare ask what he meant. Was he speaking in the short term, or of something more permanent? If Lord Stamford didn't come up to snuff with his sister, Christopher would soon have to escort his mother to Doncaster. What then? Selena couldn't bear to consider the answer.

"How did you escape?" She changed the subject, too apprehensive to dawdle in worrisome territory.

"I lied to my mother and claimed I was ill. So she'll ride home with Lady Pamela, which is a trip I'm happy to miss."

In the few assignations he'd managed, he'd regaled her with tales of domineering Regina, spoiled Melanie, and the insidious Pamela. He was surrounded by crazed females, with Kate being the only one who was sane, but she'd been banished from socializing—an edict with which she was apparently pleased, so Chris hadn't overruled his mother—and he rarely saw her.

"I wish Kate could have been here. She would have had so much fun." Before meeting Kate, she'd pictured Kate's life at Doncaster to be merry and gay, but in many respects, her situation was more bleak than Selena's own.

"I'll bring her to visit you tomorrow."

"Oh, you are the sweetest man!"

"Just with you."

He was too modest. He was kind to everyone. Her servants were infatuated with him. "Have you told her about us?"

"We'll surprise her."

"Will she be glad?"

"Very glad."

Selena wasn't as confident of Kate's opinion as Christopher was. When he'd initially stumbled into her parlor, Kate had been embarrassed, hadn't wanted him to deduce that they were sisters. How would she view their secret liaison?

As if drinking Selena in with his eyes, he was scrutinizing her. He seemed constantly on the verge of an important confession, and she was desperate to learn what it was.

How she hated being a woman! She was awful at playing the shy, flirtatious coquette. She'd inherited too much of her mother's bold nature, and she chafed at having to be silent and wait for him to proceed. If she could figure out how to broach the topic of their future, she would!

His fingers in her hair, his tongue in her mouth, he kissed her soundly, and she reveled with elation. He was such a marvelous kisser, and he quickly swept away any need to talk. He knew exactly what to do, how and when to do it, and it occurred to her that he must have had a great deal of practice. Probably, he'd kissed many girls. After all, who could refuse him?

Well, she certainly hoped that his days of *practicing* were over! When he was in the mood to kiss, she intended to be the one to whom he turned.

The embrace became more heated, more passionate, as he laid her across his arm. She was tipped back, with him supporting her as if she weighed no more than a feather. He nuzzled across her cheek, down her neck and bosom. Her dress was cut very low in the front, and he nestled in her cleavage.

"You're so pretty, Selena," he murmured. "You'll always be mine, won't you?"

As a declaration, it was vague, and every time they were together, he tiptoed closer to the edge of a significant affirmation. Would he ever blurt out what he was trying to say?

"Yes, I will."

He slithered his hand under the bodice of her gown, and with no effort at all, her breast popped out from behind the fabric. He petted the soft mound, massaging it, investigating its shape and size; then he leaned over and stunned her by sucking at the nipple. The tiny

nub hardened into a painful bud, so that every manipu-
lation had her squirming until she could barely stay on
his lap.

"Chris! What are you doing?" She hadn't really
needed to inquire. Though she was aware of many
amorous deeds, she didn't comprehend precisely how
they were accomplished. Or that they could transpire
in a carriage whilst careening down a dark lane!

"This is desire, Selena. I want to show you how it
will be between us." He pulled away and gazed at her.
"You'll let me, won't you?"

She couldn't tell him no, not when he was staring at
her as if she were the most extraordinary, most unique
woman in the world. Still, she had no ring on her finger, and she was terrified that in his ultimate proposal
he would suggest she be his mistress, which was a
position she would flatly decline, so she wasn't about
to travel too far down the road until she was clear as to
his purpose.

"Swear to me that you'll stop if I ask."

"Of course I will." His warm regard billowed over
her. "I would never dishonor you."

"I know you wouldn't."

He moved to her bosom again, laving and sucking
one breast, while he toyed with the other. The sensation
was powerful, and set her on fire, sinking in till her
veins and pores seemed to vibrate. At her core, her
womb jerked and twisted with each tug of his lips. She
was wet, her body weeping for him, and she felt as if
she might explode.

Down below, he was inching up her skirt, but she
didn't care. She was in a frantic state, so agitated that
she couldn't tolerate much more, and she was convinced

he would alleviate her distress. There had to be an end point. A person couldn't possibly endure so much turmoil. It couldn't be safe, and she worried that if the spiral went on much longer, her heart might quit beating.

"What's happening to me?" she wailed.

"Relax, darling. It's nearly over." His hand slid higher, toward the vee between her thighs, where her agony was centered. "I'm going to touch you. I'll make you feel better."

He arrived at his destination, cupping her, her legs widening as if she instinctively recognized what he planned. With her dress rucked up and her knees spread, she had to appear a wanton, but she was unconcerned. Just so the torment ceased!

He slipped a finger inside her and began stroking back and forth. Her hips immediately caught his rhythm, so that she drew him deeper, achieving a modicum of relief, but it wasn't enough.

"I can't bear much more," she moaned.

"Almost finished."

He grasped where they were headed, and she was so glad. She was beyond thought, beyond control. His thumb jabbed at a sensitive area she'd never noticed before, and it was like a bolt of lightning shooting through her.

"Oh . . . oh . . ." She couldn't speak, couldn't advise him of what was ensuing, but he seemed to know.

"Now, Selena," he commanded. "Let go."

Blinded by ecstasy, she shattered into pieces and flew across the universe. Without meaning to, she cried out—loudly!—and she was positive anyone outside the carriage would have noted her raucous exclamations.

Gradually, the feelings abated, and she grew limp as

a rag doll, flopped as she was across his arm, and he chuckled, having relished her lusty display.

"My little wanton," he cooed, "what fun we'll have together."

"What was that?"

"Passion, Selena."

"Do you think the footmen heard me?"

"I'm sure they did."

Squealing with mortification, she buried her face in his jacket. He soothed her, with words and caresses, until they rumbled to a halt at her apartment.

No servant rushed to the door, which boosted her certainty that they'd gleaned what antics were occurring. Were carriages a frequent spot for illicit activity? Was she the only one who hadn't known? She'd never look at a passing coach the same way again!

She tried to sit up, but her torso wouldn't obey, so Christopher had to make her presentable, straightening her hair, her gown, draping her shawl over her shoulders.

Circumstances had aged her more quickly than they might have another female, but she hadn't really matured until this instant, hadn't appreciated what being a woman entailed. She felt older, wiser, ready for another phase of her life to commence.

"Is this something married couples do?" she queried.

"On a regular basis."

Suddenly, matrimony held an entirely new appeal. "So it can happen more than once?"

"Yes." He laughed. "Over and over."

"When can we do it again?"

"As soon as we find a moment to be alone."

"Do you promise?"

"Yes, my strumpet. I promise."

The banter concluded, and they grinned, a world of understanding flitting between them. Their fondness for each other was genuine, precious, and couldn't be ignored or set aside. It seemed as if she'd always known him, as if Fate had specifically wended her to this place, and an exhilarating ripple of inevitability washed over her.

She leaned forward and hugged him.

"I love you," she whispered. Her pronouncement was brash and presumptuous, but she was so happy that she couldn't stop herself.

"I love you, too," he answered, but he didn't add more. He didn't pledge himself, or mention the future. He kissed her sweetly; then he rapped on the door, and a footman opened it and arranged the step.

"I'll come to see you tomorrow," Christopher declared.

"Bring Kate with you."

"I will."

She waited another second, but he didn't offer anything further, and she kept her smile firmly affixed. Turning, she climbed out, the servant courteously assisting her and giving no indication that he was aware of her scandalous demonstration.

At the last, Christopher murmured, "Selena . . ."

"Yes?" She whipped around, expectant, encouraged, on tenterhooks of suspense.

For an eternity, he assessed her; then he said, "We'll talk on the morrow. When Kate is with us."

What did he mean? Kate was her guardian, and her sister. Was he planning to propose? She couldn't bear to hope.

"All right." She nodded and fled into the building.

~ 13 ~

Marcus entered the foyer of his own house, blinking to adjust his vision after being in the bright sunshine. As an adult, he'd vowed never to reside in the mansion, and so far, he'd succeeded, making rare appearances when duty forced him. He stared up the grand staircase, pondering why he couldn't muster any connection to the drafty, ostentatious place. The property had belonged to his family for three hundred years, and Pamela spent a fortune ensuring that it was fashionably decorated.

Heritage alone should have made it welcoming, but what he perceived was the dreary remnants of a forlorn childhood, the acrimonious memories of a confused adolescence. The walls echoed with bitter treachery and betrayal of a naive young fool who'd been enamored of the wrong woman.

Occasionally, he thought about his father, curious as to whether he'd regretted the perfidy he'd perpetuated with Pamela. By all accounts, their union had been rocky and filled with strife. Had she been worth the loss of his relationship with his only son? Had he ever been repentant for what he'd done?

Marcus didn't know, and even if his father had undergone a deathbed conversion and had begged to apologize, Marcus wasn't sure he'd have cared to hear it. A pox on his sorry hide!

The butler espied him and rushed over, greeting him in an effusive way that left Marcus uncomfortable. Ill at ease with his title, he felt like an imposter who didn't merit such fussy displays. He'd known the elderly gentleman his entire life, had endured many a scolding, and even a few swats on the bottom if he'd been naughty, and it always seemed as if he were betraying the fellow by not being a more involved earl, by not embracing his legacy with more enthusiasm.

Whenever he dropped by, not just the butler but all the servants tried to be particularly obliging—in a manner they never were with Pamela—and Marcus received the impression that they were on the verge of imploring him to move in, to send her packing.

Would they be any better off if he inflicted the likes of Melanie Lewis on them?

He cheered the butler by giving him a task to perform, having him set out plenty of brandy before Marcus went to his monthly appointment with Pamela. They'd discuss expenditures and singular requests she was dying to have him grant.

What a bitter tonic she had to swallow, being compelled to solicit him for every single farthing. He wasn't positive why his father hadn't provided for her in his will, but Marcus pictured the man laughing from his grave, enjoying the petty retribution.

Marcus turned to proceed to the meeting, and much

to his surprise and delight, Kate was coming down the hall. She had on her drab chaperone's costume and gray cloak, the hood pulled up to conceal her glorious hair. Evidently, she was going somewhere, and he experienced a humorous stab of jealousy that her day was progressing without him, that she had plans and engagements of which he was unaware.

He passed a significant portion of each night with her. He could describe how she tasted, how she tensed as she had an orgasm, how she sighed when it was over. But he had no idea where she was headed, and the realization bothered him very much.

Was she off on a shopping excursion? By herself? The prospect unnerved him. She must have a footman with her! Or was she making social calls? Who did she know in London? An old friend? An aged auntie? He was upset to consider that there might be someone she cherished and adored, someone who was intimate with her as he was not.

It occurred to him that he detested the limited nature of their affiliation, and he was deluged by a desperate need to learn more about her, to share her world. When he was trysting with her, there were so many questions he yearned to ask—about her parents, her personal history, her position at Doncaster—but he was usually so overwhelmed by passion that he'd shove aside any examination, thinking he'd delve later, but would that moment arrive? In a week, she was leaving. Was he prepared?

The obvious answer was *no,* so what did that mean?

His heart ached. Was this love? How could it be? Yet how else could he explain his painful feelings? He was obsessed to the point of absurdity, and when they were apart, he was driven to lunacy by his pitiful impatience to be with her again.

It had to be love. No other emotion could possibly apply, so what was his intent?

He wasn't so despicable that he'd confess to being smitten. Kate would savor such a pronouncement, would erroneously assume it held some value, but it wouldn't. She should have a loyal husband, a home, and children upon whom she could dote. He would never saddle her with his wretched presence. He was so vile, his bad habits ingrained and offensive. If they ended up married—a curse he would never inflict on her—she would quickly grow to loathe him as she discovered what a cruel, merciless, undependable lout he actually was.

No woman should suffer such a fate. Especially his dear Kate. But he couldn't help wondering what it would be like to squire her about. How would she react if he sauntered over, grabbed her arm, and led her to his carriage?

He smiled. She'd probably hit him with her reticule, but oh, what a delicious notion it was, the two of them chatting merrily as they traipsed about town. He'd take her to Madame LaFarge's dress shop, would have her measured for a new wardrobe, and they'd drink tea at that restaurant that was the current rage on Bond Street, and they'd—

She glanced up and saw him, and he wished he had a machine that could capture her expression. A storm of sentiments swept over her: elation, terror, fear, gladness, misery. She was thrilled to have run into him, but petrified as to what he might say or do.

She had so little faith in him!

"Hello, Miss Duncan," he greeted her. "How are you this fine afternoon?"

"Lord Stamford." Keeping her eyes glued to the floor, she slumped into a curtsy.

"Are you going out?" he couldn't resist inquiring.

"Yes." He stared at her, his hot gaze inducing her to add, "To visit an acquaintance."

"Not alone, I trust?"

"Lord Doncaster has graciously agreed to accompany me."

"Good. The streets of London are unsafe for a female. There's no telling what mischief could befall you."

She appeared so disturbed, so meek, and he abhorred her subservient attitude. He approached, clasping her hand and making her rise. A swift peek around ensured that there were no servants lurking, and he neared until his boots slipped under the hem of her skirt.

"Desist. Please," she begged, her voice barely audible.

He was aggravated that she didn't want anyone to detect that they were on familiar terms. Would it be so terrible if he proclaimed that she belonged to him? Would the earth stop spinning? Would time stand still?

He was hurt by her reticence, and his pique was hilarious. It was the sole occasion—other than his misguided *amore* for Pamela as a boy—when a woman had mattered to him, and she was horrified by his regard. Her disdain was warranted, and no more than he deserved. After all, what had he done but sneak around, seducing her to ruin? Why should she have a high opinion of him?

"I don't believe I've ever seen you in the light of day." His voice was as quiet as hers, and it took every ounce of fortitude he possessed to keep from reaching out to her. As he'd deduced from the start, it was impossible to be around her and not touch her.

"I have to go."

"Not yet." He placed his finger on her chin, and raised her pretty face, compelling her to look at him. "May I escort you?"

She was taken aback by the suggestion, scared witless that he'd force himself into the middle of her jaunt. "Absolutely not. Don't you dare."

He'd been certain she'd refuse, but he'd tendered the outrageous idea anyway, and he shouldn't have. If she'd consented, what was his plan? His every move held some loftier meaning, so he couldn't innocently ride in a coach with her. Was he ready to publicly admit their affair? She'd lose her employment, so she'd have to stay in London. Was he prepared to support her? For how long? Under what conditions?

As he was a man who went out of his way to avoid personal entanglements, the questions were so alarming that he couldn't begin to answer them, so he shrugged them off, grinning and feigning levity.

"I hate it when you attire yourself in gray."

"So you've said. Frequently." She tried to slither around him, to flee. "Now if you'll excuse me . . ."

He blocked her path. "I don't excuse you."

Was he mad? They were huddled together. Anyone could pop out into the lengthy corridor and observe them.

Just then, footsteps sounded on the stairs, and they jumped apart. It was Christopher, whom Marcus liked very much, and he was relieved that they'd been interrupted.

"Hello, Marcus." With his usual energy, Christopher bounded toward them. "I'd forgotten that you'd met my cousin. She's been in hiding ever since we arrived."

Marcus whirled around and frowned at her, but she was studying the floor again, and he was wounded anew by this latest, and seemingly vital, piece of information. He'd supposed her to be a servant, but gad, she was the poor relative, the superfluous eternal houseguest who had nowhere else to live.

What a deplorable, sorry existence for someone he deemed to be so fine.

"Your cousin?" He wasn't sure if he was asking her or Christopher. "I didn't realize the two of you were related."

"Very distantly," Christopher acknowledged, "but cousins nonetheless. We're off to visit her sister."

Kate blanched at Christopher's blithe statement. Perplexed and confused, she scowled. "How did you know?"

Christopher chuckled and patted her on the shoulder. "We'll talk in the carriage."

Marcus's fierce concentration was glued to her, demanding an accounting as to why she'd never told him she had a sibling in London, but why would she have? He hadn't evinced the slightest indication that he was interested in any component of her life outside his bedchamber.

Still, he wanted to shake her, to insist she explain herself. Despite the stilted aspects of their association, he'd thought they were close, but apparently, she felt no need to share any genuine facts about herself. If pushed, what reason would she give for being intimate with him? Was it because he'd pressured her? Because she couldn't decline to obey a command from the lord of the manor?

He'd assumed she was fond of him, that perhaps she even loved him, and he was shocked to confront the possibility that his perception of their bond may have been wrong.

"You have a sister? Here in town?" Nearly pleading for her reply, his tone was confidential, more hushed than ever, but Chris responded.

"Yes, and I was wondering if we could impose on you when we return, so that we might seek your advice."

"About what?"

"Kate acts as her sister's guardian, but there's a problem with excessive and unauthorized withdrawals from the trust fund. We would appreciate your guidance on how we should investigate the matter."

Kate was so distressed by Christopher's remarks that Marcus worried her knees might buckle, that she might fall. Christopher didn't notice, but Marcus was so attuned to her that he could read every nuance, and he yearned to reach out and steady her, but he didn't dare.

"Chris," she finally spoke, "you're boring Lord Stamford with our family troubles. I wish you wouldn't."

"It's all right," Marcus said. "I don't mind."

"Well, I do," she mutinously contended. She was furious, reeling with a turmoil he didn't understand. He'd stupidly presumed that he'd learned everything crucial about her. How could she have so many secrets?

Christopher laughed off her annoyance. "Don't pay any attention to her," he counseled. "She's so tough. She forgets that she has friends, and she thinks she has to handle every crisis alone." He offered Kate his arm. "Let's be off, shall we? Selena will be growing impatient."

Kate stumbled then, but she recovered her balance without making a scene, and Marcus evaluated her. She was extremely disconcerted by Christopher's repeated mentions of her sister, but her anxiety was beyond normal behavior. She was scared of something. But what? What tidings could there be that she wouldn't want revealed? Did she know more about the fiscal discrepancies than she'd admitted to Christopher?

A vision niggled at Marcus, of her in his room, replacing the ring she'd stolen. He'd noted that it was missing again, even though he'd specifically told her she couldn't have it.

Was she a thief? Early on, he'd joked about the prospect to Pamela, but without considering the accusation to have any substance. The concept was so bizarre and so outlandish that he shoved it off, refusing to lend it any credence.

"We'll talk later," he apprised them both, but it was a warning for Kate that he would expect some answers.

As they walked away, he assessed her, challenging and taunting her with his displeasure. They exited, and he tarried at the door, watching until their carriage pulled away; then he trudged down the hall to the tedious appointment he'd scheduled with Pamela.

At the threshold to the library, the butler was leaving, having arranged the brandy tray. He bore a sympathetic expression but had no comment and scurried away, much as if he was evading the line of fire.

Marcus entered, and was greeted not just by Pamela,

as he'd anticipated, but by Regina Lewis, too. He loathed her, and his first instinct was to spin around and stomp out.

Pamela leapt to her feet, filling the awkwardness with babbling. "Stamford! How kind of you to be so prompt." She gestured to Regina. "And look who's joined us. You remember Regina, of course."

"Of course." He shot them a glare that could have melted lead, and he proceeded to the sideboard and poured himself a hefty beverage. Fortified, he sat down behind the large desk, using it as a barrier between himself and the two females.

Pamela knew better than to spring the encounter on him, and the fact that she had, meant the duo had cooked up some scheme. They were accomplices in pursuit of his marriage to Melanie, so he was determined to quash any hopes they might have of bringing the union to fruition.

He stared them down, not uttering a word, and they both squirmed. Regina was a bully who reveled in her ability to intimidate others, but she'd met her match. He waited, and waited some more, sipping his drink as if he hadn't a care in the world.

Trapped between them, Pamela was out of her league, and she cracked, breaking the silence. "Regina asked to chat with you today. She's eager to discuss Lady Melanie."

Still, Marcus didn't speak, so Pamela urged, "Why don't you begin, Regina?"

Regina shifted in her chair. "We traveled to London at Pamela's invitation, and I was encouraged to believe you had an interest in Melanie."

"Were you?" He sampled his liquor, drained the

glass, and rudely went to pour another, which he enjoyed while Regina regrouped.

"Since our arrival, you haven't shown a hint of curiosity. What are your plans toward her?"

At least she'd spared him extra aggravation by getting straight to the point, without any dillydallying, which sped the conclusion. But what should it be? It was on the tip of his tongue to blurt out that he wouldn't propose in a thousand years, that he despised Melanie, but once the pronouncement was voiced, Regina would pack them up and head out. Kate would go with them, and he'd never see her again.

He'd convinced himself that it was what he wanted, and he'd advised Kate that their liaison was finite, but with reality beating down on him, he was stricken at the thought of her departure.

His nights loomed, a solitary, quiet expanse that she'd imbued with passion and laughter. How could he persevere without her? Yet it wasn't fair to Regina to lead her on, to feign excitement where none had been generated.

He never should have let Pamela persuade him into allowing their visit. It had been folly from the outset.

"I have no *plans* for her." The women bristled, and more gently, he added, "We would be a terrible match— as I'm sure you recognize. Please avail yourself of our continued hospitality for the next week, but after that, it will be best if you return to Doncaster." He stood and downed his brandy. "I trust you will make my apologies to Lady Melanie."

He marched out, and Pamela hesitated, then chased after him, following him out of the house and into the drive. An argument was pending, and he was happy to oblige her, but he detested that she would vent their private quarrel in front of the footmen.

"Marcus!" she called when he would have clambered into his carriage.

He whipped around, his fury and antipathy abundantly clear. "Say it fast, Pamela. I'm in no mood for more of your shenanigans."

She smiled, pretending all was well. "We didn't have our conversation about my monthly financial requests."

"Each and every one is denied."

Money—or the lack of it—always riveted her attention, and any pretense of civility was abandoned. "She demanded a meeting. I couldn't tell her no."

"Why not?"

Pamela struggled for a reply he'd accept, ultimately choosing, "She deserved an audience."

"And now she's had it."

"You can't send them home."

"I can, and I have."

"You never gave the bloody girl a chance."

"She didn't merit one. I can't fathom why you selected a candidate who is so unsuitable for me."

"What—precisely—is it that you would deem to be *suitable* for your exalted self?"

"We could start with an individual who isn't a child and who has a personality."

Pamela fumed, her mouth pursed in an unbecoming grimace. "Am I to pull another fiancée out of my hat? Like a magician at a fair?"

"What you do—or don't—has ceased to matter to me."

"What about our"—she caught herself—"*your* inheritance? The clock is ticking toward your birthday."

"I don't care if you and I end up living on the streets. I really, really don't."

"Bastard!" she hurled.

"Tut, tut, my dear. There's no need to question my antecedents. I'm positive my parents were married before I was born."

Her hostility unmasked, she trembled with rage. "I won't let you fritter away like this."

"I don't see how you can stop me."

"I'll ruin you! I'll fight you in the courts. I'll take you for every penny you have. I'll . . . I'll . . ."

She couldn't conjure up any other threats, and her blustering slid off like water. There was no way to force his hand. "Why don't you find yourself a rich husband, so that I can pry your greedy fingers out of the Stamford coffers?"

"You're a cruel beast!" she seethed.

"Yes, I am."

"I hate you!" She whirled away and ran inside, slamming the door so hard that the windows rattled.

He climbed in the coach, settled himself against the squab, and relaxed as the horses trotted away.

~ 14 ~

"I wish you wouldn't bother Lord Stamford with my troubles."

"Why?" Chris queried. "He's really a very nice fellow, once you get past the bluster."

"Still, it embarrasses me. Please promise that you won't confide in him again—about me or Selena."

"We need his advice, Kate. There's something shady about Selena's money."

"I doubt you could get him to pay any attention to the situation. He assumes—as with everyone in London—that we're a couple of country bumpkins."

"We *are* country bumpkins. That's why he'll help us. We're like fish out of water."

"I've written to her solicitor, Mr. Thumberton, about the discrepancies. Your mother had the letter delivered last week. I'm waiting to hear from him about an appointment."

"That's well and good, but Stamford is available immediately."

"I don't want his assistance!" she insisted, with more bitterness than was necessary.

"Why don't you like him?"

"I just don't, and I won't have you pestering him."

"All right," he concurred, as their carriage rattled to a halt. "I won't approach him," which was a lie to soothe her ruffled feathers. Whether Kate liked it or not, Chris intended to parley with Marcus as soon as he had the chance. Despite what was whispered about him, Stamford was very shrewd, very smart, and Chris was positive he'd have many excellent ideas as to how they should proceed.

In the interim, he'd prepared to move Selena into a more suitable neighborhood, and he'd cover her bills until the fiscal mess was resolved.

He peeked out the curtain, gazing at Selena's dilapidated apartment building. "Before we go inside, I have a question for you."

"I won't answer it," Kate retorted, "until you apprise me as to how you cozied up to Selena, and how you found out she's my sister."

"I asked her if she was."

"When?"

"After I brought you there the first time, I returned on my own." She scowled, and he laughed. "Are you satisfied?"

"But why would you?"

"Because she was the most beautiful girl I'd ever seen"—he blushed at the admission—"and I couldn't resist."

Kate groaned. "Your mother will kill me."

"Why?"

"Selena is my dirty little secret, and Regina aided me
in arranging her affairs only after I swore that I'd never
reveal her existence to a single soul. If she learns that the
two of you are acquainted, she'll have an apoplexy, and
she'll blame me."

"Before all's said and done, I imagine she'll have
more than an apoplexy."

"What do you mean?"

"May I pose my question now?"

"I suppose you may."

In a dither, he straightened his cravat and shifted on
the seat. His entire life, his mother had handled the important decisions. She'd managed his assets, had hired
and fired his employees, had wrangled and finessed himself and Melanie so that things always went her way.

At age eighteen, and almost nineteen, his heritage
weighed heavily on his shoulders. He didn't like how
Regina acted or how she treated others, and he loathed
the air of tension and distrust that she'd fomented at
Doncaster.

He was ready to initiate a transformation, to render
his own solutions, but this was the biggest decision
ever. It was shocking; it was outrageous, and he'd discussed it with no one, had sought no counsel. Was it for
the best? The recipes for disaster scared him witless,
but he had to determine his own fate, had to establish
his independence.

A vision of Selena flashed in his mind, of her as
they'd danced at the masquerade ball, and his heart
swelled with pride and joy. He might be young and untried, but in this he wasn't mistaken. He could arrive at
no better choice, not for himself, and not for the people
of Doncaster.

"You're Selena's guardian."

"Yes, I am."

He cleared his throat. He'd repeatedly rehearsed his speech, but he hadn't realized it would be so difficult to recite.

"So I need to . . . that is . . . I wish to . . ."

"For pity's sake, Chris. Spit it out."

"You like me, don't you, Kate?"

"You're terrific."

"I'll be a worthy husband, wouldn't you agree?"

"Absolutely."

"I was hoping that was your opinion. Miss Duncan," he formally requested, "may I have Selena's hand in marriage?"

Kate gasped. "No. Your mother would murder us both."

"I don't care about my blasted mother!" he sharply remarked.

"This is so sudden, so unexpected."

"It is."

"You can't have thought it through."

"But I have."

"How can I grant my permission?"

"I'm inquiring as a courtesy, Kate," he gently explained. "I want you on our side, but we'll forge ahead, no matter your reply. Don't have me shame her by eloping."

She studied him as if he were speaking in a foreign language. "You've known her for what? Five days?"

"As have you. Can you seriously tell me I'm wrong?" He had to persuade her! With her as his ally, they could face down Regina. "Think of what it would be like to have Selena at Doncaster, as my countess. With her there to help me, we could institute so many changes."

The picture he painted was painful to her, and she leaned into the squab and massaged her temples. "I appreciate that you don't want to talk about Regina, but Chris, you can't have fully considered the ramifications of crossing her. She'll never allow the match, and she'll do whatever she can to stop you."

"Don't worry about Regina." He was growing more confident by the moment. "I want to be happy, Kate. Selena makes me happy. Say *yes*."

For a lengthy interval, she was silent, contemplating and reflecting, and finally she murmured, "I don't have many memories of my mother, but Selena reminds me of her."

"It would be so fitting to have her at Doncaster. I believe your mother would have liked Selena's being there."

She stared him down, searching for his resolve. "Are you sure?"

"I love her, Kate. More than life itself. Give me your blessing."

With a sigh of resignation, she relented. "As if I could refuse you."

He let out a whoop of glee, flung open the carriage door, and leapt out, but he was too impatient to delay as she tottered along behind him. At the apartment, they'd been watching for him, and before he could knock, a maid answered. He swept past her and toward the parlor, as Selena rushed out.

"Chris, you're here!"

He kissed her on the cheek, maintaining some decorum in front of her servants. "I told you I'd come at two."

"Some men visited me. They said you'd sent them."

"They're moving you on Friday."

"To where?"

"I've taken rooms for you at the Carlyle Hotel, just until we locate something more appropriate."

Kate caught up to him, and Selena sparkled with delight. "Kate! Kate!"

She ran forward and hugged her sister, and though Kate was disconcerted by the display of affection, her fondness for Selena was too strong to ignore, and she hugged her back.

"Hello, Selena. It's so good to see you again."

"And you," Selena responded. "What a grand afternoon! I have both of you all to myself!"

"We need to chat," Chris advised her, and he guided her into the parlor, as Kate trailed after them. Selena flashed her a curious look as to whether she was aware of what he planned, but Kate kept her expression carefully blank.

Too nervous to dawdle, he escorted Selena to the sofa, fell to his knee, and clasped her hand. "My darling Selena . . ."

Overwhelmed by emotion, he couldn't finish the sentence.

"What is it, Christopher?" she asked.

"You are the finest woman I've ever met."

"How sweet. *Grazie.*"

"I've known you less than a week, but I feel as if it's been a thousand years."

"I feel the same."

"Would you . . . would you . . . do me the honor of becoming my wife?"

Tears welled into her eyes. "Oh, Chris . . . oh . . ."

Terrified that she might spurn him, he hurried on. "I'm not claiming it won't be difficult. We'll have to deal with my mother, and my sister, and as my countess, you'll have many burdens. But I'll be standing by your side, and I'll always be your best friend."

"Of course you will."

"And I promise that I'll be a true and faithful husband, and I will love and cherish you till I take my last breath. Will you have me?"

She peered at Kate. "Is it all right with you?"

"Nothing would bring me more joy." Kate's eyes glistened with a few tears, too.

Selena turned to him. "Then, yes, I will have you, my dearest Christopher."

"You'll never be sorry."

"No, I never will."

Selena rested her palm on his cheek, which warmed and comforted him, and he could feel her heart beating, pounding in a rhythm with his own. In complete accord, it sealed their pact, joining them together as no vows ever could.

A ray of sunshine burst through the window, encasing them in its bright glow, making it seem as if heaven had approved. Recognizing that his world could never be more perfect than it was at that very instant, he offered up a prayer, for Selena and the many children they would have.

The door to Christopher's room was locked, so Pamela took her key and used it to admit herself.

Foolish boy! she mused. As if he could bar her, in her own house!

He'd been out for hours, arriving home very late, and she was furious. He'd missed a special supper invitation, so she'd been forced to attend with Regina and Melanie, and after their earlier debacle with Stamford, civility simply hadn't been possible.

Pamela wanted them gone, but she couldn't kick them out until she'd convinced Chris to stay in London.

In light of Marcus's comments about Melanie, drastic measures were warranted. Pamela had to stabilize her future, and she couldn't rely on him.

For fourteen years, she'd been beholden to one Stamford male or another, and where had it landed her? With no property, no assets, and not a penny to her name. That's where! Not even her clothes were her own.

She'd laid her cards on the table with Regina, had pledged to deliver Marcus's head on a platter, in exchange for Regina's permitting her pursuit of Christopher. The old bat had enthusiastically agreed, having grasped that if there was anyone in London who had a chance at persuading Stamford, it was Pamela.

Yet, after his curt disavowal of Melanie, Regina had accused her of false negotiations, of reneging on their bargain. With Regina so irate, Pamela couldn't count on her keeping her word. Regina couldn't be trusted, and Pamela realized that she'd finally stumbled upon someone more ruthless than herself.

It was time to assume control of her own destiny. She desired Chris. For his fortune, and his title, but for himself, too. No man could satisfy her as he did. She was pining away, fantasizing and moping.

She had taught him so much, had given so much of herself, but he continued to be cool and detached, keeping a subtle wall erected between them. Their interactions were highly charged and passionate, but when they were concluded, he buttoned his trousers and departed, leaving her with the impression that his fondness wasn't increasing, and she couldn't bear the notion.

Before Regina herded them to Doncaster, Pamela had to secure her situation. Christopher needed a reason to remain behind, and she intended to be that reason.

She could make him love her! She just knew she could. As an unsophisticated child, he couldn't fight her steely determination. Despite the cost, she would have him for her own, and no one was going to stand in her way.

A footman had notified her that he'd rung for a bath, and she could distinguish the scent of soap and hot water emanating from his dressing room. She sauntered over and peeked in. He was relaxing in the tub, his glorious blond hair washed and pushed off his forehead, his skin slippery and wet.

"Hello, Chris."

"I thought I heard you." He sighed. "Pam, when I lock my door, most people would take it to mean that I don't wish to be disturbed."

"You would keep *me* out?"

"What do you want?"

"Can't you guess?"

She slithered out of her robe, her lush figure vividly outlined by her negligee. He scrutinized her torso, his torrid gaze following her as she walked to the dresser and deposited the wine and glasses she'd brought.

While he might pretend no interest, might act aloof and grumble over her presence, his body couldn't lie.

If she reached under the bathwater, he'd be hard as a rock.

Her back was to him, so he couldn't see what she was up to as she removed the cork from the vial of love potion the apothecary had sold her. The mixture was dark red, and it had an earthy odor. She dumped an equal amount into each goblet, added some wine to conceal the drug, then faced him.

He'd exited the tub and was wrapping a towel around his waist, shielding his privates from view, but she could detect the tempting bulge where his erection prodded the fabric.

She smiled. "Will you join me in a nightcap?"

He accepted the glass but didn't drink from it. "You have to quit visiting me," he scolded. "I can't have my mother finding out about us."

"What if she did? Would it be so awful?"

"If we're discovered, there will be a big fuss, which I couldn't abide."

"Let's not worry about it now."

She sampled hers, liking the musky flavor the tincture had supplied. As if the tonic was urging her on, she eagerly gulped it down. Her serving was empty, but he still hadn't raised his, and she began to fret that he wouldn't. He could be such a Puritan!

"Don't be a spoilsport," she coaxed. "I've missed you all day."

She traced the rim of his cup, seducing him with her eyes. From the first, he hadn't been able to resist her, and this occasion was no different. He considered refusing; then he swallowed it down.

He smacked his lips, and ran his tongue over his teeth. "It tastes odd."

"It grows on you." She gestured to his goblet. "Try another sip."

Shrugging, he complied. "It's not so bad."

She smirked, silently cheering her scheme and buoyed by the prospects for success. "To us, darling. May all our dreams come true."

∾ 15 ∾

Kate sat in her room, staring out at the night sky. Rain was falling, hitting the ground in muted thumps, the flowers in the garden drooping. Thunder rumbled in the distance, and a cold breeze fluttered by, cooling her heated skin.

While she was trying to be glad for Selena and Christopher, their news had her so unhappy that her heart ached. Their joy illuminated the poor choices she'd made in her life. The dissatisfaction that bubbled below the surface was leaking out, inundating her in misery.

She had nothing and no one to call her own. Why hadn't she demanded more for herself? Why hadn't she picked a different path?

As she looked down the road to her return to Doncaster, it was such a grim, forlorn vision. Was this all there was? Would she putter away forever little more than Regina's unpaid servant?

On Kate's dresser, she espied the bottle meant to hold a love potion. In case Melanie ever asked for it, it now contained red wine. But Kate had drunk the original. Had it been magic? Could it have caused so much despair?

Lying next to the vial she could see the note and single pink rose Marcus had had delivered. His ring was on her finger.

Come to me at midnight, the message read, and he'd signed it with the initial *S.*

Her time with him was condensed to minutes and hours, her imminent departure looming like a black hole, yet for once, she couldn't go upstairs.

He seemed to realize that she wouldn't visit of her own accord, that she'd need to be cajoled, although his coercion hadn't worked. In a subtle fashion she didn't understand, the events of the afternoon had changed things between them. A veil had been lifted, revealing her actions for what they were. She'd been operating in a trance, mesmerized to folly, not thinking clearly or making sound decisions.

Why had she been fornicating with him? Her conduct violated every tenet she believed, everything she valued about herself.

By running into him in the light of day, in his elegant foyer, a shift had been created in their relationship. It was obvious they didn't belong together, that they had naught in common, and she had to extricate herself from the conundrum into which she'd leapt.

She'd wandered far outside of the bounds of her humble existence, and she had to find her way back, so that when she quit London and went home she could reestablish herself in the country with a modicum of contentment. If she didn't, her quiet routine at Doncaster would slowly drive her mad.

Long before he arrived, she heard his footsteps approaching. She hadn't locked her door, for she couldn't keep him out if he was determined to enter. He would never allow her to ignore his summons, so she'd been expecting him to appear. It was beyond him to let her go until he was good and ready. He was powerful and stubborn, a selfish, omnipotent king, and the mere thought of defying him made her tired.

Flouting his wishes was like sailing into a hurricane. It was impossible to weather the experience unscathed.

He didn't bother to knock, but spun the knob and marched in. She stood, dreading the confrontation, but prepared for it nonetheless.

"What is your sister's name?" he challenged.

Feet braced, hands on hips, he was livid, condemning her, which was so absurd. About what did he have to be furious? She'd complied with his every request, had raced to ruin, had enthusiastically tried each decadent, wicked behavior he'd suggested. What more could he want? How much more had she to give? She felt ravaged, as if he were the devil who'd pilfered her earthly remains and who was now extorting her immortal soul, too.

"Why this abrupt interest in me and my family? Have you discovered that you're human?"

The slur slid by him. "Tell me."

"How can it matter?"

"Tell me!" he snapped, beyond patience.

"Selena Bella."

"How old is she?"

"Sixteen."

"Why didn't you confide in me about her?"

"What purpose would it have served?"

"Perhaps I want to know."

"Other than my foolish and misguided attempts to please you in bed, when have you evinced the slightest curiosity about me?"

"Who was your mother?"

"A rash, impetuous fallen woman, who shamed everyone who cared about her."

"And your father?"

"A man of absolutely no consequence, at all."

She wasn't about to discuss her father, wasn't about to divulge that he'd been the Earl of Doncaster, that she'd once been treated like a princess and because of her mother's recklessness, and her father's weakness, she'd been left alone in the world to fend for herself. She'd choke to death before she'd explain any of it!

"So . . . you were born on the wrong side of the blanket."

"Only you would reach such an insulting conclusion."

"What do you mean?"

"My mother was wed too young, to a man she despised, and she craved an excitement my father couldn't furnish. When I was eight, she ran off with her paramour, and I never saw her again."

"Selena is her illicit child?"

"My mother birthed no bastards, so you can put your suddenly pious mind to rest."

"Your mother married her lover?"

"After my father's death. Will there be anything else? Is there any other detail of my most private and personal affairs that you must probe?"

"I've advised Regina that I won't choose Melanie. I've told her to pack up and depart."

"Bully for you."

Quite sure he was lying, she studied him. Earlier in the evening, she'd spoken to Regina, and she had mentioned no such thing. In fact, Regina had claimed he was coming around. Those were her very words: that they'd conferred over terms and he was *coming around.*

Regina wasn't prone to fantasy or delusion. If she said he was about to marry Melanie, then he was. Why would he deny it? Or was he simply endeavoring to spare her feelings?

Had he considered, for one measly second, what their lives would be like when he became Melanie's husband? She had a vision, of them ensconced at Doncaster, enjoying Sunday dinner, Marcus seated at the head of the table, and she felt ill.

If he could wound her so deeply, she would never forgive him. Never in a thousand years.

"Why are you angry with me?" he queried, which had her supposing that he was the most dim-witted individual she'd ever met. Couldn't he recognize how his very presence cut like a knife to the bone?

"Why are *you* angry with me?" she countered.

He crossed to her, so that they were tangled together. His hands were in her hair, pulling at the strands so that she winced at the pressure.

"You didn't come to me as I asked."

"I'm certain you'll survive."

"Don't ever tell me *no.*"

"I'm not doing this with you anymore!" she wailed. "Can't you get it through your thick skull?" She was so forlorn, so depressed, her emotions scraped raw. She'd never loved before, so she hadn't grasped how painful it could be, how draining and exhausting. It hurt to look at him, and she ached as if she was being lashed by his nearness. "I just want to go home. I want my life to return to normal."

"I can't let you. Not yet."

Anchoring her to him, he wrapped her lengthy tresses around his fists, and started kissing her.

She'd planned to resist, but as with the other occasions she'd been with him, she couldn't. With a groan of dismay, she relented, folding her arms around him and hugging him close. He was a poison in her system, and she'd been contaminated by her desperate desire for him, but her addiction had to be purged.

He picked her up, spun her, and deposited her on the bed. She could have fought to escape, but what was the point? She was incapable of fending him off.

She'd heard that there were animals who would walk peacefully to their doom, who would jump off a cliff or perish in a swollen river, so long as the trusted beast leading the herd guided them to destruction. Now, she comprehended precisely how those poor creatures felt as catastrophe approached. She wasn't afraid or alarmed, but resolved to follow wherever he went.

He yanked on the straps of her negligee, and when he couldn't remove it fast enough, he clasped the neckline and ripped it off, shredding it to the hemline. The pieces fell away, and she was naked and prostrate before him.

Not even the obliteration of the prized garment, one of the few items she possessed that had been her mother's, disturbed her. She was on a slippery slope, careening downward, and she had no idea what would transpire when she hit bottom.

"You can't stay away from me," he insisted. "We shouldn't be separate. We shouldn't be alone."

"But this is killing me. I can't bear much more."

"I won't permit you to avoid me. There's too little time remaining."

"I can't keep on. You want too much from me. More than I am, more than I have inside me. When you're through, there'll be nothing left."

"Yes, I want it all! Give yourself to me. Don't hold anything back!"

"I love you," she blurted out, shaming herself even further. "How stupid is that?"

Her declaration stunned him, but he didn't offer a similar sentiment. Though she hadn't expected him to. He was who he was: a solitary, influential man, who— for reasons she still didn't understand—had focused his potent attentions on her.

He dallied with women for one purpose, and one purpose only, and that was sexual congress. He'd never concealed his intentions, or professed that their conduct had a loftier objective. His goal was physical satisfaction, as quickly and as often as he could manage it, and any hopes she might have had to the contrary were idiotic.

This fleeting, brief affair was all she would ever have of him, and the bleakness of her situation overwhelmed her. Tears surged and coursed down her cheeks.

Why had no one ever loved her? Why couldn't he?

He was stricken by her maudlin exhibition, detesting that he had to witness it, but she was beyond caring. Had she asked him to barge in? He could deal with her upset or go!

"My beautiful Kate," he murmured, "you can't
be sad."

"I hate you."

"No, you don't."

"Yes, I do," but they both knew she was lying.

How could she *hate* him? He was the sole ray of
sunshine in her dreary existence.

"I've never been loved before, Kate." The admission
shocked her, not so much that he'd voiced it, but because
he'd confessed such a personal detail. She'd never
encountered anyone who so meticulously guarded his
thoughts.

"Well, I wish I hadn't been the first."

"Let your affection rain down on me. Drown me
with it, so that I can reminisce after you leave."

"Oh, Marcus."

Perhaps he didn't cherish her, but she could act as if
he did. A bit of pretending would make her own circumstances less dismal.

He kissed away her tears. "Show me how much I
mean to you."

She couldn't refuse his request, for she, too, wanted
him to recollect. She was so weak, so pitiful, in her
need to please him! Yet she relished the embrace, her
busy fingers stripping him of his clothes, until he was
as naked as she, and she stretched out, their nude torsos
melded.

He was hard, eager, and she moved down, to his
belly, his groin. His cock extended out to greet her, and
she stroked him; then she sucked him into her mouth.

This was what she craved, this mindless, uncontrol-
lable spiral where there was just pleasure. She had no
extra energy to worry about Melanie or Regina, Selena

or Christopher, or to grieve over Marcus and how she would carry on without his bittersweet company.

Rapidly, he was at the edge, prepared to leap over, and he drew her up and rolled them so that she was beneath him. He smiled, what minimal fondness he possessed flickering through.

"I will always love you," she told him. "Never forget."

"I never will."

"No matter what happens. No matter where I end up."

"Hush. Don't let's talk about the future."

He was correct to ignore their pending separation. Why lament? He would never beg her to stay, and if he did, she'd never accept. Their fates were sealed, their destinies dragging them down different roads.

He entered her, and she arched up, wrapping her legs around him, needing to take him as deep as she could.

There was a finality and graveness to their actions that they both sensed. Each touch, each caress, held a significance it hadn't before. They were building memories, storing them away.

Her orgasm was imminent, and she shattered, losing herself in the wildness of the exploit. He joined her, and they hurled over the precipice together, tensing and crying out as the inferno swept through.

To her surprise, he didn't extricate himself, as he had in the past. His phallus throbbed inside her, his seed spewing into her womb, and the feeling—the *rightness*—increased her gratification, and she soared higher than ever.

She didn't know why he'd been so reckless, yet she wasn't sorry. Not at the moment, when he was still buried within her, when he was still shuddering with the throes of passion.

In the morning, she imagined she'd panic, that she would rue and curse his name, but for now, she was elated.

Their ardor waned, and he slid out of her and spooned her to him, her backside nestled to his front. He tugged a blanket over them and snuggled with her, but he didn't speak, choosing not to mention what he'd done, so she didn't raise the issue, either.

Her heart was heavy with mixed emotions, the silence so acute, the impression of conclusion so intense, that she was left to wonder if this wasn't farewell, but he was unable to tell her so.

He draped his arm across her, patting his thumb across her knuckles and stumbling on his signet ring. When he'd arrived in her room, she'd been wearing it and had forgotten that she was, and he chuckled.

"You can't have this, my little thief."

"I didn't—"

"I know; I know. You didn't steal it."

She sighed. Any defense was a waste of breath. How could she explain that it kept popping up, despite her best efforts to be shed of it? If she babbled a word about love potions or unseen forces, he'd deem her a lunatic.

He took the ring off her finger and put it onto his own, curling his hand into a fist as if he suspected she'd filch it again the instant he wasn't watching.

"I have another ring for you," he said.

"I don't want it."

"I'm giving it to you anyway. It will be a gift from me, something to remember me by."

She rubbed her abdomen, speculating as to whether he hadn't already bestowed a *gift,* and trying to decide what she would do if catastrophe arose, and she was sure it would. Since she'd met him, her life had been one disaster after the next, so she was positive that the worst was bound to transpire.

"You're a tyrant."

"Yes."

"You never listen to me."

"Why should I, when you're being silly?"

"What will I do with a fancy piece of jewelry? How will I account for it to others? Will I say that I found it on the street?"

"Kate!" She'd exasperated him. The lesser mortals who inhabited his world never quarreled with his edicts, or declined to obey his orders, and he was aggravated that she would. "I want you to have it."

And that was that. He wouldn't take *no* for an answer, so she'd have to agree. She'd keep it hidden, but it would be a memento that she could sleep with under her pillow. If calamity struck, and there was a babe, she could sell the ring for the money she would need after Regina branded her a harlot and banished her from Doncaster.

He linked their fingers, squeezing tight, and she felt as if they were the last two people on earth, as if she was tethered to him and if he released her, she might float away.

"I'm going to stay with you tonight," he declared.

It was pointless to argue. "All right."

"Let's rest a bit, and then I'll love you again."

"I'd like that."

Was it to be their final rendezvous? As he reposed, as he slumbered, she closed her eyes, noting every detail. She focused solely on his large, warm body cuddled to hers and refused to ponder the morrow or what it would bring.

Pamela lurched down the hall, frantic to locate her bed-chamber, but not certain where she was in the huge mansion. Her head pounded as if there were a blacksmith with a hammer inside it, her stomach roiled with nausea, and she hoped she wouldn't vomit on the priceless rugs.

What had happened? She'd been in Christopher's room, had slipped him the drugged wine, which they'd both drunk. She'd pulled the towel from his loins and . . .

She had a hazy memory of being on her knees, of having him in her mouth, but she couldn't determine if it was a dream or reality. What had occurred—or not—after that was a mystery, but it must have been exquisite. She'd been transformed by a new and formidable affection.

A vision of her beautiful Christopher flashed, so blond and radiant—like a god—with his smooth boy's torso, his lean, lanky physique. She ached with loving him. It was a living, fomenting beast inside her. She was consumed by a yearning so potent, and so severe, that she didn't know how she would cope with it simmering inside her.

Chris . . . Chris . . . Chris . . . His name echoed through vein and pore. She couldn't wait to be with him, once again, so that she could show him how desperately she cared.

She'd awakened on a sofa in the main parlor, though she had no recollection of how she'd come to be there. Freezing, and with a cramp in her neck, she'd staggered up the stairs. Dawn was breaking, and she was anxious to be sequestered in her suite before any of the staff saw her.

But where was she? And why couldn't she get her bearings?

That blasted potion! It had to have been much more powerful than she'd been led to believe. She felt as if she was suffering from a near-fatal hangover.

Down the corridor, a door was furtively opened, the occupant creeping out, and Pamela halted, huddling in the shadows, terrified she might be observed in her deplorable condition. Who—besides herself—could possibly be wandering about at such a hideous hour?

To her amazement, it was Marcus, slithering out and no more interested in detection than she. Why was he in the house? Why was he in a guest's bedroom? Whose was it? Was it even occupied?

She was too muddled to recall.

It was clear he'd been trysting, but with whom? Had he stooped to philandering with the servants? Which hussy would dare?

He was attired just in his trousers, no shoes or stockings, his shirt off and dangled over his shoulder. He dawdled in the threshold, gazing into the room with such a mixed expression of anguish and joy that she could barely stand to watch.

The bounder was thoroughly smitten! There could be no other explanation for his combined air of melancholy and elation. How could he be? How could such an outrageous, shocking event transpire, without her being aware?

In farewell, he kissed his fingertips and sent the gesture winging toward his paramour. For several agonizing seconds, he tarried, in abject misery, his shoulders bowed, his despair and woe rolling off him in waves. Then he walked to the servants' stairs and the short climb that took him up to the master's chambers.

Pamela lingered, not breathing, not moving a muscle, until she heard the faint sound of his tread on the floor above; then she stole over and peeked inside.

Sprawled across the mattress, her glorious auburn hair scattered over the pillows, was Melanie Lewis's chaperone. She was naked, sleeping, the quilt rising and falling with each respiration. She appeared young, fetching, innocent, but looks were deceiving, because there was no doubt she'd been debauched by Stamford.

The space was a mess, blankets and garments strewn about. They'd fornicated with a reckless abandon, with the sort of blissful connection that only the luckiest of lovers ever achieved.

This is what he's been doing? Pamela rippled with fury. All this time, she'd been waiting for him to buckle down, to get serious about Melanie, to rescue them from ruin, but instead, he'd been dabbling with the hired help. She was so incensed that she worried she might explode.

Unnoticed by the inhabitant, Pamela tiptoed away. At the stairs, she stumbled to the next floor, and groped her way to Regina's door.

She banged loudly, the noise making her head throb, but she continued until the shrew growled, indicating that she'd stirred; then Pamela strode in.

Regina was scrambling out of bed, her nightgown twisted, her mobcap askew, her feet hitting the rug as Pamela sidled up to her.

"What is the meaning of this?" she snarled as she recognized her intruder.

"You've been demanding I deliver Stamford. Well, you must do your share to bring him to heel."

"For God's sake, it's the middle of the night. About what are you babbling?"

"Stamford has been sneaking into the mansion, so that he can fuck your pretty little governess."

Regina almost collapsed. "What did you say?"

"He's enamored of that trollop you refer to as a chaperone. They've likely been carrying on ever since you arrived."

"Are you sure you're not mistaken?"

"I saw them," Pamela lied. "No wonder your mousy daughter can't catch his eye. He's too busy tumbling your servants." Lest she commit assault, she whipped around and marched away. "I want her out of my house. Today! Do you understand me?"

"Yes," Regina hissed, "I understand."

"After she's gone, if you can't manage to have Melanie fully compromised in the next twenty-four hours, I'll arrange it for you."

"I can handle me and my own without any half-hearted assistance from you."

Pamela snorted in derision. Regina couldn't find the dining table if someone didn't show her the direction every morning. "In the interim, I suggest you throw on some clothes, and haul your fat ass down to the rear garden, before he slinks out to the mews and rides off."

"Don't order me about, Pamela. Lesser people than you have tried, and they've always been sorry."

"Shut up. I'm so sick of you. If you plan to corner

him into an agreement, you'll not have many more chances. After your governess departs, there's no telling when we'll be able to lure him over here."

Regina turned and strutted back to bed.

"Go after him!" Pamela shrieked.

"I'll not embarrass myself by running around in the dark, hysterical and barely dressed—like some people I know."

"The woman is the key!" Pamela shouted. "He's absolutely besotted. See if you can do something right for a change. Use her to lay him low."

"I intend to," Regina claimed, "but at a decent hour. Now leave me be." She clambered onto the mattress and pulled the covers up to her chin.

Pamela stormed out and slammed the door behind.

~ 16 ~

Marcus sat behind his desk, assessing the pile of pilfered loot Regina had displayed. There were common
household items, as well as priceless heirlooms,
including silver candlesticks, a gilded picture frame,
many coins, and, most shockingly, a diamond cravat
pin from his dresser.

Wary, determined not to believe a word spewed
from her obnoxious mouth, he asked, "Are you claiming Miss Duncan is a thief?"

"Considering the objects in front of you"—Regina
gestured to the cache—"there is no need to utter the
accusation aloud."

"Where did you find them?"

"In her room. Tucked under the bed."

"With what intent?"

"Probably to sell for cash, although frequently, she
hoards what she purloins. She gains an odd thrill from
doing wrong, from being in possession of something
she oughtn't to have."

"And you're telling me this because . . . ?"

She was cold and calm as a snake before it strikes, and he took a breath, held it, refusing to give in to the urge to squirm. From the moment her note had been delivered to his club, calling for a meeting to discuss Kate, he'd been consumed with dread.

What could the old bat have up her sleeve? She had to have learned of their liaison. But how? From whom? And what would she demand? Not marriage. She was too greedy, too set on Melanie's advancement, so Kate was in the bulls-eye.

Kate would be the method by which Regina achieved her goals, and no matter what choices he made, they would be bad ones. Catastrophe was about to unfold, and his beloved Kate would be devoured.

Was he ready to hurt her? Could he?

He went to the sideboard, poured himself a stout whiskey, and returned to his chair. Sipping on the potent brew, he was bolstered by the brief interruption. "You've admitted that your Miss Duncan is not honest. You've restored what she filched. Such a paltry issue could have been broached with the housekeeper, so I fail to see why it was necessary to drag me here."

"Let's be frank, shall we?"

She oozed bitterness and sarcasm, and he responded in kind. "By all means. Let's be *frank*."

"I know about your affair with her."

His initial instinct was to deny any connection, but Regina was so blunt and assured that he had no doubt as to her possessing accurate information. What purpose would be served by disavowal except to delay the inevitable?

"Who told you?"

"Lady Pamela."

"Of course." He'd deal with her later. "I'm still not clear as to why you required an appointment with me. If you think it appropriate to comment on my private life, you have more gall than any woman I've ever met."

"It's obvious you harbor deep feelings for her."

He bristled with fury. What had Pamela said? Why would she presume to understand so much about his association with Kate?

"I harbor *deep* feelings? For Miss Duncan?" He scoffed, and with his repudiation of her, he'd likely damned himself to hell, but he forged on. "If that's what you suppose, then you don't know me, at all."

"I know enough." Bending down, she retrieved a pouch off the floor, pulled out a ledger, and rested it on the desk. "Let me come straight to the point. Kate is a thief."

"So you've alleged." He shrugged, though he was dying inside. How often had she taken his signet ring? He'd lost track.

"She has some terrible personal problems, that stem from her mother's abandonment of her when she was a girl. Are you aware of her history?"

Crudely, he maintained, "We didn't spend much time talking."

"Her mother ran off with a lover. As a result of the shame, her father committed suicide."

He hadn't heard this piece of the story, and the wall he'd planned to keep erect, to deflect any bombs Regina might hurl, started to fall. "She was orphaned?"

"I was her only living relative, and it was my Christian duty to care for her."

If Regina were a Christian, he would become a god-less heathen! "She's not your employee?"

"No."

"You raised her?"

"As a member of the family, with my own children as her companions, but she never recovered from the loss of her parents. She steals."

"Yes, yes. She steals. She steals. So what?"

Regina pushed the journal closer, but he wouldn't glance at it.

"She has a sister."

This wasn't news, and he accepted it blandly. "I thought she was alone in the world."

"Her sister is illegitimate."

Feigning boredom, he peered at the clock on the mantle. "You need to hurry, Regina. I've a game of dice commencing at four. I don't want to be late."

"Kate is her guardian and approves expenditures from the trust."

"And . . . ?"

"She's been embezzling." Regina patted the book. "Look at the numbers. Money that should have lasted for decades is almost gone."

"You'd have me believe that you magically found papers proving as much?"

"I won't defend how I stumbled upon them, but they're genuine."

He still hadn't peeked down and wouldn't, but he gave up any pretense of distance by using Kate's name. "You're contending that Kate's pocketed the entire amount?"

"I'm not *contending* she has. It's a fact. The scheme is simple. The girl sends her bills to Kate, and

Kate fakes new ones, for a much higher figure, then pockets the difference."

He was arguing for form's sake. The previous afternoon, hadn't Christopher mentioned some abnormality with the trust?

Oh, Kate! he wailed inwardly. *What have you done?*

"Why would she?" he prodded. "She's scarcely flaunting a fortune. What could be her motive?"

"She's not right in the head. She has reasons we couldn't begin to comprehend."

"Fine, Regina. Kate's a crook, an embezzler. Why are you confiding in me?"

"With the sums involved, this is a serious felony. She could be hanged."

After a painful lull, he inquired, "Or?"

"I could conceal it . . . so that no one would ever learn of her crime."

"How?"

"I would reimburse the funds, out of the Doncaster coffers. It would be a hardship, but I would make the sacrifice."

"In exchange for what?"

"For your marrying Melanie."

He chuckled. "You assume you can coerce me into it?"

"I'm positive I can. With your darling Kate as my bait."

"You're certainly convinced that I'm smitten. It's quite a gamble on your part."

"It's no gamble." She picked up the ledger, tucked it into her satchel, and balanced it on her lap. "There's a man at Doncaster who loves Kate, who's always loved her. He's older than she, and initially, he was married to another. Now, he's a widower, with two toddlers. She's fond of him, and she adores his daughters. He'd like to propose once she's home."

The tidings sucked the air out of the room. His collar felt too tight, and he couldn't catch his breath. "Have you told Kate?"

"Not yet." She was silent, letting the gravity of the information sink in. "He's a good man, with a steady job in our stables. He has a decent house behind the manor, and an excellent salary. He'll be kind to her." She paused, flogging him with her words. "I can erase the irregularities in the trust, and she can go back to the country. She'll have a husband who cherishes her, and babes to mother. What other opportunity does she have? What alternative would you select for her?"

Regina's questions poked at him like the blade of a sharp knife, but he wouldn't permit her to detect how disconcerted he was. "Why would you imagine I have any interest in what becomes of her?"

"Precisely." Regina stared him down, her low opinion of his character abundantly clear. "What can you offer her? Are you prepared to marry her yourself?"

"God, no." He could barely suppress a shudder. There was no more horrid punishment he could inflict on Kate than to saddle her with the burden of his being her husband. He was who he was, and she deserved so much better.

"Will you make her your mistress? When you tire of her—as we both realize you will—what then?"

How he wished she would shut up! Candidly, he stated, "I don't know."

"Would you rather throw her to the dogs in the judicial

system? Will you be responsible for having her incarcerated, perhaps executed?"

"*I* could pay off the trust fund discrepancies."

"Yes, you could, but I ask again: What then?"

What then? indeed. Would she stay in London? As his what? She was no doxy, to be used badly and discarded.

Downing his whiskey, he walked over, poured himself another, and drank that, too. His hands were shaking, his pulse pounding. Regina was much more shrewd than he'd surmised, and he hated that she'd cornered him by utilizing Kate.

He gazed out the window, at the roses in the garden. How had this happened? He had so few valid options, and his great affection for her had been reduced to such a glaring, unpalatable conclusion.

"This is checkmate, Stamford. The choice is yours. What shall it be?"

Wasn't it best to send Kate to Doncaster? To a man who loved her? She should have a normal life, where she would be free of his wicked influence. Though it killed him to ponder her wedding another, he would survive it. He couldn't hurt her any more than he already had.

"Have someone fetch her. I'll break it off."

"A wise decision."

Regina retrieved some documents and passed them over. "Sign these first."

"What are they?"

"The marital contracts." He stiffened, surprised by her temerity, and she chortled. "Do you take me for a fool? I'll have your agreement in writing or not at all."

"With all due respect, madam, I can't abide the notion of marrying your daughter."

"So? How can it possibly matter? You make no bones about how one girl is the same as the next. Melanie is no better or worse than any other."

"A stunning endorsement of her stellar qualities."

"I'm a realist."

"Are you?"

"Absolutely. You should view this as a blessing. With the stroke of a pen, your assets will be secured, and your search for a bride will have ended."

Swiftly, he read the terms, and he was so detached, having limited concern as to how events would play out. His sole worry was that Kate's future be guaranteed.

He ascribed his name. "That should suffice."

"I'll apply for a Special License, with the ceremony held here in London, a week from today."

"I want it accomplished quickly and quietly, and don't bother me with any of the details. I also demand that you keep your daughter away from me. Considering the circumstances, I have no stomach for any of her juvenile pandering."

"As you wish."

She nodded, then went to the hall, calling for a servant to find Kate and order her to join them.

"Have you purchased more of the potion?" Melanie queried.

"Yes."

Kate handed over the latest vial, which contained merely red wine, but Melanie didn't need to be apprised of the contents. Kate wasn't about to obtain more of the dangerous concoction. In light of her own experience, she declined to be liable for others imbibing the mysterious tonic.

She couldn't bear much more torment, couldn't endure many more conversations where Melanie waxed on about how it would be when Marcus was her spouse. The topic was too excruciating, and Kate could no longer discuss it civilly.

Didn't anyone—besides herself—see what a mistake this was? What if they managed to persuade him? Had they contemplated the union that would be created? What type of crazed people would intentionally impose that much gloom on themselves?

A knock sounded, and she answered it, recognizing that Melanie never would. Melanie had always treated Kate as her personal servant.

"What is it?" Kate inquired of the maid who tarried in the hall.

"Lord Stamford and Lady Regina request that you immediately attend them in the library."

Kate frowned. "Are you sure they didn't mean Lady Melanie?"

"No, miss. They were quite explicit in asking for you."

"For me?"

"Yes."

Her heart thumped with dread. Marcus and Regina were together? Commanding her presence? What could they want? It couldn't be anything good.

She glanced at Melanie.

"What have you done now?" Melanie snapped.

"Nothing."

"A likely story."

Kate smiled at the maid. "I'll be right down." She

closed the door and leaned against it, needing a few seconds to collect herself.

"You might as well blurt it out," Melanie goaded. "I'll learn of it soon enough."

"There's naught to tell," she mumbled.

Her thoughts awhirl, she was terrified as to what the encounter portended. How could she go in blind? If she could guess their purpose, she'd be better prepared to defend herself, although if the subject was her scandalous behavior, there weren't many excuses she could provide.

"You're constantly causing trouble," Melanie scolded. "It's about time you received your just desserts. When I'm wed to Stamford and have my own house, you'll not be allowed such liberties. Mother should have reined you in years ago. I don't understand why she permits you to gad about."

Kate assessed Melanie, wondering how she'd earned such enmity, and for once, she was out of patience and beyond circumspection. "Shut up, Melanie."

Melanie leapt to her feet. "How dare you speak to me so rudely! I'll advise Mother of what you said. She'll have you whipped!"

"I'm certain she'll be eager to proceed."

Kate strode out, refusing to be distracted by Melanie's tantrum. All the way down the hall, Melanie's yelling was discernable. A loud thud reverberated from her having thrown something at the wall, but Kate kept walking.

The stairs were an intolerable gauntlet, that went on forever. At the bottom, disaster awaited, so she took each step slowly, feeling as if she were marching to the gallows.

The butler lurked at the entrance to the library, briskly knocking to announce her arrival. He flashed a glare of such scorn and rebuke that she had no doubt he'd been eavesdropping.

What had he heard? She yearned to have the floor open and swallow her whole!

Knees quaking, but head high, she strolled past him and into the opulent, masculine space. Marcus was behind his desk, Regina in the chair opposite. Neither stood, and Marcus wouldn't look at her.

Coward! She hurled the mental reprimand toward him.

She crossed to them, but she wasn't invited to sit, making it plain how far they were separated from her by rank and station. This was not a friendly chat. She was in for castigation, and punishment would follow.

There were numerous objects scattered on the desktop, and she studied them, her face carefully blank as she tried to deduce what they signified.

Regina ended her speculation.

"I found these items hidden in your room, and I've shown them to Lord Stamford."

It was the last attack she'd anticipated, and her eyes widened with shock and dismay, so she appeared guilty before they'd even begun.

She forced herself to remain calm. "Are you calling me a thief?"

Regina rose, a hulking, angry menace, who towered over Kate in both size and stature. "We are Lady Pamela's guests, and you've shamed our family. I demand that you apologize for your larceny, and that you swear to Lord Stamford you'll not disgrace yourself again, so long as you reside here."

"I've never seen any of those things before," she attempted to claim.

Regina peered at Marcus and shrugged. "Have I convinced you? She's mad."

Marcus finally located the courage to meet her gaze, and his disappointment was so evident that she felt as if he was stabbing her with it. "Kate," he gently admonished, "don't make this worse than it already is. Just admit what you've done, so we can move on."

A potent fury surged through her. Regina had told him she was unbalanced, that she was a thief, and without any consideration, he'd believed Regina's lies.

Kate wanted to weep, to shout and rail. Didn't he know her, at all?

He was so willing to think badly of her, to cast her aside, to have Regina as his partner, so Kate wasn't about to demean herself by begging him to have faith in her. If he'd pulled out a pistol and shot her dead, it would have been so much more bearable than this . . . this . . . betrayal.

"I have nothing to say," she replied, sick at heart and wounded to her very core.

As if Kate were the heaviest burden in the world, Regina sighed, feigning great concern. "I'll dispatch her to Doncaster at once, and I'll carry through with the plans we discussed."

"Good." He nodded, and Kate's ire flared anew.

They'd *discussed* her, had they? They'd parleyed and nattered about her as if she were a prized cow off to slaughter, or an African slave in bondage.

"I'll be excited to hear all about it," she chided. "I'm absolutely on pins and needles."

"It's for the best, Kate," he insisted.

"Oh, I'm sure it is," she bitterly retorted.

"And I hope you'll return the money you took."

"What?"

"To avoid a scandal, Regina has agreed to replace the funds in your sister's trust, but I'd like to prevail upon you to restore them of your own accord."

Regina was alleging that she'd pilfered Selena's trust? How could Marcus imply that she would behave so despicably? She couldn't steal from her own sister! She was so lacking in a criminal state of mind, that if such a dastardly deed had occurred to her, she'd have had no idea how to implement it!

She stared him down.

He was cool and composed, imperturbable, and the love she'd had for him instantly metamorphosed into a white-hot hatred so intense that it nearly blew her down with its severity.

"I'd give it back," she sarcastically declared, "but she has so much, while I have so little. Why should I?"

Distraught over her flip response, he gaped at her, unable to fathom how he could have failed to detect her felonious disposition. She yearned to shake him, to slap away his smug, calculated expression, to hit him and hit him, over and over again, until he fell to the floor in a bloody heap.

Regina clucked and tutted over Kate's remark. "Honestly, Kate," she scolded, "I expected better from you."

"Did you?" Kate rejoined. "Did you really?" She trembled with such malevolence and hostility that Regina flinched and shifted out of range.

Regina gestured to Marcus. "Tell her the rest."

Kate waited, then waited some more, but he couldn't spit it out. He blushed, embarrassed by whatever he was about to recount.

"Well?" Kate queried, and still, he couldn't answer.

Regina butted in. "Your affair with him has been exposed."

"So?" Kate sneered. "As you're neither my mother nor my guardian and I am fully of age, I don't see how it's any of your business."

"You live in my home"—Regina sputtered with rage—"you eat the food at my table, and you maintain it's not my *business* if you act like a harlot?" She scowled to Marcus. "Before she met you, she was an innocent. She had no background to help her defend against male duplicity."

"I'm aware of that fact," he assented uneasily.

"You've had innumerable experiences with seduction, haven't you, Stamford?"

"I suppose."

"Don't be so modest. Kate is hardly the first you've debauched. You enjoy quite a reputation as a libertine and scoundrel."

"I've never been a saint," he admitted.

"It's well known that you regularly lure women into every manner of dissolution. Why . . . you practically regard it as a challenge to corrupt them."

"I wouldn't go that far."

"A man will pretend fondness, won't he, Stamford, in order to coax a female to immorality?"

"It happens all the time."

"You're no different from any other, are you?"

"Probably not," he allowed.

"I'm positive Kate assumes you're in love with her. Wouldn't you suspect the same?"

"It's possible."

"Have you ever loved her?"

He glanced down. "No."

"Do you love her now?"

"No," he repeated, his voice barely a whisper.

"She likely presumes that you have honorable intentions toward her. She might even imagine that you'd marry her. Would you?"

"It would be the worst folly ever."

Regina paused, letting his disavowal fester, ensuring that the momentous impact was sufficiently devastating. Kate had never been more humiliated. She wanted to die, wanted to curl up in a ball and cease to be.

"Did you hear him, Kate?" Regina ultimately asked. "He doesn't love you. He *never* loved you."

"Yes, I heard him, Regina."

She'd always understood that Marcus was isolated and solitary, that he deliberately kept himself separate from others, but she'd never recognized him to be cruel. Why would he feel the need to participate in her crucifixion?

When had he become Regina's puppet? Why had he acquiesced in such brutality? He'd drowned whatever spark of affection she'd harbored for him. Must he grind her into the rug until there was nothing left of the person she once was?

"I believe we've gotten her attention," Regina snarled to Marcus, "so tell her the rest of it, or I will!"

He continued to study the floor. "I'm marrying Melanie, Kate. One week from today. It's been arranged."

There was no more horrid, or more painful, comment he could have made, and though she struggled to sustain her equanimity, she couldn't stop the single tear that plopped down her cheek.

"Like gravitates to like, Kate," Regina crowed. "How foolish of you to reach so far above your station."

Kate felt as if the death knell had sounded, his words killing any soft portion of her that had ever existed.

She glared at him, begging him to look at her, but he wouldn't. Was he mortified? Sorry? She snorted with disgust. Most likely, he was simply dreading the hideous encounter and desperate for it to be over, yet she dawdled, pathetically wishing that he'd smile at her a final time.

"Will that be all?" she quietly inquired.

"Yes," Regina replied, "that will be all. Proceed to my bedchamber and wait for me. I'll be up in a few minutes."

Numb and ill, Kate trudged to the door and was about to exit when Marcus called to her back.

"Kate!" he implored, her name wrenched from his lips.

She halted and frowned at him over her shoulder. "What?"

"I hope you'll be happy in your new situation. I really do. Good luck, and all the best to you."

She had no idea about what he was talking. He appeared sincere, yet terribly sad. It almost seemed as if he was regretting what he'd just done, but why would he?

As Regina had so bluntly indicated, he'd merely drifted to his own kind. He inhabited a sphere that used to be hers, but it wasn't any longer, and he'd picked someone of his own class, someone appropriate and fitting to be the wife of an earl.

Why should she be surprised? Why should she be crushed? Why should she feel as if her broken heart might quit beating?

"Go to hell, *Lord* Stamford."

She spun on her heel and walked out.

~ 17 ~

Regina burst into her bedchamber, her rage so intense that not even her sense of triumph could dampen her dark surge of anger.

Kate was lucky they were in town and surrounded by so many others. If they'd been in the country, if they'd been alone, Regina might have been driven to commit murder.

Kate was perched on a chair, her meager belongings packed, her portmanteau at her feet. She'd donned her cloak and was ready to depart. Pale as a marble statue, she looked icy, frozen, detached from reality, and so mentally distant that Regina wondered if her mind hadn't snapped.

Melanie hovered beside her, flitting around like an irritating gnat.

"What's Kate done, Mother?" Melanie inquired. "She won't tell me."

Regina ignored the question and retrieved her walking stick from the wardrobe; then she went to Kate, halting in front of her.

"Stand up," she ordered, and Kate rose, exuding a belligerence and lack of remorse that enraged Regina further. "Apprise Melanie of your perfidy. I would have her learn of this betrayal from your own treacherous lips."

"I've been having an affair with Lord Stamford. I'm being sent home."

"What do you mean?" Melanie queried.

Melanie was too naive to grasp the implications, so Regina explained, "She's been sneaking into his bed at night, entertaining him as a prostitute would."

Melanie gasped. "Deny it, Kate."

Kate was mutinously silent, so Regina continued. "We've been in a dither over why Stamford wouldn't court you, but he was occupied, slaking his manly lust with her. She has the morals of an alley cat, just like her mother."

Melanie bristled. "After all our kindnesses toward you!"

"She fancied him to be in love with her. With *her!* Can you believe it?"

"Don't say so, Mother. I can't bear it."

"He liked her more than you; he wanted her more than you. Her! The daughter of a whore."

"How dare you!" Melanie seethed.

"Harlot!" Regina hissed.

She raised her cane and cracked it across Kate's face. Kate hadn't expected the blow, so she was unprepared. The rod smacked against bone, and she crumpled to the floor, a whimpering ball of shocked agony.

Regina brought it down, over and over, whipping it across Kate's shoulders, buttocks, and legs, reveling in how each strike landed with precision. To her credit,

Kate didn't resist the beating, but stoically accepted the punishment as her due. Regina kept on, until her arm was tired, until she was perspiring from the effort. In disgust, she stepped away and tossed the cane on the rug. Kate remained huddled on the floor, too stunned to move.

"You can't stop now," Melanie complained. "She has to pay for how badly she's behaved."

"She'll *pay* forever," Regina sneered.

"What will happen to her?"

"She's about to disappear, so she won't be back to plague us."

"Are you positive?"

"Trust me: She shan't return." Regina straightened her hair, her gown. "I don't want your brother to know about this. He can't have a chance to intervene. Don't tell him."

"As if I would," Melanie huffed. "Get her out of here. I'm sickened by the sight of her."

Regina fetched her coat and hat as she advised Melanie, "I've come to an agreement with Stamford."

"About what?"

"He's decided to have you, after all. The wedding is a week from today. In London."

Melanie was astonished and alarmed. "You can't be serious."

"I was never more so."

"When will he propose?"

"Propose?"

"Yes. When will he ask for my hand?"

Girls—with their foolish, romantic notions! "He's a busy man. He doesn't have time for such folderol."

"But I've been planning on it!" she griped. "I've selected the dress I'll wear for the occasion and everything. I'll just die if he doesn't!"

After so many trying hours, Regina was in no mood for Melanie's whining. She pulled herself up to her full height. "You'll marry him, and you'll be happy about it."

Defiantly, Melanie contended, "If he doesn't propose, I won't go through with it. You'll never make me. Never in a thousand years!"

Regina was still roiling from the thrashing she'd administered, and briefly, she considered using the cane on Melanie. Where had the child located the nerve to be so rebellious?

"We'll see," Regina threatened, but took no action. In her current state, she couldn't predict of what she might be capable.

She spun away and grabbed Kate by the arm, hauling her to her feet. She was battered and bruised, a cut oozing on her cheek, and she sucked in a tortured breath.

Good! Perhaps her ribs were broken.

"We're leaving the house," Regina notified her. "Will you walk out on your own, or shall I drag you like the rubbish you are?"

"I'll walk," Kate mumbled.

"We'll utilize the rear stairs. You'll acknowledge no one; you'll talk to no one. Do you understand?"

"Yes, I understand."

Regina started out, aggravated by Kate's slow and unsteady strides. She lugged her along, wanting only to be finished with the entire sordid business.

"When will you be back?" Melanie demanded as they trudged into the hall.

"Later," Regina replied. "I have many tasks to perform before this debacle is concluded."

She ushered Kate down and out to the mews, thankfully not encountering anyone. The hack she'd hired was ready, the driver in the box and awaiting directions. They climbed in and were off without incident.

As they traveled toward their destination, Regina was relieved that Kate was quiet. After all, about what had they to chat?

The carriage rumbled to a halt, but Kate didn't indicate that the cessation had registered, and Regina commanded, "Get out."

"Where are we?" she was cogent enough to question.

"I've dropped you at your sister's, which is more than you deserve. I should have thrown you into the gutter to fend for yourself." She opened the door and pitched Kate's bag into the street. "Don't ever contact us. Don't write; don't inquire; don't return to Doncaster. If you dare, you'll be sorry."

Kate dawdled for such a lengthy interval that Regina wondered if she'd have to physically push her out. Ultimately, she stirred and queried, "Why have you always hated me? What did I ever do to you?"

"I don't hate you," Regina declared. "I don't care about you, at all. You're nothing to me. You never have been. Now be off—before I take a stick to you again."

Kate stumbled out, groaning as her muscles protested. Regina knocked on the roof, signaling the driver to proceed. In a matter of seconds, she was away, and she peeked out, catching a glimpse of Kate, collapsed on her sister's stoop.

"Whore!" Regina muttered.

She checked her timepiece, glad to note that she'd be gone when the solicitor's men rolled up behind her.

Selena rushed out, terrified by the frightened summons of her maid.

"Kate!" she cried. "What happened? What is it?"

She knelt down, gripping Kate's hand. It was obvious she'd been beaten, but by whom? And why? Who would do such a thing to a woman? Who would do such a thing to anyone?

Onlookers had gathered, curious as to the pathetic, crumpled figure, so Selena and the maid carried Kate inside and laid her on the sofa in the parlor.

"Kate!" Selena was desperate to rouse her. "Who is responsible for this?"

"Regina," Kate managed.

Christopher's mother? Selena trembled with revulsion. "But why?"

"I didn't steal your money, Selena. I swear it."

"Of course you didn't," Selena concurred. "Who would raise such an absurd accusation?"

"Regina said so, and Marcus believed her."

"Marcus? You mean Lord Stamford?"

"I loved him," Kate groggily confessed. "Did you know that?"

"No, I didn't."

"Regina attacked me, because I loved him."

"Oh, Kate . . ."

"I would have fought her, but she knocked me down before I could. Then she hit me and hit me."

"Hush." Selena glanced at her maid and gestured for her to find Edith.

"He's about to marry Melanie."

"You must have misheard."

"It's true. He was very clear."

"Then he's a fool."

"Yes, he is." She chuckled, half out of her mind with pain and melancholy.

Edith entered as Kate clutched at her ribs and seemed to pass out. Selena used the interlude to have Edith bring hot water and towels, as well as ointments and warming pads for Kate's swelling bones and joints.

Selena spent the next hour calming and soothing her. Kate's panic waned, but was replaced by heartache and sorrow. Selena forced some laudanum down her, and she rested on her side, staring blankly out the window. An occasional tear dribbled out and flowed down her cheek, as Selena patted her hair and murmured soft words of support.

"It's over," Selena told her. "You'll never have to go back there. You'll never have to see her again. I guarantee it."

Silently, she vowed that the outrage would be avenged. If it took till she was a hundred years old, she would ensure that Regina paid for the assault. Regina thought she was omnipotent, but she'd made a fatal error in assailing Kate.

Regina wasn't aware that Selena was about to become Countess of Doncaster. Her perfidy would be thwarted, her despicable deed revealed for the odious, horrid crime it was.

A rapping sounded outside, but Selena was so absorbed with Kate that she scarcely heeded it, so she was irked when Edith led two men into the salon. They were attired as gentlemen, but they exuded a tough, coarse attitude that boded ill. They resembled well-dressed ruffians, or pugilists at a fair.

"What is it?" Selena rose, instinctively positioning herself between them and Kate. Kate sat up, but she was too dazed to speak.

"They're here for your sister," Edith explained.

"For what reason?"

"They have a warrant, signed by a Mr. Thumberton, who is having her arrested for theft of the funds in your trust."

"What utter nonsense! She's done no such thing!" Selena approached the pair. "Get out of my house."

One of them politely tipped his hat. "Sorry, miss, but we have orders to seize her."

Selena nearly flew at him, but Edith prevented her. "You can't argue with them, Selena. It's the law. You'll only land yourself in trouble."

"But . . . but they can't just make off with her. We can't let them. This is wrong."

"You don't know that," Edith gently chided.

"Oh, but I do! Kate would never deceive me!"

As if Selena were invisible, the duo circled around her, advancing on Kate and roughly jerking her to her feet. She winced.

"Brutto stupido!" Selena bellowed. "Can't you tell she's injured?"

"It can't be helped," one of the knaves contended, as the other pulled a rope from his pocket and bound her wrists. "She's a dangerous felon."

Without another comment, they marched her out. Kate was too stunned to react, and Selena followed behind, frantic to hinder them, but Edith kept her from trying anything rash.

The men hoisted Kate into a wagon and dropped her on the hard planks of the bed. Kate moaned in agony, and Selena shrieked with indignation.

"Where are you taking her?"

"To Newgate. Where would you suppose?"

"What is Newgate?" Selena asked Edith.

"It's a prison," Edith whispered, and she clucked her tongue in dismay. "It's an awful place."

The pair climbed up onto the wagon, clicked the reins, and the horses started off. Selena ran alongside, unable to see over the wooden panel.

"Be strong, Kate," she shouted. "Don't give up hope. I'll come for you as soon as I can."

Marcus dawdled at his desk, staring at nothing. The sole noise was the tick of the clock. He sipped his whiskey, reliving—over and over—the hideous scene with Regina and Kate.

He was to be married in seven days. To Melanie Lewis! His stomach roiled. How had he tumbled into such a wretched predicament? What must Kate have thought?

The air still reverberated with her presence. She'd looked so small, so young, a beautiful, tragic figure wedged between his disinterest and Regina's wrath. He'd meant to do right by Kate, to save her from ruin and have her safely established in a new life at Doncaster. Why, then, was he feeling as if he'd betrayed her?

His conduct left a bitter taste in his mouth. Regina had been so cogent in her arguments that it had seemed logical to acquiesce to her plan. Yet, despite Regina's evidence to the contrary, he didn't believe that Kate had stolen from her sister, and he couldn't understand why he'd been so willing to assume the worst.

He was plagued with doubts. Why hadn't he furnished Kate with a chance to defend herself? Why hadn't he questioned Regina, or at least scanned her documents? Why hadn't he deliberated and pondered—as was his usual habit? He'd simply cut Kate loose, cast her to fates Regina insisted were real, but how could he be certain?

He closed his eyes, and attempted to picture where Kate was at that very moment. Although he hadn't been apprised, he knew she'd departed. He was so attuned to her that he could perceive her absence. The drafty mansion was dead of energy, forlorn and gloomy without her.

Was she on her way to Doncaster? When would she arrive? Would she hate him forever? Would she ever forgive him?

"I'm sorry, Kate," he murmured to the empty room. "So sorry."

Footsteps approached, and he steeled himself, smoothing any hint of emotion from his expression. Pamela staggered in, attired in her nightclothes even though it was late afternoon. It was obvious she'd been awakened to answer his summons. She was bedraggled, her hair down and tangled, and she was pale and drawn, as if she'd been sick at her stomach.

"This better be good, Stamford," she snarled as she stumbled over and sank into a chair. "I was asleep, and it would be best for both of us if I still was. My head is about to explode."

Dispassionately, he scrutinized her, and he struggled to remember why he'd ever imagined himself in love with her. The explanation had to be the impetuosity of youth, for when he peered at her now, he felt nothing, not a glimmer of camaraderie, not a glint of esteem, not a flicker of sympathy.

She'd made her bed, and she was about to lie in it.

"You haven't seen Christopher, have you?" she inquired, glancing about as if he might be hiding in the drapes.

"No, why?"

"Last evening, I slipped a little something into our drinks—a tonic to enhance the mood—but I'm terribly woozy from it. I'm worried that he might be under the weather, too."

"You've been fornicating with Christopher?"

"*He* has been fornicating with me. He can't resist." She raised a brow. "You'll shortly be hearing a great deal more about Christopher and myself."

"I've no idea about what you're talking."

"The boy is absolutely infatuated."

"With you?" Christopher had mentioned that he had a secret, that he'd met someone special, but he was very clear in stating that she was a *girl*. Pamela had to be out of her mind.

"Oh yes. I've discussed the matter with his mother, and she was extremely amenable. You can expect an announcement very soon."

"An *announcement* about what?"

"I'm about to become a countess again."

He chuckled. "You're mad as a hatter. You actually suppose Regina would let *you* have her only son?"

"Why wouldn't she?"

"Maybe because you're a thirty-year-old widowed, dissolute harpie, whom Regina can't abide."

"I don't feel well enough to sit here and be insulted by you." She stood, ready to stomp out in a huff.

"I haven't excused you."

"As if I need your permission!" She took one bold step, then another.

"Stop!"

She evaluated him, and something in his gaze forestalled her. She wavered, then plopped into her chair, but her exasperation was plain.

"What is it?"

"I'm glad you presume you'll have somewhere to stay."

"Why?"

"Because your days of residing here, and leeching off me, are over."

She gasped. "What?"

"Even as we speak, the housekeeper is packing a trunk for you. It should tide you over for a while, but you'll need to supply me with an address, so I'll know where to deliver the remainder of your belongings."

"I refuse to go!"

He shrugged. "Then I shall physically toss you out onto the street."

"But this is my home! This has been my home for fourteen years!"

"Well, you'll have to find a new one. You claim you're about to be the next Countess of Doncaster, so you may have others to impose upon." Grimly, he smiled. "Although I don't think you should depend on it."

"You can't just evict me!"

"I can, and I have."

"But . . . but . . ."

"You'll be off as soon as you're dressed."

"No!" She leapt up and shouted, "I won't permit you to do this to me. You've no right. No right at all!"

He didn't rise with her, but sipped his whiskey and watched her tremble and rage, and he was surprised by his limited emotion. It was as if, with Kate gone, any lingering spark of humanity he'd possessed had been snuffed out.

"You shouldn't have told Regina about myself and Miss Duncan. I'm curious as to how you learned of it."

"Who the hell is Miss Duncan?" She studied him, puzzled over Kate's identity, but recollection rapidly dawned. "Ah . . . she's the bit of fluff you were tumbling upstairs."

"Had you ordered the servants to spy on me?" He hoped not. It would be a shame to have to fire somebody because of her.

"No. I saw you myself." She turned cunning, then cruel. "Is that what this is about? I discovered your peccadillo, so you're having a tantrum?"

He unfolded from his seat, working to keep his temper under control. "How dare you tell anyone my private business. Especially Regina Lewis."

She realized that she'd struck a nerve, and stupid female that she was, she was determined to use it to her advantage. "You've really lowered your standards."

"Have I?" He was lethally calm.

"You're utterly smitten," she crowed. "How droll! I can't wait to share the news that you've finally been caught, and it's by Regina's maid!"

She chortled with glee, her nasty disposition flooding over him, and in a flash, he was round the desk and gripping her by the throat, tightly enough to cut off her air. "If you mention her name to a single soul, I'll kill you."

He shoved her away, and she lost her balance and fell to her knees, and she hovered, rubbing her neck and steadying her breathing. She glared up at him, malice rolling off her in waves, but she had the foresight to hold her tongue, and in a way, he was relieved that Kate might be on the road to Doncaster.

Pamela could be a treacherous adversary, but she'd never have the courage to seek revenge at himself. She'd retaliate against someone weaker, someone more vulnerable. Kate would have been an easy target.

Slowly, Pamela crawled to her feet, biting down on the insults she was dying to hurl, but she recognized that she'd pushed him too far.

"What am I to live on?"

"I'll have my solicitor contact you regarding an allowance."

"How much will it be?"

"I'm considering five hundred."

"A month?"

"A year."

It was a pittance, and once he'd cooled down, he'd relent and grant her more, but it pleased him to have her fretting.

"You can't mean it!"

"What have you done to earn more? Besides spreading your legs for me and my father?"

"I hate you!"

Then again, maybe he wouldn't increase the amount. "So you've said. Many times. Now get out."

"I've always hated you."

She spun and ran out the door.

Christopher tarried in his mother's sitting room, rif-
fling through the documents on her desk and rudely
snooping through the satchel she routinely carried. He
was perplexed as to where she was and what could
have distracted her so that she'd left it behind, but he
wasn't concerned over his prying. After all, *he* was
the Earl of Doncaster. Any records dealt with his people
and his properties, and suddenly he was frantic to ascertain what information she kept hidden from him.

To his amazement, the first item he stumbled upon
was Kate's letter to the attorney, about Selena's trust
fund discrepancies. Why hadn't Regina dispatched it?

A feeling of dread washed over him. There was a
malevolent ambiance in the house that he didn't like.
All afternoon, he'd been searching for Kate, but her
bedchamber was empty, her clothing missing, and he
was growing alarmed. Where would Kate go? Why
would she leave without a good-bye?

The butler had revealed that she'd been summoned
to an appointment with Regina and Stamford. He'd
claimed not to know what was discussed—an out-and-
out lie, Chris was sure—but after the meeting Kate had
vanished.

He couldn't imagine what Regina and Stamford
could have wanted with Kate and was worried that
they'd forced her departure. But why would they?

Farther into the satchel, his curiosity was rewarded in
spades as he encountered a ledger listing the disburse-
ments from Selena's trust. Kate's tidy handwriting was

visible on every page, and he scanned the columns. The sums didn't square with Selena's level of poverty, so he was more confused than ever.

Where had the money gone?

He pulled out an envelope, stunned to find Kate's father's will. It seemed odd that Regina would be lugging it around, so he skimmed through it. Kate was to have been reared by an old friend of her father's—and not by Regina, as his mother had regularly contended—and she'd been bequeathed her *own* trust fund, as well as assets for a dowry.

Staggered, he collapsed into a chair. Regina had tortured Kate with stories of how her parents had beggared her, with how every penny had passed to the Lewis family and not a farthing directed to Kate's welfare. She'd flailed Kate over her penury, over what a burden she was, over how Regina had to provide for her when her own parents hadn't bothered.

Why was no one aware of Regina's shenanigans? Where were the guardians and acquaintances who'd been charged with Kate's interests? Why had no one assisted her?

Regina must have tricked them all. How and why? When they'd initially moved to Doncaster, Kate had been a child. What had generated Regina's animosity toward her? Or, considering his mother's parsimonious habits, had it simply been greed?

Clutching the portfolio, he exited, crossed to Melanie's room, and entered without knocking. She was pacing, a kerchief dabbed to her reddened eyes, and in the middle of a protracted bout of weeping.

She glared at him. "Did you hear me invite you in?"

Any normal brother might have asked the cause of her upset, but he didn't care enough to inquire. "Where's Mother?"

"How should I know?"

"Have you seen Kate?"

She snorted in disgust. "She's been sent back to Doncaster. In disgrace!"

His blood boiled. "Why?"

"She's been having a torrid affair with Lord Stamford. She's shamed us all."

"Not me," Chris insisted. "She couldn't possibly. No matter what she did."

"You are such an idiot."

"As opposed to you, I've always regarded Kate as my friend."

"Well, Stamford is to be *my* husband," she maintained.

"He is not." Stamford had said as much himself. He had no desire to marry Melanie.

"He is, too!" she whined. "I'm to be wed to him next week, after Kate has been fornicating with him like a common slattern. Oh, how could he do such a thing to me? I'll never be able to gaze at him without picturing *her*! I'm sick, I tell you! Just sick!"

She slumped into a chair, fresh tears welling, and he sneaked out so she could wallow in her misery.

The conversation had him more anxious than ever. Regina had probably delivered Kate home, unaccompanied, on the public coach. Was Stamford cognizant of Regina's capacity for cruelty? If so, why would he permit her to abuse Kate so horridly? Particularly if he'd been involved with her? What type of gentleman would be so crass?

Chris would never have picked him as the sort who would seduce Kate, or abandon her after, but with women, who could predict how a man might conduct himself? His actions with Pamela were a prime example of male folly.

He'd philandered to excess, had continued even after he'd met Selena, after he'd fallen in love. He'd been too willing to seek the pleasures of the flesh, so he wouldn't judge Stamford too harshly. At least not until he'd had a chance to question him as to what had occurred, but heaven help him if he'd mistreated Kate.

Panicked, Chris bounded down the stairs, eager to determine whether Stamford was still on the premises.

He arrived in the foyer when, to his great dismay, Pamela emerged from the library. She was disheveled and blindly careening toward him, so there was no way to avoid a confrontation, but gad, he couldn't bear to speak with her!

Their rendezvous the previous evening had left him so groggy and disoriented that he wondered if she hadn't drugged him. He didn't remember much of what had happened, and what he recalled was foul and humiliating.

Stamford had warned him that she'd had dozens of lovers, that she burrowed through men like a plow in a field, and Chris was appalled that events had proceeded so far. Where she was concerned, he'd been so spineless! But currently, he had pressing business to attend to, and he couldn't be delayed.

She espied him and rushed over, pulling him into a tight hug. "Chris! Oh, Chris! Save me!"

She was making a general spectacle of herself, and he was mortified.

"Lady Pamela, please." He tried to pry her loose, but she was fiercely attached and wouldn't release him.

"My darling, my darling," she kept repeating, sounding almost deranged. "Where have you been? I've searched high and low. I was so desperate to locate you."

She was kissing his cheek, his neck, his chest, and he was revolted. Had she no dignity? No sense? Two maids hovered down the corridor, witnessing the tawdry scene.

"Stop it, Pamela," he commanded sharply. "You're embarrassing me."

"I can come to Doncaster with you, can't I? You won't desert me; I know you won't. Fate brought us together! We can't be torn asunder by mere mortals!"

She was babbling incoherently, and he was frightened. She didn't seem sane, and he wrenched free and held her at arm's length.

"Pamela, listen to me."

"What a fabulous countess I'll be. The people of Doncaster will adore me! They will! I'll show you!"

"No, Pamela, you're talking crazy."

"It's meant to be, Chris. We drank the potion. We can't change our destiny."

"But I'm in love with someone else. I'm engaged to be married."

His admission interrupted her keening diatribe. She began to tremble. "What did you say?"

"I'm betrothed."

"No." Vigorously, she shook her head. "No, you can't be. You can't be!" She dropped to her knees and grabbed his jacket, her fists clasping at the fabric. "You're lying!"

She was screeching, imploring him to deny it, when

Stamford appeared from the library. Chris shot him a pleading look.

"Pamela," he barked, "leave the boy alone."

She heard him, but pretended not to have. "Chris, I'm begging you! Don't forsake me."

"Pam!" Stamford shouted. "Get hold of yourself."

In a few quick strides, he was down the hall, and he yanked her to her feet. She wrestled to escape, but he wouldn't ease his grip.

"Don't touch me, you beast! You churl!"

He drew her close, so that they were eye to eye, and he spoke softly but furiously. "As this is no longer your residence, I am not required to suffer such a distasteful display of histrionics in my foyer. Desist at once, before I take a belt to you!"

"I won't, I tell you!" She was defiant and insolent to the end.

"I am granting you an opportunity to dress before you depart. If you wish, I can evict you in your night-clothes." He paused, and there was no doubt as to his resolve. "There's the door. The choice is yours."

Her glorious bosom heaving, her body quivering with wrath, she weighed her options, and recognized that he was serious.

"I will never forgive you!"

He laughed. "I don't care."

She jerked away, gave Chris a final, frantic appeal for help, then fled up the stairs.

~ 18 ~

"Why is Lady Pamela so upset?"

Christopher was angry, spoiling for a fight, and Marcus studied him, the massive library desk positioned between them. "I notified her that she has to leave my house, her funding is cut off, and she'll have to find another situation."

"Why?" Chris repeated.

"Because she's overstayed her welcome."

"That's not an answer."

"All right. How about this?" Marcus hated to be so blunt, but candor was necessary. "She was trying to manipulate me. Will that suffice as an explanation?"

"I have no interest in what happens to her."

"Still, you need to be wary."

"Of her?"

"Yes. She claims she's about to marry you, that she's talked to your mother and it's been arranged."

"Is she really so dense that she'd presume Regina would agree?"

Marcus shrugged. "With women and their schemes, who can say?"

"I'm engaged," he unexpectedly confessed, "but not to Pamela."

"To whom, then?"

"Kate's sister."

Marcus suffered a surge of resentment, incensed that the lad had the nerve to forge on toward happiness, when Marcus had been too craven to reach out and seize what he wanted.

How had he let Kate get away? He'd been so willing to toss her over, but if he'd thought through the details, he could have arrived at a better conclusion.

"Have you informed your mother?"

"Not yet, but soon."

"It will be difficult."

"I'm sure it will."

"I'll help you," he amazed himself by offering. He never interfered in others' problems, never grew involved or went out on a limb, but if matters proceeded as they were destined, Chris would soon be his brother-in-law, and he wanted them to be friends.

"I'm not certain I want any *help* from you," Chris shocked him by replying.

"Why not?"

"What have you done to Kate?"

"To Kate?" He hemmed and hawed, stalling, so that he could devise the appropriate response.

"If you pretend you don't know who she is, I swear to God, I'll come round this desk and beat you to a bloody pulp."

Gad! After the two horrid appointments he'd recently

endured, that's all he needed! The two of them brawl-
ing on the rug, like a pair of miscreants! Considering
Chris's youth, physical fitness, and overt outrage, Marcus wasn't positive he could win!

"I know her," he quietly confessed.

"So what did you do to her?" Chris asked again.

He took the coward's route. "Nothing."

"Where is she?"

"I've no idea."

"Her room is empty."

"Is it?" he cautiously broached.

"Melanie insists that you and Kate were having an
affair."

Regina had apprised Melanie? He blushed bright
red, reflecting on what a hideous beginning it would be
for their union. "Well . . ."

"As the head of my family, and Kate's only male
relative, I demand to know your plans toward her."

"I have none."

"Why am I not surprised?" he chided. "Guess what
else my sister told me?"

"What?"

"All of a sudden, you've decided to marry her. Just
like that." He snapped his fingers. "Out of the blue."

"Yes, I have."

"How has my mother coerced you into it?"

"Why would you assume she had?"

"I'm not stupid. There's no way you'd have consented of your own accord."

Chris dropped a leather satchel on the desk between
them. It landed with a heavy thud, and Marcus stared,
surmising that the contents would be vile.

"What's this?"

"It's my mother's business portfolio. She hides her private papers in it, the things she doesn't want anyone to see." He opened the flap and pulled out many documents, scattering them for Marcus's perusal. "I finally had the chance to snoop in it, and look what I found." He held up a letter. "This is from Kate, to a solicitor. A Mr. Thumberton."

"I'm acquainted with Thumberton." He was a renowned attorney, who worked for many of the best families.

"You recall my mentioning Kate's sister—my fiancée—and the irregularities with her trust fund."

"Yes. We were to discuss it, but we hadn't gotten around to it."

"Thumberton is the trustee."

"Kate wrote to him?"

"Yes. Regina was to have had the letter delivered. Why is it still in her pouch?"

Marcus's pulse pounded a tad faster. "I haven't a clue."

"Someone has been embezzling from the trust. I have the feeling you suspect it was Kate."

"Your mother said it was!"

"And you believed her?"

"No! But she had a ledger book as proof. It was there, in plain sight."

Chris retrieved a journal from the stack. "Was this the record she produced?"

"No. It was a different size, a different shape."

Chris scanned the pages. "This is in Kate's handwriting, and there's no evidence of theft."

"Then what was your mother waving around?"

"You tell me."

Marcus was confused. The sole answer was that Regina had faked a copy of the expenses, that Regina was the perpetrator, but the prospect was so outlandish that he couldn't accept it.

She was a dowager countess, a rich woman with her fingers in the pies of several fortunes. By comparison, the amount in the trust was a pittance. Why steal it? Why blame it on Kate?

"You think it was your mother?"

"Don't you?"

"Why would she?"

"Because she's cruel. Because she's deranged. She's always hated Kate, and with Kate so vulnerable, it was easy to deflect suspicion."

"I agree that she hates Kate, but why?"

"Are you aware of Kate's background?"

"Much of it," which was a gross understatement. He scarcely knew anything about Kate. While most females of his acquaintance yearned to wax on about themselves and would never shut up, Kate had been particularly reticent.

"Then, you realize that her father was Earl of Doncaster."

"She never told me!"

"Her father was the earl before mine. When she was a girl, her mother ran off with another man, and her father committed suicide. We came to Doncaster, and Regina claimed that she'd been named Kate's guardian, but now that I've read these documents, I've learned it wasn't so. What other deceit has she practiced?"

Marcus was stunned. Kate was the daughter of an earl? His funny, sexy, lonely Kate? Why had she kept it a secret?

The air seemed to leave his body. He grew weak, his knees giving out, and he fell into his chair. He'd sensed, deep down, that Regina was lying!

"Does Kate have an old beau at Doncaster? A widower with two small children who'd like to marry her?"

"Who would spread such twaddle?"

"Your mother."

Chris scoffed. "No one's ever loved Kate."

Except me, Marcus thought bleakly, the terrible, marvelous notion sweeping over him. He was deluged by it, and he wondered how he'd ever be able to make this right. "Regina convinced me that Kate took the money, but she offered to replace it—if I married Melanie."

"So you buckled under to protect Kate?"

"Yes."

Chris chuckled miserably. "If I were you, I wouldn't be too excited about the assets in Melanie's dowry."

"Why not?"

"They're supposed to be Kate's. Regina falsified those, too." He patted the portfolio, indicating that the papers were inside, should Marcus wish to study them. "All these years, Kate could have been wed. This very minute, she could be the lady of a grand estate, instead of Regina's abused handmaiden."

"You still haven't explained why Regina detests her."

"I don't know. I've never known."

Marcus was awhirl as he tried to absorb the information, and he stood, not grasping what his next act should be, but recognizing that he had to do something. He couldn't loiter in his library, twiddling his thumbs.

"We have to find Kate." Suddenly, he was overcome by the strongest feeling of dread, and it was imperative that they locate her. Though the perception was silly—Kate was likely safe and on the road to the country—he couldn't put it aside.

"Would your mother convey her to Doncaster, as she promised?"

"I wouldn't bet on it. She couldn't risk anyone asking Kate about the missing funds."

"Where would Regina have taken her?"

"I couldn't begin to guess."

Marcus's heart sank, as he wrestled with gruesome images of Kate and what Regina might have done to her. The prospects were alarming and endless. How could they commence a search?

Just then, the butler knocked and peeked in.

"Excuse the interruption, milord; there's a young lady here, inquiring after Lord Doncaster. She's awfully upset. I couldn't send her away."

"Who is it?"

"A Miss Selena Bella, sir. She apologizes for disturbing you, but she says it's urgent."

Chris was already racing out to the foyer, and Marcus followed, sliding to a halt on the polished marble floor as he came face-to-face with Kate's sister. She was taller, darker, and more willowy, but there could be no doubt of the relation. They were both great beauties, but while Kate was more unpretentious, more down-to-earth, this girl exuded a regalness and nobility that belied her age.

As she saw them, she dropped into a respectful, graceful curtsy.

"I beg your pardon, my lords," she started, but Chris raised her up, declining to have her bowing to them.

"Marcus, this is Kate's sister, Selena"—Christopher beamed as if she'd hung the moon—"and my fiancée."

"It's a pleasure to meet you, Selena." Around the two of them Marcus felt ancient and weary. They were such a perfect couple, so youthful, so attractive, and so visibly smitten.

"Lord Stamford." With the imperiousness of a queen, she extended her hand. "Kate has told me so many marvelous stories about you."

There wasn't a chance in hell that Kate had uttered a kind word about him. "You, my dear, are an impossible liar."

She looked up at Chris, trying to maintain the courteous banter, but the hood on her cloak fell back, and it was obvious that she'd been crying.

Christopher was horrified. "What is it?"

"It's Kate," she said. "Your mother beat her, then dumped her on my stoop."

Marcus nearly collapsed. "Is she hurt?"

"Very badly."

"Oh my God," Chris murmured. "I was afraid something like this might happen."

"Where is she?" Marcus demanded, even as he counted the numerous ways Regina would pay.

"Some men arrested her. They claimed they had a warrant, that she'd stolen money from my trust. But she hasn't!" Selena loyally decreed. "She would never commit such a hideous deed!"

"They took her to . . . to jail?" Marcus was aghast.

"Yes." She began to cry again, huge tears rolling down her pretty cheeks. "They dragged her out of my house. I couldn't stop them."

"Which jail, Selena?" he pressed. "Tell me which one."

"A place called Newgate. Have you heard of it?"

Marcus shuddered, then glared at Chris. "Your mother had better hope she's all right."

He spun and hurried outside, Christopher and Selena hot on his heels.

Pamela assessed Elliot's crowded parlor, wondering how he could afford to host such a large gathering.

After being evicted by Stamford, she'd been frantic as to where she should go and Elliot had seemed the logical choice, at least until she could resolve things with Christopher and his mother. Without hesitation, Elliot had welcomed her.

As of yet, no one was aware of Stamford's perfidy, nor had anyone learned that she'd sought refuge with Elliot. She strolled through the brimming salons, smiling and chatting, and playing the part of Elliot's hostess, a role she'd often assumed in the past.

However, when she was so distressed, it was difficult to exude courtesy. She felt ill, overheated, and a tad reckless. How she loathed being female, having no power, no assets, no authority over her own life! What she wouldn't give to be independently wealthy, to rub Marcus's nose in it! The bastard!

Up ahead, she espied Regina and Melanie, and she rose on tiptoe, straining to see Christopher, but he wasn't with them, and her spirits plummeted.

Where could he be?

She sneaked up behind Regina, determined not to let the older woman slink away.

"Where's Christopher?" she challenged.

Regina turned and scrutinized her. "Lady Pamela," she gushed in a voice that was much too loud, "is it true you've had a spot of trouble with Stamford? Has he kicked you out of your own house?"

Everyone within twenty feet heard the sly comment, and many of them gasped with glee. Several crept off, eager to disseminate the news. Gossip would spread like paint spilled across the floor.

She quivered with rage. "We need to talk. Come with me."

"At the moment, I'm busy. If you'll excuse me . . ."

Regina attempted to move away, and Pamela blocked her escape. "If you don't attend me this very second, I shall let slip a despicable falsehood about Melanie that is so atrocious she'll never be able to show her face in public again."

"You wouldn't dare."

"Wouldn't I? She's been residing with me for weeks. No matter what I say, it will be believed."

"Lead the way," Regina ultimately snapped, her antipathy blatant and impossible to conceal. Pamela proceeded to Elliot's library and shut the door.

"Where is Christopher?" she repeated, desperate to speak with him, to apprise him of what Stamford had done.

"I have no idea," Regina contended. "He's been out since early afternoon. I left a message for him to join us here. Will that be all?"

"No, that won't be *all!* We must make plans."

"About what?"

"About announcing my engagement to him."

"*Your* engagement to him?"

"Yes. When will we?" She had to have her finances settled, to be assured that Chris was hers.

Regina laughed. "I'd thought you were acting

strangely, but if you imagine you're about to marry my son, you're absolutely deranged. Are you sickly? Should I summon your friend, Mr. Featherstone, and have him call for a physician? Perhaps a draught would soothe your nerves."

Pamela stepped closer, menace rolling off her in waves. "We had an understanding."

"You and I? About Christopher?" Regina refused to be cowed, refused to yield any quarter.

"You said if I delivered Stamford to you, I could have Chris. It was all arranged! We agreed!"

"How—precisely—did you *deliver* Stamford?"

"I told you about the girl, about his affair."

"So?"

"You can't renege! I want Chris, and I intend to have him for my husband."

Regina chortled, her derision and scorn palpable. "You're mad, Pamela. Totally insane!"

"I'll create a public stink. I'll embarrass you into it. I'll sue to force your compliance."

"If you want to make a fool of yourself, have at it. There isn't a person in England who'd heed you. Now, good evening. Don't bother me again." She went to the door, then halted, peering over her shoulder and glittering with triumph. "By the by, Stamford offered for Melanie. We'll be announcing *their* betrothal tomorrow morning. The wedding is in a week, but were I you, I wouldn't count on receiving an invitation."

She strutted out, and Pamela tarried in the quiet, a flood of fury washing over her. How many duplicitous events should she be expected to endure in a single day?

"Betray me, will you, you fat sow?" She was seething, her mind whirling with revenge. So . . . Regina presumed that Stamford was about to wed her precious daughter.

"We'll see about that!" Pamela chuckled, and she stomped out to find Melanie.

Elliot gazed around his teeming parlor, packed as it was with reveling guests. He was thrilled that he could draw such a crowd, yet frantic as to how he'd pay for the gala. Night after night, he threw lavish parties, but the bills were stacking up.

He had to have Melanie's dowry, whether she wanted to provide it to him or not, and no one—especially her mother—could be allowed to hinder his acquisition of it. His fiscal problems had to be fixed, and if committing a slight ravishment would save him, he would meander down that dirty road.

From across the ballroom Pamela approached, and he gnashed his teeth. To his dismay, she'd shown up on his stoop, weeping, cursing Stamford, and pleading for sanctuary.

Elliot had furnished accommodations, but oh, how he prayed she wouldn't stay long. In light of his penury, she'd send him straight to paupers' jail!

She was in a frenetic state, her color high, her emotions at a fevered pitch, and there was a wild gleam in her eye that had him uneasy.

Over the course of several hours, she'd penned and dispatched a dozen insistent letters to young Christopher Lewis, advising him of where she was and begging him to fetch her. She kept asking if the boy had been invited to the soiree, checking to learn if he'd arrived, and not seeming to remember that she'd inquired minutes earlier.

Her obsession had been noted by all. People were

whispering, pondering—as was he—whether she hadn't swung off her rocker, which was just his luck! To be sheltering a poverty-stricken crazy woman!

As she neared, he sipped his brandy, feigning calm, and pretending to be glad for her presence.

She slipped her arm into his and grinned. "Would you still like to marry Melanie Lewis?"

He almost spit out his drink. "Yes."

"When the orchestra strikes up the next song, she's sneaking upstairs. I gave her directions to your bed-chamber. How much time will you require to push her beyond redemption?"

"Will you appear to *discover* us?"

"With Regina by my side. I want her to witness Melanie's downfall for herself."

Considering his station and Melanie's, it would be thoroughly damaging for them merely to be caught to-gether and alone, but Regina Lewis would wrangle Melanie out of such an innocuous incident. If he wanted Melanie's ruination to rest firmly on his shoulders, he'd have to do something rash, something reckless, from which there could be no escape other than an immediate wedding.

"I'll need thirty minutes. I want to have her naked before you walk in." He hoped she'd no longer be a vir-gin, either.

"A wise man." Pamela snatched a glass of wine from a passing waiter and raised it in a toast. "To your pending nuptials, Elliot. May you and your little bride be very, very happy."

19

Kate crouched in the corner of the dark cell, unsure of how long she'd been there. Vaguely, she wondered if it was still the same day of her arrest or if more time had passed.

It was so difficult to tell.

There was a dreamlike sensation to what had befallen her, and she couldn't focus on the particulars. Nothing seemed real. Not her life at Doncaster. Not her weeks in London, or her affair with Lord Stamford.

Marcus . . . How could you have done this to me?

The beloved name whispered through her tortured mind, and she shoved it away, declining to have it take root and grow. She couldn't dwell on the past, or on what had transpired previous. There was only now, and the bleak future.

What would become of her? Would she be hanged? Transported? The possibilities were too bizarre to grasp. She felt out of her body, as if she were watching another woman suffer.

Hazily, she recalled the Stamford town house, her quiet room at the end of the hall. Would anyone realize she'd disappeared? Would anyone care that she was gone?

Regina would concoct a story about her leaving. Christopher might be suspicious, Selena might worry— they might even search—but ultimately, they'd move on.

There was no one else who'd be concerned. No one else, at all. How sad that in twenty-five years she'd made such a pitiful mark.

Bitter tears welled into her eyes, and she forced them down. She had to concentrate on her predicament, and she couldn't waste energy lamenting her fate. What had happened was over, finished, and she had to figure out how to carry on from this moment forward.

The foul, cold, damp place was her world, and she had pressing needs, but no idea how to meet them. Since the cell door had clanged shut, no food had been delivered, no blanket offered. Although there were occasional screams and groans, they drifted by from far off.

Did the guards even remember that she'd been jailed? Would she tarry, hunched over on the wet floor, until she starved to death?

To her surprise, she wasn't distressed by the notion. What would it matter if she died? Who would mourn? Wasn't it better to perish here, out of sight, so that those who'd once known her couldn't witness how low she'd plummeted?

She considered standing, walking about, and investigating her surroundings, but as she attempted to climb up onto her knees, the pain in her back and ribs was so intense that she gave up. Every muscle cried out in agony, every bone ached and throbbed, and when she steadied herself by balancing her palm on the wall, she recoiled from the slime she encountered.

What good would it do to explore? What was she expecting to find? A key? A hidden passage? A map that delineated the escape routes?

Miserably, she chuckled, her voice sounding rusty and broken, and it occurred to her that perhaps she was already dead, that this was hell, and she would remain into infinity.

Is so, what had been her sins? Loving too deeply? Wishing too fervently? Trying too hard? Or was it because she'd coveted more than she had? Maybe, as Regina had claimed, she'd reached too high, and was being punished for her reckless yearning.

There was no reason to examine the small space, no reason to pray, no reason to hope. She sank down and huddled into a tight ball.

Melanie gazed out across the teeming, swirling crowd of dancers, Lady Pamela's comments ringing in her ears. She had a vision of Lord Stamford, with his imperious, aloof smile and his arrogant, haughty attitude. He was cruel, he was heartless, and if she married him, she would spend her life forlorn, detested, and ignored. She couldn't bear the thought of his being able to treat her so abominably.

Why, the despicable knave wouldn't even propose! What a merciless fiend he was, to deprive her of such a victorious moment! He was an insensitive, unfeeling brute, and she wouldn't have him for her husband. She wouldn't! Regardless of the consequences, she would defy him and her mother.

She crept out of the ballroom, rushed to the stairs, and

ascended. At the end of the deserted hall, she opened the
last door, and tiptoed into the room.

As Pamela had promised, it was empty. A lamp
burned on the dresser, casting stark shadows, and terribly uneasy, Melanie went to the bed and stared at it.

She was nervous as to how men and women acted
when they were alone. She'd heard vile, hideous rumors, but she had no method for determining if the
tales were true. It wasn't as if she could ask Regina!

She shuddered. In revulsion. In fear.

What would her mother say, what would she do,
when she learned of Melanie's decision?

She'd observed how Regina had disciplined Kate. It
was lunacy to cross or betray Regina, and Melanie had
never before dared. This would be the first time.

How would Regina respond?

I'll have a husband to protect me, though, Melanie
mused woefully, pondering whether Elliot would be up
to the task. He was harmless and polite, the sole individual in London who'd been kind to her. Would he be
a match for Regina?

Footsteps echoed in the corridor, and her heart
pounded with dread. Was it Elliot? So soon?

Oh . . . she wasn't prepared!

She'd brought a glass of wine with her, and she set it
on the table by the bed. From her reticule, she retrieved
the vial of love potion Kate had procured. Assessing its
color, she held it toward the lamp. It wasn't as dark a
red as the prior batches. She removed the cork and
sniffed. It didn't smell the same, either, but it was too
late to wonder if the concoction had a similar potency.

Just as Elliot entered, she dumped the contents into
the glass and stirred it with her finger. While she would

save most of it for him, she took several swigs, frantic to receive some of the potion's effects.

She hadn't told him about Stamford's proposal, hadn't mentioned that the contracts were signed, the date selected, and she wasn't about to. If Elliot suspected that Stamford had folded to Regina's incessant demands, she was convinced he'd decline to assist her.

Without a word, he approached. He appeared so large, so much taller than she recollected. He was glaring at her as if he was angry, and she felt threatened by him, when she never had before.

A frisson of alarm slithered up her spine, but she shook it off. She was being silly. He was here at her request. This was what she wanted, how she planned for it to end. He was her friend, and he wouldn't hurt her.

Still, she could barely keep from stepping away. He reeked of alcohol, his fetid breath washing over her like a poisonous cloud, and she speculated as to how much he'd imbibed, though he didn't seem foxed. He was alert, vigilant, but studying her in a manner that was frightening.

"Lady Pamela," he began, "said that you were eager to speak with me."

"Yes, I need to ask you . . . that is . . . I have to . . ."

She blushed. She had no idea how to confide in him, no concept of what needed to transpire. She was ready to ruin herself, so that Stamford couldn't have her, so that he wouldn't want her, but she had no notion of what such conduct entailed. Elliot would perpetrate some coarse, distasteful deed upon her person, but she wasn't certain what it was.

"Usually," he goaded, "when a woman comes to a man's room, she has something in mind besides talking."

"You're correct," she was able to reply, shielding her trepidation. "Elliot, I can't marry Stamford, and I'm so afraid my mother will make me."

"I'm positive she will. That's been her scheme all along."

"But if I landed myself into a predicament," she ventured, "where I had to wed someone else, I wouldn't have to acquiesce. She couldn't force me."

"Too true." He shimmered with a triumph she didn't comprehend.

"Would you like a drink?" she inquired.

She bumbled about, offering him the wine, hoping he'd swallow it without her having to coax him. She had no qualms about slipping him the drug. She was resolved to proceed, despite how unpleasant or revolting it might be. If she was willing to hazard so much, it was only fair that he love her.

Without argument, he grabbed the goblet, gulped the mixture, then tossed the goblet onto the rug. He seized her wrist, squeezing so that she couldn't get away, and he led her toward the bed.

Instantly, her body rebelled, and she dug in her heels, trying to halt their progress, but to no avail. He was bent on his destination, and she couldn't stop him.

"You foolish girl," he chided, "quit fighting me."

"I'm confused . . . I'm worried . . ." She'd thought she was clear on her goal, but deep down, she recognized it was wrong, and it was happening too fast.

"Turn around," he ordered.

"Why?"

"Just do it."

She should have refused, but suddenly, she felt very

young, out of her element, and she spun, showing him
her back. He started unbuttoning her dress, slackening
it so that the bodice flopped free, and she clutched the
garment to her bosom.

He yanked her hands away and tugged the gown off
her torso.

"What are you doing?" she queried, which was stupid, since his intent was unmistakable.

"I'm disrobing you."

"Must I remove my clothes?"

"Yes."

He made swift work of her attire, stripping her until
she was clad solely in her thin chemise. She was cold,
from her near nudity and from fear, and she trembled.

Her nipples reacted to the cool temperature, harden-
ing into taut buds that jutted against the sheer fabric,
and he stared at them like a hungry wolf. She draped an
arm across her breasts, across her crotch, but her attempts at concealment were useless. He could see all.

"Climb onto the bed and lie down," he instructed as
he shed his coat and cravat.

"Why?"

"Why would you suppose?"

"I haven't the foggiest."

She hesitated, and he grew irritated. "Do you want
to be Stamford's bride or don't you?"

"No!"

"Then shut up and do as I say."

"Will you marry me after we're through?"

"We'll have no other option."

He shoved her, and she relented, clambering up,
and reclining on the pillows. As he rummaged about,

eliminating the remainder of his clothes, too, she studied the ceiling, and she shivered, feeling sick to her
stomach, and curious as to when the love potion would
kick in.

Would it take effect immediately? How strong would
it be? Would there be a dramatic difference in his behavior? Or would it be subtle, difficult to detect?

Inside her own body, there was no indication that
the tonic was activated, and she panicked. If her emotions didn't engage, and quickly, she couldn't bear to
continue!

He slinked onto the mattress, and she braved a hasty
glance at him. His upper anatomy was bare, but from
the middle down, he was wearing a pair of drawers, the
string cinched at the waist. As if he never ate, he was
emaciated, his ribs sticking out, his skin a pasty, gray
color.

He stretched out on top of her, his weight squishing
her, until she was suffocating, but he didn't notice her
distress. She wrestled, anxious to push him off, but her
efforts irked him.

"Hold still."

"I can't breathe."

"You don't need to breathe."

"Please!" she begged, not sure for what she was
pleading. She didn't want him to cease, yet she didn't
want to forge on.

He chuckled and reached for her chemise, jerking at
the straps so that her breasts were visible. When she
struggled to cover herself, to reclaim some modesty, he
clasped her wrists and pinned them over her head.

"Stop fighting."

"I don't like it when you look at me."

"I plan to do much more than *look*. Let's see how these little duckies taste, shall we?"

He dipped down, and she braced, certain he would kiss her, but instead, he fell to her nipple. Horrified and repulsed, she watched as he suckled her as a babe would its mother.

He bit and nipped, pinched and squeezed, until she was aching from the rough treatment; then he shifted to the side and dragged her chemise the rest of the way off.

She was naked, and after a protracted evaluation of her figure, he smirked. "You're a tad chubby, but I guess you'll do."

She'd never been more humiliated, and she wished she could die! His foul gaze coursed over her, and she closed her eyes, praying that whatever he intended would end swiftly and soon.

Down below, he was touching her between her legs. She tried to keep them pressed together, but she couldn't impede his groping. His fingers were at the vee of her thighs, and he rammed them into her, stroking them until she almost retched.

"A tight puss!" he crooned. "That's what I like."

He fussed with his drawers, and she tensed, realizing that his actions boded ill. Her scuffling increased, but she couldn't escape. He was positioned so that she was open, exposed, her privates displayed for his perverted enjoyment, and she wailed with embarrassment.

"I don't believe I've ever fucked a virgin," he mused.

His words sounded cruel, vulgar. "What do you mean?"

He didn't answer, but persisted with his filthy torment. His fingers had been removed, but he'd replaced them with something bigger, something thicker. He flexed his hips, poking it into her.

"Desist! At once!" she commanded. "You're about to rip me in half."

"Not bloody likely," he muttered. "You're dry as an old hag. Relax, would you?"

Relax? Was he serious?

He renewed his motions until she tore inside, and whatever he'd been ramming was fully impaled. She arched up and howled in agony, but he clamped his hand over her mouth to stifle her shout. Then he began thrusting in earnest, and she was in hell! She was trapped beneath him, unable to breathe, his putrid respirations making her gag, as he kept on and on.

As if she were invisible, he was unconcerned as to her comfort or welfare. Perspiration beaded on his brow, and suddenly, he halted, his body paralyzed. He emitted a growl, of primal pleasure and male glee, and she felt something hot spurting far inside.

Just as abruptly, he collapsed onto her, and she suffered a frantic moment when she worried that he'd had an attack of the heart, that he'd perished. But he pulled away and rolled onto his back, exhaling as if he'd run a long race.

"I must have had too much brandy," he groaned. "For a while there, I didn't think I'd be able to finish."

"We're . . . we're done?"

"Yes."

"That's it? That's all there is?"

He glared at her. "What were you expecting? Candy and bad poetry?"

"But . . . but . . . I thought . . ."

What precisely? That it would be more romantic? More affectionate? Less physical?

This had to be the *secret* of the marital bed. What if he insisted on trying it again? What if the behavior was mandatory? What if she had to perform the abominable ritual whenever he requested it?

Her stomach roiled.

She stared at his scrawny, withered torso, at his mussed hair and untrimmed nails. The event was concluded, yet he wasn't paying her any more attention than he had when it was occurring. She'd been naught but a receptacle, a vessel for his manly lust, and the greatest disappointment she would ever experience swept over her.

"You don't love me, do you?"

He frowned. "What?"

"You don't love me. You never will."

"Of course I don't love you. How ridiculous! Be a good girl, would you?" He nodded toward the dresser. "Fetch me a wet cloth."

Desirous of being away from him, she scurried off, though her anatomy protested. At her center, she was raw and throbbing, and she stumbled over and dipped a towel in a bowl of water. Gulping down tears of disillusionment, she wrung it out and returned to him.

He wiped himself, and she dared to peek at his loins, stunned to discern that they were covered with blood. She peered down at her own crotch, finding blood there, too.

"I'm wounded!" she shrieked. "You tried to kill me!!"

"Be silent!" he growled. "And lie down."

She should have hurled an insult, then stormed out,

but she was trembling, her knees weak, and she felt as if she might swoon.

"Lie down!" he barked again, causing her to scramble onto the mattress.

For an eternity, she was quiet, analyzing the ceiling, the floor, looking anywhere but at him.

"What now?" she ultimately asked.

"Now . . . we wait."

"For what?"

"For your mother," he said calmly. "Be sure you're smiling when she walks in. I want her to see how glad you are."

"She's coming? When?"

"Very soon."

She shuddered with dread, incapable of imagining the scene. There was a knitted throw by her feet, and she reached for it, desperate to warm herself, but to shield herself, too.

"Leave it," he snapped. "From the instant she enters, let's give her an unimpeded view of what we've done."

~ 20 ~

"Where is she?" Marcus demanded, out of patience.

"I've told you, milord," the prison warden claimed, "there's no record of anyone by that name being brought in."

"Look again."

"I've been over the list a dozen times. She's not here."

"A twenty-five-year-old woman doesn't simply vanish into thin air."

"That's true, but you're assuming your information is correct, and that this is—in fact—the institution to which she was transported." He flashed a wan smile at Selena, hoping he hadn't insulted.

Marcus frowned at Selena. "Where did they say they were taking her?"

"Newgate Prison," she responded without hesitation.

"So where is she?" Marcus repeated, and he grabbed the warden by his jacket.

"Now see here, Lord Stamford," the man blustered. "There's no need for violence."

"You call this *violence*?" Marcus lifted him up, the seams on his coat popping as his feet dangled in the air. "I'll show you *violence*!"

He slammed the warden into the wall, banging him into the plaster with a loud thud that had his clerk rushing in from the other room.

"What the devil . . . ?" the clerk bristled on witnessing his supervisor hanging from Marcus's fist. Christopher stepped forward to prevent any interference.

"Get out!" Marcus seethed without slackening his grip.

The clerk scurried away, and as help was summoned, Marcus could hear a commotion in the outer office, but he ignored the uproar. He felt as if he were outside himself, gazing down at a crazed lunatic who was assaulting a public servant, and was stunned by his state of emotion. He—who never cared for others—was angry enough to commit murder, and if anything dastardly had happened to Kate, he just might.

"You have five seconds to explain how a hurt, frightened gentlewoman could be wrongly incarcerated in this jail without anyone knowing."

"Well . . . well . . ." the warden stammered.

"Have you any idea of how powerful I am?" Marcus asked. "Can you begin to comprehend what I will do to you? To your family? I'm sure you value your employment. If you don't tell me where she is, how long will you hold on to it?"

"There are so many prisoners," the warden squeaked. "Perhaps we missed having her identity recorded."

Marcus's heart sank. If she'd been tossed into the

teeming throng, how would they find her among the thousands of people? The place was packed to the gills with the most wretched souls in London. She could be tried, convicted, and hanged before they located her.

A brief meeting with solicitor Thumberton had proved that Regina had presented fake documents in her scheme to have Kate arrested. Over an extended period of years, she'd gone to great lengths to conceal her theft, of not only Selena's money but Kate's inheritances as well. If Regina was capable of such unmitigated duplicity and deceit, what else might she perpetrate? Had Kate actually been delivered to Newgate? Or had Regina engineered a more dire fate?

Regina had much to lose, so she couldn't allow Kate to surface, couldn't give Kate the opportunity to defend herself.

It was entirely possible that Kate's abductors had mentioned Newgate as a ruse, so that those raising questions would presume that the law had been involved, that Kate had been appropriately seized and confined.

Had Kate ever made it to Newgate? Or had she disappeared en route? In a few days, would a body be discovered, floating in the Thames?

He shuddered and tightened his grasp on the warden's neck, shutting off his air so that he was turning blue and prying at Marcus's fingers.

"Please . . ." the warden begged. "I don't . . . I can't . . ."

"If you haven't found her in the next ten minutes, I'll kill you."

Behind him, footsteps pounded, and several burly

guards raced in, intent on effecting a rescue. Marcus spun to confront them, dropping the warden in the process, and he crumpled to a heap, panting and rubbing his throat.

They milled around, perplexed as to what their role should be. They couldn't manhandle a lord, but they couldn't have him pummeling the warden, either. One was more brave than the rest, and as he advanced, Selena gasped.

"It's him," she insisted, pointing. "He took Kate from my house."

"You're positive?" Marcus queried as Chris positioned himself to block an escape.

"I've never seen the lady before," the oaf contended, shifting uncomfortably. "She's daft."

The warden wobbled to his feet and reasserted control by shooing the others out. "Let's discuss this privately."

"By all means," Marcus agreed, quiet and composed until the warden closed the door; then Marcus hit the guard, lashing out so quickly and so firmly that the man fell like a stone.

He attempted to rise, and Marcus punched him again and kicked him in the ribs.

"What have you done with her?"

The incoherent fellow didn't answer. Blood poured from his face, his nose was probably broken, and Marcus gripped him by his shirt. "This is your last chance."

"I don't know who—"

Marcus struck him a third time, the blow smashing the bones in his cheek. He was a wailing, defeated lump, and Marcus bent over and clutched him by the neck. "Is she here?"

"Yeth . . ." he muttered, pushed beyond the spot where he could lie.

"Where is she, Jimmy?" the warden inquired.

"Itho . . . itho . . ." With his injuries, he couldn't pronounce the word, and Marcus glared at the warden.

"What is he trying to say?"

"I believe he's informing us that she's in an isolation cell."

Marcus straightened, a hundred hideous thoughts careening past. "Why would she be?"

"Well, she might have been deemed a danger to herself or others."

"Or?" Marcus prodded, a niggling suspicion dawning.

"I suppose someone could have . . . could have purchased a more serious detention."

Marcus leaned down and clasped the guard's hair, tipping his head back. "Who paid you?"

"A woman," the man managed to spit out.

"Was she very obese?"

"Yeth. . . ."

Although he'd never given the stories any credence, rumors abounded as to such atrocities. A wealthy person could enjoy an easier internment, so why couldn't it be arranged that a poorer person suffer a worse fate? Felons were occasionally thrown into the judicial system, then vanished.

Were their records lost? Or had something more sinister transpired? What had been Regina's objective for Kate? Very likely, Kate was to have been murdered and disposed of by the knave lying at Marcus's feet.

After all, who would have checked on Kate? Who would have missed her?

Too bad for Regina that she'd miscalculated. She had no idea that people loved Kate, that Selena and Christopher, and he—mostly he himself—would search to the ends of the earth to find her.

Within seconds, they were marching down the hall, and Marcus ignored the smells and moans of human agony. They paraded through the main sections of the prison, across sweltering courtyards, through dank, filthy tunnels; then they descended into the bowels, the stairs slippery and dark, the light dimming behind them, the cries of despair fading.

They stopped at the last door. The warden had escorted them, and he rotated the key in the lock, though he wasn't strong enough to pull it open. One of his lackeys tugged it aside, and Marcus stared into the forbidding chasm, sickened that this was where they'd hidden her.

Would they have starved her? Tortured her? Left her to rot? His rage surged anew.

The warden entered first, holding up a lamp. Brave, determined Selena squeezed in after him. Marcus tried to enter, too, but there was so little space that he and Chris were forced to tarry in the corridor.

"Kate?" Selena called softly. "Kate, it's me."

There was a rustling and murmurs, Selena fussing and cooing, but no reply from Kate, and Marcus squeezed his eyes shut, praying that she would respond.

"This was all a mistake," Selena whispered. "You're to be released."

"Selena?"

When he heard Kate, his relief was so great that his knees buckled, and lest he sink to the floor, Chris steadied him.

"Yes, *mia cara*. It's really me." Selena's voice was wobbly, and Marcus could tell she was on the verge of tears. "Everything will be all right now."

Kate said something Marcus couldn't decipher, and Selena explained, "I went to Christopher. He and Lord Stamford helped me. They're just outside."

"Lord Stamford helped you?" Kate sounded confused. "Why would he?"

Marcus was crushed, hating himself for being such an ass, for putting her through hell, and he gazed at Chris, feeling petty and small under the younger man's scrutiny.

"He accompanied us because he was so worried," Selena told her. "We were all so worried. Can you walk?"

"I think so."

There was another rustle and shifting about, and the warden emerged, then Selena, who was leading Kate. Even though there was scant illumination, Marcus could detect a gash on her cheek, blood from it splashed on her clothes. Her movements were stiff and faltering, the severity of her beating obvious.

On viewing her, Christopher gasped and rushed forward. "Oh, Kate, oh! I'm so sorry. So terribly sorry."

Marcus approached, too, considering himself more impotent than he'd ever been. He was desperate to sweep her into his arms, to profess how much he loved her, how much he'd always loved her. He'd carry her up the stairs and out to his carriage; then he'd whisk her away from this awful place, would keep her safe forevermore.

He had to let her know, had to make her understand, and he reached out to her, meaning to speak, to confide his churning emotions, but the words swelled in his throat, choking him with how much he cared.

"Kate . . ." He murmured her name, unable to say anything else, and his hand wavered before her, but she didn't grab for it.

She assessed him as if she wasn't sure who he was, as if she was afraid of him. He could see the hurt and betrayal, the disappointment and sorrow. Any fondness she might have felt for him had been shattered.

He could have had her for his own, but folly had steered him to the wrong choices. How many times in his life had he destroyed what he cherished, what he valued? He hadn't believed her, hadn't trusted her, and his lack of faith had condemned her to this horrifying end.

With a nauseating conviction, he comprehended that he didn't deserve her continuing affection, wasn't worthy of her friendship, or even her courteous regard.

She turned to Christopher and fell toward him. "Get me out of here, Chris."

"Yes, Kate. At once. We're leaving immediately."

"Take me home. Please. Take me to Doncaster."

"I will, Kate. I will straightaway."

Her remaining strength gave out, and Chris caught her as she collapsed. He swooped her up and started off, Selena and the warden fast on his heels. Marcus dawdled, following slowly, watching the touching tableau from a distance.

His heart breaking, his spirits dashed, he recognized that he didn't belong with them, wasn't part of them, and shouldn't interject himself into their private family tragedy. When his assistance was neither wanted nor needed, he shouldn't interfere.

He was someone separate and distinct, and nothing about the ghastly event had changed that fact. Yet as he trudged after them, he felt more alone, and more lonely, than he'd ever been.

∽ 21 ∽

Her temper flaring, Regina dawdled in Elliot Feather-stone's parlor. Christopher still hadn't arrived, and Melanie had vanished.

Though Regina hadn't meant to spoil her children, they had been. They didn't remember the past, didn't realize how lucky they were, but they were about to be reminded of who was in charge, who gave the orders. Like it or no, they were accountable to Regina.

A flurry erupted in the foyer, with people straining to see what was occurring, and suddenly, Stamford and Christopher burst in together, an exotic brunette trailing after them. The men weren't dressed in their formal wear, but in casual clothes, with both attired as they'd been earlier in the day.

They were an impressive sight, her son and future son-in-law. One dark and the other golden blond, they were tall, confident, determined, and they instantly dominated the room.

Stamford honed in on her, and as they stomped over, she could discern that they were livid. Stamford in particular was incensed, and as he neared, his anger was so blatant that she actually flinched, worrying that he might assault her. In Featherstone's entryway! With all of fashionable London looking on!

Only Christopher's calming hand on his arm prevented Stamford from initiating an attack.

"Madam," Stamford tersely bit out, "I would have a word with you in private."

She wasn't about to have him bossing her. "Melanie and I were just leaving. Whatever it is, it will have to wait till tomorrow."

"Mother," Christopher cut in, "I have your satchel. We've turned the contents over to Mr. Thumberton."

The news was gravely dismaying, but she cautiously shielded any reaction. She'd been so distracted with Kate that she'd forgotten about the portfolio. It was the first time in years that she'd failed to secure it. What was to be done?

It contained mountains of evidence that could convict her, and she sifted through possible excuses, even as she was crafting an offense. She wasn't about to sit idly by and allow the two of them to bully her. If they supposed they could, they were fools.

"The jig is up, Regina," Stamford gloated. "Shall we debate it here, with everyone watching?"

Several guests tittered at the prospect, and she spun and glared at a footman. "Escort me to the library."

She led the way, refusing to have them presume they were in control. Inside, she moved behind the desk, using the imposing piece of furniture to bolster her air of authority as she whipped around to challenge Stamford.

"Have you no manners?" she barked. "I won't have

you badgering me, nor will you spoil my plans for the rest of the night. Get on with it!"

"How much did you pay them?" he snarled.

"You're babbling in riddles. To what are you referring?"

"How much did you pay them to have Kate disappear?"

They'd found her? And so fast, too!

The discovery presented another set of problems, but she'd work them out. She merely needed a few minutes to assess her alternatives, yet as she stared into his eyes, she'd never observed such banked fury, and she was uneasy.

Perhaps he'd had genuine feelings for the little strumpet, so she had to tread lightly. Heightened sentiment would make him a more vicious adversary.

"I have no idea about what you're talking," she claimed. Christopher stumbled in, the willowy brunette clinging to him, and Regina frowned. "Who are you to come in with us? This is a family discussion. Be gone!"

The girl had the audacity to advance on the desk. "Who am I?" she mimicked. "Who am I? *I* am Selena Bella, daughter of Caroline Duncan, the former Countess of Doncaster, and sister to Kate Duncan, daughter of the late earl. I will see you hanged for this atrocity. I swear it on my life!"

"You have the gall to show your face among your betters?" Regina chastised. "How dare you!"

"Enough!" Christopher roared, approaching, too, and he positioned himself in front of the whore, shielding her from Regina's wrath. "Mother—for once—you will guard your caustic tongue, or I will gag you."

"Shut your mouth, Christopher. You will speak to me with respect, or you'll not speak to me, at all."

"Selena is my fiancée."

Regina laughed, raking Bella with a contemptuous sneer. "Don't be ridiculous. I would never agree."

"The decision shan't be up to you," Christopher contended.

She ignored his bluster and scowled at Bella, waving dismissively. "My permission is denied. Now, why don't you scurry back to that hovel where you reside? Don't darken our doorstep again."

"Donna brutta!" Bella hissed, and she lunged as if to pummel Regina with her fists. Christopher grabbed her and stopped her.

At the rabid display, Stamford said nothing but skirted the desk to tower over her. He was attempting to awe and frighten, but she wouldn't be cowed. Who did he think he was, blustering and trying to scare her? He didn't know with whom he was dealing.

"Sit down," he commanded, looking as if he were about to commit murder. Her own!

"I prefer to stand."

"Sit! Down!" he bellowed with such vehemence that the force of his shout had her tumbling into the chair. She'd never encountered anyone who was quite so irate. Had she misjudged him?

By all accounts, he was a drunkard, laggard, and ne'er-do-well who flitted about with no concerns or passions. His bother over Kate was something Regina hadn't calculated. Not that she'd imagined Kate would ever be located. Who would have cared enough to search?

"Don't raise your voice to me!" she warned, though without as much bombast as she'd previously exhibited. He was in a frenetic mood, capable of lashing out, and the slightest error on her part could result in a sound thrashing.

"You'll be lucky if my *voice* is all I raise." He bent over her, trapping her in her seat. "Here are the terms. You have no other options."

"What . . . what terms? You'll make no demands on me. I won't tolerate it."

She tried to rise, and he yelled again. "Sit down! And by God, if you get up before I'm through, I'll beat you to a bloody pulp."

She bristled with humiliation. No one had whipped her since she was twelve and had grown big enough to defend herself, but regardless of her girth, she was no match for him.

"What are your conditions?" she derided, hot with ire.

"My marriage to Melanie is off."

"No!"

As if she hadn't spoken, he continued. "To avoid a scandal for your children, I shall be designated as their guardian."

"No," she repeated, but he kept on.

"Chris and Selena will marry, and you will not object. Nor will you attend the wedding."

"How will you prevent me?"

"The financial affairs at Doncaster will be placed under my control until Chris reaches his majority at age twenty-one."

"I forbid it!" She couldn't lose Doncaster! Despite what others believed, she'd never intended to surrender the reins of power to her son. She wouldn't relinquish the affluence or clout the property had provided.

Stamford smiled, a wily, conniving smile that chilled her. "Mr. Thumberton is already drafting the papers."

"I won't sign them!"

"Your signature won't be required." He smirked. "Investigators are on the trail of the money you've pocketed. What they don't manage to find you will refund of your own accord."

"Sod off, Stamford," she crudely snapped. "You have no proof I've stolen anything."

Christopher chimed in. "Give over, Mother. You were too meticulous at recording your crimes. We have all the evidence we need."

Stamford resumed. "You shall retire to Cornwall, quickly and quietly. You will withdraw to the town from which you were allowed to slither so many years ago. We will use estate funds to purchase a modest house for you, and you'll be furnished with a small stipend, but that is all."

Cornwall! The very name had her shuddering. She thought of the poverty, the coarse, downtrodden people, the toil that had been necessary to survive. She'd escaped from the dreary, gloomy spot, and she wouldn't go back. They couldn't make her!

"I'll not return to Cornwall. Not for any reason."

He persisted with his tirade. "You are to depart at dawn. If you refuse, the full force of the law will fall upon you."

She was dumbstruck. She'd never envisioned being caught, and she'd always presumed that if she was, she would be able to talk her way out of any trouble.

She hadn't reckoned on Stamford, on his ill will and malice, on his determination to have her brought low. Who could have predicted his attachment to Kate?

"What can you do to me? I am Countess of Doncaster, and if you suppose that you'll prevail, then you underestimate me at your peril."

"If you decline, you will be publicly prosecuted for your crimes. Embezzlement. Battery. Fraud. Kidnapping. Attempted murder. Pick your felony, Regina. For which would you like to be incarcerated?"

"My son is your peer, and he will never let you mistreat me!" She glanced at Christopher and was shocked to see him staring at her with no emotion. He and Bella were holding hands, united in their condemnation of her.

Would he abandon her? Would he side with Stamford against his own mother? How could he?

Oh, the treachery! The betrayal! He was so lacking in loyalty!

She would get even with him! She would get even with all of them!

"What is your response?" Stamford goaded.

She was frantic to wiggle out of his trap, and she had to buy herself some time. "I'll never agree!"

"Then I shall personally attend your hanging."

"My . . . my hanging!" Instinctively, her fingers stroked her throat, caressing her neck as if she could feel the noose tightening.

"And I plan to enjoy it. I'll bring refreshments and guests, and I will sit in the front row. I'll even ask the executioner if I may pull the rope."

She was cornered, ensnared in a conundrum of her own creation, and nervously, she gnawed on her bottom lip. "I'll need a few days to consider."

"No. This offer is good for the next minute."

He studied the clock on the mantle. The atmosphere in the room was oppressive, the air beating down on her until she couldn't breathe. She began to perspire, her heart palpitating, as she endeavored to figure out an advantageous argument, but she was disordered by his threats.

Too rapidly, the interval was concluded, and he assessed her. "What is your reply?"

"Bastard!"

"I take that as a *yes*." He stepped away so that she could stand.

"I'll kill you for this," she vowed.

"You'll never have the chance."

She looked at Christopher, hoping for a softening, some hint of compassion or pity, but she couldn't detect a flicker of sympathy.

"You shouldn't have hurt Kate," Christopher nagged. "I'll never forgive you."

How dare he castigate! How dare he condescend! Her rage spiraled till she was quaking. "I cast you out! You are no longer my child!"

She wasn't sure what reaction she'd expected, but Christopher merely shrugged. "So be it, Regina."

Stamford gestured to the door. "Proceed directly to my house and start packing. I want you gone before I arrive."

Without another word, she fled into the hall, her fury billowing out like a wave of locusts.

Pamela loitered in the corridor, curious as to the parley in the library. Marcus had roared, and Regina had complained, but Pamela couldn't decipher their actual comments. She wished they'd hurry! Regina had an appointment in Elliot's bedchamber.

Suddenly, Regina stormed out. She appeared positively homicidal, and Pamela could barely stifle a giggle of glee. In view of what was about to transpire, she couldn't have arranged for a more perfect mood.

Regina spied her and yapped, "I'm leaving. Have you seen Melanie?"

"Why, yes, I have," Pamela slyly remarked. "She was sneaking upstairs. With Elliot Featherstone."

"What?" Regina gasped, and those nearby snickered at the delicious innuendo.

"I'll show you where they went," Pamela suggested, more than eager to deliver Regina to her fate.

Regina charged off, as Christopher emerged from the library, and Pamela was momentarily distracted. There was a slender beauty walking beside him, but Pamela ignored his companion, to rush forward and hug him.

"Christopher, darling. I've been searching everywhere for you."

"Pamela, please. You're making another scene."

He peeled her away and held her at arm's length, while she struggled in vain to mold herself to him. "But Chris, we have to talk."

"Not here," he said. "And especially not now."

The girl edged closer, as if to situate herself between them. Pamela glared at her. "Who are you?"

"I am Miss Selena Bella. *Who* are you?"

"I am Chris's *friend*."

"Not anymore," Miss Bella snidely stated. "Come, Christopher."

"Be gone, you impertinent waif." Pamela had moved to shove her away when Chris intervened.

"Pamela, Selena is my fiancée. We're to be married."

The pronouncement had her sizing up Bella, taking her measure, and Pamela seethed, hating her confidence, her poise and dignity, her gracefulness, her . . . her youth!

She couldn't have heard him correctly, and she scoffed. "You're joking."

"No, I'm not, and you will display the courtesy that is her due."

He was serious! Her heart pounded with alarm. This couldn't be! Chris was hers. She was enamored, obsessed, smitten beyond any sensible limit. She needed him, needed his protection and position, and she had to be alone with him so that they could sort everything out.

She glanced up the stairs, and Regina was almost at the top, and Pamela was frantic to observe her expression when she witnessed Melanie's downfall. Pamela couldn't miss it.

"But Chris, it's your sister." She clutched at his jacket. "You must help her. I can't predict what your mother might do!"

He was out of patience. "What gibberish are you spreading?"

Out of nowhere, Marcus materialized, stepping between them. "For God's sake, Pamela. What is happening to you? Are you completely mad?"

"Marcus—"

He cut her off. "Whatever it is, Pamela, I don't care."

"But you have to see this," she insisted. "You have to

learn how your precious Melanie has betrayed you. Your pride will never recover."

She spun away, not giving them a chance to question her, not wanting to forego the excitement. Certain both men would pursue her, she hastened after Regina, passing her and guiding her to the end of the hall.

"They're in here," Pamela claimed, praying that Elliot had been successful. If he wasn't naked on the bed with Melanie, she'd strangle him. "What must they have been thinking?"

Regina frowned, and she prepared to knock, but Pamela reached in front of her, and turned the knob.

"Let's go in, shall we?"

The door swung open and . . . there they were, arrayed on the mattress. They were a strange couple. Elliot was so much older, his body shaky and wasted from years of dissipation, while Melanie was so pretty and plump, rounded with her blossoming womanhood. She was shivering, with fear and cold, her pert nipples contracted into pointy buds.

It was disgusting; it was debauched; it was too scandalous for words. If they'd posed themselves, it couldn't have been any worse.

Regina shrieked and burst in. "What is the meaning of this outrage?"

Elliot laughed and, in false modesty, made a feeble attempt to conceal his privates. "Regina, dear girl, what can I tell you? We were overwhelmed by passion."

"Are you mad?" Regina howled. "She's engaged to Stamford!"

"She's what?" Elliot gulped and paled, his cockstand withering to a tiny stump, and he lurched away from Melanie as if she had the pox. He scanned the floor for his clothes, obviously trying to figure out how he could slip into them with the least amount of humiliation.

Melanie was trembling in terror, yet she had the temerity to respond, "Elliot and I are in love."

"Love, bah!" Regina screeched, and she raced to the door, desperate to shut it before anyone followed her in, but Christopher and Marcus were already entering.

"I'll be damned," Marcus chuckled, as Christopher muttered, "Oh my lord!"

Christopher's adoring strumpet had wandered in behind him, and he shoved her into the corridor so that she couldn't view the sordid spectacle.

Elliot leapt off the bed, his flaccid breasts drooping, his phallus a limp worm. "I didn't know, Marcus. I swear to God!"

"For pity's sake, Elliot," Marcus retorted. "Cover yourself!"

"Don't murder me!" Elliot whined.

"As if I'd expend that much energy. Just get dressed. Please!"

"I will; I will." He scurried about, scooping up his trousers and tugging them on.

Regina whipped around and screamed at her daughter. "You pathetic fool! Don't you realize what he is? What he's after? Have you any understanding of the enormity of your folly?"

"It's what *I* wanted," Melanie contended. "Me! It was my choice."

"Oh . . . oh . . ." Regina was moaning, wringing her hands in dismay. "How could you do this to me? How could you?"

"Well, Regina"—Pamela grinned and clucked her tongue in *faux* sympathy—"I guess there'll be a wedding, but Marcus won't be the lucky groom. And you had so many wonderful plans for him as your son-in-law."

Regina went still as a statue. Then, a strange rumbling sound started, and it seemed to emanate from inside her, as if her wrath had been brought to a boil and was about to foment out of the pot.

"You!" she smoldered. "This is your fault."

"You're blaming me?" Pamela reproached. "I'm not the one in bed with Elliot. I'd say the wanton trollop ruined herself."

"You . . . you . . . you . . ." She advanced on Pamela until they were toe-to-toe, but apparently, she'd been goaded beyond thought, beyond speech.

Pamela preened. "Betray me, will you, you wretched hag?"

Regina looked wild, a furious pulse hammering at her neck, angry spittle on her lips. Awareness swept over her—that she'd been tricked, that she'd been bested, that she'd been outdone—and Pamela chortled with malice.

"Next time," Pamela counseled, "maybe you'll think twice before stabbing your partner in the back."

She saw Regina's arm rise and flex, saw her fist clench, but it took a moment for the deed to register. Regina's intent was so shocking, and so unanticipated, that Pamela had no opportunity to react or move away. After all, women of her class didn't brawl like tavern whores.

Her last conscious memory was her surprise at how

fast a human punch could fly, at how ferociously it could land.

A bone cracked, blood surged, the room went black, and she dropped like a stone.

~ 22 ~

A soft knock sounded on the door, and Selena's heart raced.

"Are you ready for me?" Christopher called.

By stretching up off the pillows, she was able to see herself in the mirror. Her brunette tresses were combed out and flowing free, her negligee clinging to her shapely form. She tugged at the bodice, lowering it so that more of her cleavage was exposed.

She looked like her mother, like Kate, too, but different from them. She was a woman in her own right. A woman desperately in love.

A blushing bride.

"Yes, Chris, I'm ready."

He slipped inside, dressed solely in his robe, the belt loosely cinched at the waist, and as she watched him approach, she shimmered with joy that he was her husband.

How lucky she was! How blessed!

Out of all the females in the world, he'd chosen her,

and she vowed to herself that she would always make him happy, that she would always make him proud. She would be a worthy wife, a cherished confidante, a loyal friend, an admirable countess.

Suddenly shy and uncertain, he paused. At a loss for words, he smiled, as nervous and jumpy as she was herself.

Though they'd been alone on many occasions, had trifled and embraced as if there were no tomorrow, they'd restrained themselves, had stopped before taking the final step in their relationship.

Embarrassing as it was to admit, Christopher was the one who'd insisted they delay till their wedding night. During their frequent trysts, she'd repeatedly begged him to progress further, but he wouldn't dishonor her.

She patted the mattress, and he eased himself down, a hip balanced on the edge, a palm braced on either side of her. Tenderly, lovingly, he caressed her hair, her arm, her thigh, and he brushed a kiss across her lips.

"You're so beautiful," he murmured.

"So are you." She reached inside his robe. His skin was warm and silky, and she couldn't wait to feel it pressed to her own.

"What gorgeous babies we'll make."

"Yes, we will."

"I hope we have a dozen."

She prayed that they'd all be sons who resembled him. "Then we'd better get started."

"Are you afraid?"

"No!" she bravely claimed, then frowned. "Yes," and she groaned. "Oh, I don't know!"

He chuckled. "It will be wonderful."

"I'm sure it will be." How she loathed being a virgin! She was anxious to be relieved of her chastity.

"We'll go slow."

"Don't you dare! If I'm not deflowered in the next five minutes, I can't predict what I might do."

He laughed again, then sobered, and he studied her, his devotion and affection shining through. "Any regrets?"

"Just that Kate wasn't here for the ceremony."

After the various upheavals, they'd been terrified that something horrid might occur to keep them apart. Not wanting to tempt fate, they'd obtained a Special License and had been married in Lord Stamford's parlor, with only Marcus, the vicar, and his wife as witnesses.

There hadn't been time to order a dress, arrange a supper, or send an announcement to the papers, so there definitely hadn't been an opportunity to bring Kate from Doncaster. Not that she'd have come in her condition. It would take a long while for her to recuperate, both physically and mentally, from her London ordeal.

Edith Fitzsimmons had accompanied Kate on her journey to the country, and had remained at the estate until Selena could arrive and care for Kate herself. Edith regularly apprised Selena of Kate's recovery, and of all her injuries, Selena suspected that Kate's broken heart would be the last to heal.

"She'll be standing with you at Doncaster."

"I'm counting on it."

Once their personal affairs were settled, they planned another ceremony, a grand fete worthy of the Earl of

Doncaster, though Chris's family wouldn't be allowed to attend. Lord Stamford had Regina under lock and key, and he intended to keep her confined and out of mischief until her house was ready in Cornwall.

Melanie and Mr. Featherstone were to be married, and soon, though Featherstone was grousing about being tricked into matrimony, and how he shouldn't have to wed Melanie when her dowry wasn't as it had been portrayed. No one listened to him, and in fact, many had been heard to guffaw aloud when he voiced the preposterous complaint.

Selena's mother-in-law and sister-in-law were crazy, but Chris had banished them from Doncaster, so she wouldn't ever have to deal with either of them. Recalling his edict, pronounced amidst much whining and posturing by both women, made her smile.

What a fine earl he was going to be!

"What are you grinning about, you minx?"

"I'm so very, very happy."

"So am I." For an eternity, he assessed her, and he blushed. "I have a confession."

"What is it?"

"Whilst you are a virgin, *I* am not."

She raised a brow. "After the shenanigans in which we've engaged, I scarcely presumed you were. How many lovers have you had? Are you a rampant libertine? Should I be worried about your fidelity?"

"No. There's only been one other."

"Who was it?" She wasn't positive if she wanted to be informed or not, and an image flashed of Lady Pamela. After observing her odd behavior that hideous night at Mr. Featherstone's, Selena was certain it was she.

She hoped Lady Pamela had been an excellent tutor.

His blush deepened. "I can't say, but you should know that I . . . that I . . ."

"It's all right, Chris. It's in the past."

"I wish I'd waited till I met you."

"Hush." She laid a finger across his lips. "I'm glad *you* are aware of what is to happen, for I haven't the foggiest idea."

"Well, I do, my dear bride. Let me show you."

He eased her onto the pillows, coming over her, and covering her with his body.

Their previous trysts had transpired on sofas and in carriages, so she hadn't had the chance to learn how glorious he would feel, how she would thrill at the sensation created by his pressing her down.

As he massaged her breasts, he began kissing her, and down below, a spark of desire was kindled. When he finally pulled down the bodice of her negligee, and dipped to her bosom, she was writhing with anticipation and begging him to hurry.

He nipped and bit at her nipple, sucking until she thought she would die from the stimulation, and she nestled him closer, urging him to feast.

His hand trailed up her thigh, her hip, and she was so eager that he touched her once, again, and she soared with ecstasy. Throughout the tumult, he held her, cooing soft words, and as she spiraled down, he was preening, tickled by his prowess, by his ability to inflame her.

"You are so sexy," he remarked.

"Am I?"

"Yes, and I am so lucky." He drew her nightgown down and off so that she was naked, and he gazed at her.

"Do I please you?" she asked.

"Oh, Selena, so much in every way. Shall we finish it?"

"You'd better!"

He loosened his robe, and she yanked it off so that he was naked, too, but as he moved over her, she stopped him.

"I'm dying to look at you."

"Be my guest."

He shifted away, so that she could explore, and she ran her fingers across his chest. He was lean and smooth, graceful as a large African cat. Between his legs, his phallus was long, hard for her, and her virginal insecurities leapt to the fore.

"Are you sure it will fit?" she queried.

"I promise."

"I don't know what to do with it."

"I'll teach you."

She reached down and gripped him, judging weight and texture, girth and length, and as if he was in pain, he groaned.

"Have I injured you?"

"No. It feels very, very good. Too good."

He retrieved her hand and kissed it. "When I'm aroused, it's agonizing to endure your fondling."

"But I want to give you as much pleasure as you give to me."

"You will, darling, but let us consummate our vows, and after, I won't be so impatient. Then, you can play until dawn."

"An excellent notion."

He widened her legs, grasped his cock, and centered it. Her sheath was moist from her climax, and he rubbed the blunt crown across it, wetting it, edging it in.

"This will hurt," he explained.

"You told me it would."

"I'd avoid harming you—if I could."

"Don't worry. I'm not afraid."

He nodded, proud of her composure, her unruffled acceptance of the inevitable, and she was surprised, herself, at how calm she was acting. Inside, her heart was thundering so rapidly that she fretted it might burst.

"I love you, Selena."

"I love you, too, Christopher. I always will."

"Put your arms around me."

She hugged him, and he began flexing, prodding into her, farther and farther. Her goal was to be extremely mature and sophisticated about the entire affair, so she'd meant to relax, to make it easier for *him,* but the process was too foreign, her body too untried. She tensed.

"Almost there," he soothed, and he thrust and burst through her maidenhead.

She felt the pain, the rush of blood, and she cried out. Kissing her, he swallowed the sound, sharing her distress, and he held himself very still, until the sting lessened. He started to move, pushing into her and retreating, and she quickly adopted his rhythm.

Sweetly, gently, he rocked himself to a conclusion, and as he stiffened, as he wrenched to the end, she reveled in his release, in the sensation of his seed spewing across her womb. He shuddered and collapsed, and she decided it was the most precious, most divine moment of her life. Tears filled her eyes.

His passion spent, he rose up on an elbow and smiled at her, but on seeing her upset, he frowned.

"What's this?" he said, swiping the tears away with his thumb.

"It was so beautiful."

"Yes, it was."

"I didn't realize how special it would be."

"It's difficult to describe until you've been through it." He slipped out of her, and snuggled himself to her side. "I didn't hurt you too badly, did I?"

"It was wonderful." She traced his face, his lips, memorizing every detail, so that she would never forget a single aspect of the instant she'd become a woman. "What now?"

"First, we take a bath"—he wiggled his brows—"together."

"Ooh, I like that idea."

"Then we try it again."

"Again?"

"Well, you had mentioned that you're eager to learn what I enjoy."

"So I had." She laughed and jumped off the bed. "I'll ring for that bath."

Elliot sawed away between Melanie's thighs, wishing the end would arrive, but he couldn't manage to generate sufficient stimulation. His cockstand waned, growing more and more limp, until the necessary rigidity dwindled, and he couldn't shove it inside her.

Who could have imagined that fornicating with such a pretty girl would be so distasteful?

Disgusted, he stopped and flopped onto his back.

"Are you finished?" she carped.

"Yes."

"Thank God."

She scurried away, leaping to the floor and concealing herself in her robe, as he stared up at the ceiling,
speculating as to how long he'd be able to persevere
before he strangled her and put them both out of their
misery.

Over by the dresser, she was fiddling with her jewelry,
which he planned to sell to clear up a gambling debt.
He hadn't advised her yet, and he probably wouldn't. It
would simply vanish.

"How long are you intending to lie there?" she
snarled.

"I'm not certain."

"Leave at once."

"I will. When I'm ready."

"It's two o'clock in the afternoon," she complained.
"I shouldn't have to suffer your attentions in the middle of the day."

"You'll *suffer* them whenever I'm in the mood."

"You're a beast. I can't abide this torment. It's foul
enough that you traipse in here every night, drunk and
stumbling about."

He sighed. How could such a marvelous scheme
have gone so terribly awry? All he'd wanted was some
fast cash, a method of stabilizing his finances. Was that
too much to ask?

Instead, he'd been saddled with an impossible, impertinent child, and without her fortune as an incen-
tive, the notion of binding himself to her had been so
repugnant that he'd actually considered absconding,
running off to France or America, and if he'd had a
penny to his name, he would have.

Despite his dire fiscal situation, he'd pondered the

prospect anyway, but with Stamford acting as Melanie's temporary guardian, Elliot was convinced that Marcus would have chased him to the ends of the earth.

She was nagging again, and his head throbbed.

"About what are you jabbering?"

"You remember the gown we discussed. When can I buy it? And I must have the matching hat."

As he'd explained to her—over and over!—she wasn't at Doncaster, and her greedy mother wasn't controlling the purse strings. He hadn't the wherewithal to spoil her as Regina had, but Melanie couldn't seem to grasp that by aligning herself with him she caused her life to take a drastic turn.

"I've previously informed you that I haven't the funds for such folderol."

"What am I to do? Tramp about London looking like a pauper?"

He rolled his eyes. When she'd moved in, his servants had carried trunk after trunk up the stairs. He'd been in her room. It was packed to the rafters.

"Money doesn't grow on trees. You can't snap your fingers and make it appear."

"I don't care where you find more. Just find some!"

"Why don't you visit your brother to see if he's decided on a settlement for us."

"You know he hasn't."

Elliot still wasn't positive of what had happened to the assets in her dowry, but if his luck got any worse, he'd go out in the yard and shoot himself!

"Check with him anyhow," he chided. "Maybe if you pester him, he'll hurry up, merely to be shed of you."

"Why must I handle it?"

He glared at her. "Need I remind you that I thought I was obtaining a rich wife?"

"And is it my fault the titles were mixed up? That ownerships are in dispute? How was I to know? Are you supposing my mother confided in me about anything?"

"Don't mention Regina to me." Since before the wedding, Stamford had kept her away, a boon for which Elliot would be eternally grateful.

"I'll do more than *mention* her. I'm going to ask her to come live with us. She could rectify our financial dilemma straightaway, which is more than I can say for you."

"Is that right?"

"Yes, that's right."

"Shut up, Melanie."

"I won't. You dragged me into this mess, and you'll drag me out of it. I insist!"

He'd had enough. Of her impudence, of her attitude, of her condescension. He climbed off the bed, and she whipped around, refusing to gaze upon him when he was nude. As she'd made explicitly clear, she found the male body repulsive and grotesque.

He approached her from behind and squeezed her shoulder, forcing her to face him.

"Drop down on your knees."

"I won't."

"Now!"

Her antipathy was palpable, but he was resolved, and she grudgingly descended, which positioned her directly in front of his phallus. It began to swell, and she glanced away, unable to hide the fact that she was sickened by the sight.

"Somewhere in our vows, I heard the term *obey*," he stated. "We'll hit it off much better if you behave as you're told."

"I've knelt as you demanded. What is it you want from me?"

She was mutinous, a vicious adversary, and if he wasn't cautious, she'd likely strangle him in his sleep when he least expected it. "You must learn to do something with that mouth besides sass."

He grinned, more aroused than he'd been in a very long while.

Regina stared out the window of the modest, dreary house Christopher had purchased for her. The barren Cornwall coast stretched to infinity, the wind lashing the rocky shore, a few scraggly trees bending with the onslaught. She spun away, wearied by her view of the clouds blowing in, of the icy rain that never ceased.

The hovel in which she'd resided years earlier, as a new bride, was located just down the road. How she'd hated that spot, and she couldn't quit obsessing over how short a distance she'd traveled in her life. She'd never actually believed Doncaster was hers, had always suspected that her fortunes could be reversed. In preparation for this very day, she'd hoarded her stashes of pilfered money, but it had been for naught.

Stamford had recovered every farthing.

Oh, to be brought down! By Stamford of all people. With her treacherous, disloyal son as his accomplice. The shame! The humiliation! How it galled! How it kindled her fury!

There was a rapping on the parlor door, and without waiting for permission, Edith Fitzsimmons entered, strutting in as though she owned the place. Stamford had sent her to stay with Regina, and she had instructions to manage Regina's household, to act as Regina's warden and jailer, to tattle and gossip regarding Regina's every move.

When will you leave? Regina had once inquired.

When Lord Stamford tells me I may, the bossy woman had proclaimed.

Fitzsimmons held out a letter. "Lord Stamford has written. He's still searching for the silver candlesticks you stole from Doncaster. Are you ready to inform him as to where they are?"

"Stamford can choke on a crow."

Fitzsimmons smiled her grim smile. "It will be my pleasure to convey your response in my next report."

She was enjoying Regina's incarceration, liking to brag how she'd befriended the harlot Selena Bella. Fitzsimmons relished the punishments Stamford dished out, and she never stopped haranguing as to how she wished Regina had suffered a more dire fate.

Fitzsimmons turned to go, and Regina was tempted to let her depart without further discussion, but Regina yearned to have the final say, the last word. Fitzsimmons was entirely too insolent, too eager to help Stamford.

Regina was anxious to bring her down a peg, to box her into a corner. There had to be a way to manipulate her, to gain the upper hand, but so far, Regina hadn't detected it.

"I'm leveling another complaint," Regina said. She loathed it that others had hired her servants, that none of them were beholden to her for their wages. They were disrespectful, curt, and slow. "An hour ago, I ordered a plate of petit fours, and I haven't received them."

Edith chuckled maliciously. "We've used up our allotment of sugar. We can't afford more until the first of the month, when Stamford posts your check. There are no candies remaining, nor will any be prepared for you."

"I demand that they be provided."

"You may *demand* all you like, but they won't be supplied. We exist on a limited income. You'll have to make do without."

Make do without. . . .

The comment reverberated through the room, and Regina shuddered. It was her worst nightmare coming true. She couldn't bear to be poor, couldn't tolerate scrimping and saving. She'd spent her life trying to avoid that very catastrophe.

Her stomach rumbled with hunger, but Edith walked out, shutting the door with a firm click, leaving Regina to stew and plot revenge.

Pamela hovered behind a hedge at the Stamford town house, watching as the Doncaster coach pulled up to the curb.

Chris . . . I've found you at last!

Her emotions were at an all-time low. Where had he been? Why had he kept himself away from her? Didn't he know how much she loved him? Didn't he realize that their separation was killing her?

They'd both imbibed of the magic potion. Surely, it had had some effect on him! He couldn't forsake her!

She hated to be out and about, hated having people

recognize her, so she tugged on her hood, shielding her identity.

Her black eyes had healed, but the bend in her nose, where Regina had broken it, would never disappear. It was blatant, obvious, and whenever others espied it, they laughed and pointed, mortifying her by reminding her of the degrading assault.

How her situation had plummeted since that igno-minious evening!

With Elliot wallowing in wedded bliss, he'd evicted her as a guest, so she'd been forced to seek asylum else-where. Regrettably, High Society could be brutal, and she'd quickly discovered how few friends she really had.

She'd been reduced to taking shelter at the Carlyle Hotel, but her meager allowance wasn't anywhere near sufficient to meet her obligations. The manager was posing embarrassing questions about her bills, about when they might be paid.

Stamford had offered to purchase a small house for her, but as it had been located far outside the fashion-able neighborhoods where she expected to reside, she'd refused to accept it.

Just thinking about his domineering manner had her bristling. How dare he drive her to living like a com-mon vagrant!

The carriage door was opened, and she rushed from her hiding spot. "Chris . . . Chris . . . it's me, Pamela."

She gazed up, her love shining through; only it wasn't Chris who emerged. It was the little brunette, who'd been with him at Elliot's, and on her left hand, she was wearing a diamond the size of Ireland. What could it mean?

He wouldn't have . . . Gad! Pamela couldn't finish the thought.

The girl climbed out, and Pamela was struck anew by how beautiful she was, how poised and confident for someone so young.

"Lady Pamela," she greeted, a definite Italian lilt to her speech, "how marvelous to see you. I was so hoping we'd have a chance to talk."

"You were?"

"Yes." As if they were bosom companions, she linked her fingers with Pamela's and squeezed tight. "Chris told me everything you did for us. I'm so very grateful."

Suspicious, Pamela frowned. "What did I do?"

The girl glanced to the side, at the footmen with their curious ears, and she leaned in and whispered, "Silly, you can't have forgotten. You taught him how to make love to a woman so that he could better ease my virginal fears."

Pamela blanched. "That's what he said?"

"Don't be so modest," Selena gushed. "Due to your selfless assistance, our wedding night was glorious. Absolutely glorious. Thank you."

"But I . . . but I . . ."

Imperious as any princess, the impudent hussy swept away, waltzed up the steps of what had once been Pamela's home, and was welcomed inside by Pamela's old butler. The door was closed behind her, sealing her in, and the sole indicator that she'd been there was a lingering hint of her expensive perfume.

Like a beggar, a supplicant, Pamela loitered on the walk, staring up at the mansion, its polished windows gleaming in the sun. She was barred from it, from her

previous existence, and there was nothing—nothing!—
she could do to reestablish herself.

   She'd lost it all: the position, the prestige, the fortune, Christopher. With a wail of despair, she stumbled
away and ran down the street.

~ 23 ~

Kate meandered across the grass, dew soaking the hem of her skirt. Off in the distance, the sun was setting, an orange globe in a lavender sky. It was a balmy evening, with no hint that autumn had arrived, the harvest festival just around the corner. Her shawl was draped lazily off her shoulders, and her straw bonnet dangled from her fingers.

Up ahead, she could see the Dower House that Chris had opened for her, where she lived in a self-imposed, spinsterish seclusion. Beyond, through the trees, were the chimneys of Doncaster Manor. To the delight of everyone in the area, Selena and Chris had taken up residence there as husband and wife.

As if she'd been born to it, Selena had fallen into her role of countess. The tenants and villagers adored her, and the local gentry were tripping over themselves to befriend her. She'd rehired many of the employees who'd worked for their mother, as well as those whom Regina had fired, and was redecorating, gradually ridding the mansion of Regina's influence.

Kate was so proud of her.

With Regina gone, a huge pall had been lifted from the estate. People were happier and more secure. Christopher had instituted impressive modifications in the running of the farms and stables, and the staff whispered about how, despite his upbringing, he'd grown to be a fine young man.

No one asked about Regina or Melanie, where they were, or what had happened during their stint in London. Not a single soul could bear to foul the air by mentioning their names.

Absurd as it sounded, Melanie had written many illegible letters, eager to express her personal misery, and her loathing of her husband. For some reason, she presumed that Kate would care to be apprised of her situation. When the first missive had been delivered, Kate had been so curious that she'd read it, but it had been filled with such rancor and malice that she'd thrown it in the fire and hadn't glanced at another.

"Poor Melanie," she murmured, feeling no sympathy. What had the girl been thinking? How could she have believed that Elliot Featherstone was the answer to her prayers? What crazed impulse had driven her to such a reckless act?

Kate shook her head and proceeded on. To guide her path, a maid had hung a lamp by the rear door. Her servants were accustomed to her pensive nocturnal wanderings. She was often restless and edgy, and the treks cleared her mind and eased her woes.

Inside, a tasty supper would be waiting. She would sit in the quiet dining room, her spoon scraping across the elegant china, the clock ticking too loudly on the mantle.

Selena had begged Kate to stay in the manor, but her experiences there had been so bitter that she couldn't, and if she was honest, her refusal had been due to more than sour reminiscence.

Selena and Christopher were so in love that it hurt Kate to watch them together. Before traveling to London, she hadn't realized that she would have liked the same sort of life her sister enjoyed with Christopher. But since her return, she couldn't ignore the empty spot inside her. She had constantly yearned for love but had never found it.

The Dower House was fancier than she required, the rooms larger, the furnishings more grand, but it had been an uncomplicated and convenient choice as she'd struggled to decide what to do with herself. Chris claimed that her father had bequeathed her several excellent properties as a dowry.

On those occasions when she was being particularly morose, she pondered moving to one of them. It was intriguing to imagine herself as the mistress of her own home, as having a place where she belonged, but she couldn't resolve to go.

It tantalized her, though, that opportunity to start over.

She opened the gate, pushing when it stuck in the grass, and she squeezed through. The extra effort had her ribs throbbing, and she rubbed her hand across them. The physician had informed her that they might permanently ache, like a rheumatism on a rainy day, and she sighed, detesting that she would perpetually carry a souvenir of that horrid incident.

Memories tried to sneak in—of her terror in the jail cell, of the agonizing weeks it had taken to recover—but she shoved them away. She couldn't reflect on that atrocious event, couldn't ruminate, or make sense of it. Not yet, anyway. Maybe in the future. Or maybe never.

Down the lane, the woods were encased in brilliant hues of red and gold. As she admired the pretty sight, motion caught her eye. A man was coming toward her, walking from the manor on foot, and she narrowed her gaze, wondering who it could be. She never had callers, so perhaps he was merely a guest out for an evening stroll, as she was herself.

For just an instant, he'd resembled Marcus Pelham, but she was sure it was a trick of the light. Yet from her fleeting consideration of the foolish possibility a ripple of excitement coursed through her, and she mused over his enduring ability to unsettle her.

Why was it that he still had an effect? She rarely thought of him, never waxed nostalgic, or dreamed of what might have been, for her recollections were too disconcerting. Every splendid encounter they'd shared had been ruined by his betrayal.

She went on, but the man kept approaching, ultimately striding out of the shadows. Her breath hitched, and she stopped, too flustered to continue. Her heart thudded, her sore ribs pounding with each beat, to painfully and vividly remind her of her grim history.

He advanced until they were toe-to-toe, and she was stunned by the shimmer of gladness that rushed through her. She tamped it down, declining to pay it any heed.

"Hello, Kate."

"Lord Stamford."

She nodded in recognition, but made no curtsy or other deferential gesture. As if he'd anticipated a warmer greeting, his smile faltered, but he quickly shielded any reaction, and she wasn't surprised. He was a master at hiding his feelings.

"How are you?" he asked.

"Fine," she lied.

He assessed her worn, functional gown. She had some money now—Chris had arranged it—and she could have ordered new clothes from the seamstress in the village, but such an expense seemed frivolous. Other than her frequent visits from Selena, she hardly saw anyone.

"I always hated that dress," he said.

"Yes, you did."

"You look awful in gray."

"As you mentioned, many times."

"You've lost some weight."

"So have you."

He was much thinner, as if he'd been ill, or as if the past few months had been difficult, but she wouldn't speculate as to whether he'd suffered a catastrophe. Once, she'd been susceptible to his charms, and she doubted she'd changed overly much. She wasn't about to revert to the position where she'd been so vulnerable and desperate to curry his favor.

That imprudent woman no longer existed. She'd been entombed in a dark, small hole at Newgate Prison, and she'd been abandoned when the altered, wiser, more cautious Kate had emerged.

He was staring at her, as if he'd meant to utter a profound remark, as if there was a load he needed to get off his chest, when she couldn't fathom what it might be. Hadn't every item of importance been spoken between them? What could be left?

A breeze rustled through the forest, tousling her

hair, and a strand blew across her cheek. As if he still had the right, he reached out to brush it away, but she flinched, avoiding him. If he touched her, she couldn't predict what might happen, and she wasn't willing to take the risk.

Never again, she vowed, intent on protecting herself at all costs.

"Did you want something?" she queried, keeping a tight lid on her emotions.

She wouldn't permit him to detect how his presence had stirred a cauldron of brewing, detested yearning and regret. He could search to infinity for a hint of the fondness she'd harbored for him, but he'd never find it.

The silence grew awkward, and finally, he shrugged. "I guess not."

"I appreciate your checking on my welfare, but go away. You're not welcome here."

She whirled away and departed, idiotic tears surging into her eyes, and she prayed he hadn't witnessed them. Anymore, she was so accursedly sentimental!

His hot regard cut into her from behind, and though every fiber of her being was urging her to halt, to chat or inquire as to how he was, she forced herself onward.

"Kate . . ." he murmured.

Don't listen to him! she scolded. *Keep going!*

He hesitated, unable to spit out his comment. The suspense was excruciating, and she couldn't stand it. She paused, but didn't peek around.

"What?"

"I've missed you."

"So?"

"Please . . . I . . ."

There was agony in his voice, remorse and sorrow,

too, and she couldn't bear to be apprised of what he was bent on telling her.

"Don't say it," she pleaded. "Whatever it is, just leave it be."

"Turn around, Kate. Look at me."

"No."

"You have to hear me out."

"I don't *have* to do anything. My days of hanging on your every word are over." She sounded so curt, so resentful, when she didn't mean to be surly. She simply didn't understand why he'd come, and she was terrified to learn the reason.

Around him, she couldn't let her guard down. Not for a single second.

"Your sister advises me that you're heartbroken, you're lonely and unhappy, and you've shut yourself off from everyone who cares about you."

Her temper flared. How could Selena stoop to discussing her with Stamford? Kate had ceased to be any of his business, and he wasn't entitled to information.

"My sister is mistaken."

"Is she?"

"I merely want to be left in peace, a request you don't seem to comprehend."

"It appears to me that she's correct. You're grieving, so you've isolated yourself, but it's wrong for you to withdraw as you have."

He had the gall to lecture her about behavior? He, who reveled in detachment? How dare he comment! His effrontery was infuriating.

She whipped around, and the tears that had swarmed began to fall. She pressed her hands to her face, trying to stop them, but there were too many. "When I was in that cell in Newgate, would you like to know what occurred to me?"

"What?"

"I was thinking that I was so insignificant, I could vanish. After all, who would hunt for *me*? So I would remain there forever." She swallowed down a torrent of anguish, needing to speak of that time aloud, needing him to be aware of how badly he'd hurt her. "No one had ever been concerned about me, no one had ever loved me, only I hadn't realized it till then." She laughed bitterly. "In a way, I ought to thank you, for now I grasp how alone I've always been, how alone I always will be."

"That's not true."

"It is." She gestured toward the Dower House. "How could it possibly matter if I choose to be by myself? I went to London, and I could have died there, but I managed to make it home. Selena's arrival has made things a tad less complicated, but as far as I can see, nothing has changed here, and nothing ever will."

He stomped across the grass, nearing until he was directly before her, until his heat mingled with her own, and he rested his palms on her shoulders.

"I love you, Kate."

"No. No, you don't." She shook away the splendid, dangerous declaration. "You've never loved anyone."

He studied her features, and he reached out and traced across her cheek, touching the small scar Regina had imprinted with her cane. As if he couldn't figure out how the mark had come to be there, he frowned. Had he no clue of what had transpired? Of how terrible it had been?

In light of what she'd endured, she was overwhelmed by the recognition that he wasn't familiar with the enormity of her struggle, and she cried in earnest. He snuggled her to him, her tears wetting his shirt. She could have fought him, or wrenched away, but she didn't. She felt as if the air had whooshed from her body, as if—should he release her—she would crumple to the ground.

He attempted to kiss her on the mouth, but she yanked away, and he brushed her cheek instead.

"You used to love me, too," he vehemently claimed. "I'm convinced you did. How can I make you love me again?"

"There's naught you can do."

Shocking her, he dropped to his knees and wrapped his arms around her waist, his forehead wedged to her stomach.

"I'm sorry," he said. "I'm so sorry."

It was the last statement she'd expected from him. "You're sorry? What for?"

He peered up at her, and she was still so attuned to him that she could read his mind. She could perceive melancholy, sorrow, heartache, and she shifted uneasily. Was that why he'd lost so much weight? Why he was so fatigued and drained? Had he been suffering? Mourning their separation?

No, it couldn't be. She started to tremble, anxious to ward off the spark of hope that ignited in her breast.

"I apologize for my conduct, for how I let *her* treat you."

He didn't utter Regina's name, and for that, Kate was grateful. "Why did you side with her, and against me?"

"It wasn't like that. She told me that you had an old friend here at Doncaster who would marry you, who would be kind to you and watch over you."

"And you believed her?"

"I assumed that anyone would be better for you than me."

"I'm sure you're right." She couldn't abide his being prostrate before her, begging for her understanding, her compassion, when she had none to share. She was too raw, too wounded. She stared off at the purple horizon. "Get up, Marcus. Go home."

She pushed him away and stamped off, and he shouted after her. "Not until you say you've forgiven me. I can't bear that I've shattered your affection." She could hear him rising to his feet. Bleakly, he contended, "You're the only person, in my entire life, who ever cared about me."

"Well, you never let anyone! Big, tough Marcus Pelham! He's so strong; he's so independent. He doesn't want anybody. He doesn't need anybody."

"I need you."

She whirled around. "You accused me of being a thief!"

"I admit it."

"You just sat there, while she spewed her lies. You never defended me. You let her blather on and on, and every word was a despicable lie."

"I was mistaken. I knew it the moment you walked out the door."

"Then why didn't you help me?"

"She said you took things." He shrugged, pleading for a sympathy she wouldn't convey. "I remembered the occasions you had my signet ring, and I thought maybe it was the truth. She promised she'd replace Selena's money, that—if I wed Melanie—she'd repay the missing funds."

"So you agreed?"

"She swore that she'd send you to Doncaster, that you'd be safe." He was adrift, confused, like a little boy who couldn't find his way. "I deemed it best for you to be away from me, for you to have someone who could make you happy. But I was wrong, Kate. You need me. *I* can make you happy."

She clenched her fist, and she could feel his signet ring on her hand. Shortly after she'd moved into the Dower House, it had shown up on her dresser, and she wasn't certain how. She'd been forlorn, saddened, at her lowest ebb. Its presence had terrified her, and she'd decided to pitch it in the lake, had even marched out to the bank and tarried, but in the end, she couldn't throw it away.

She wore it constantly now. It was her sole memento of the affair with him, the sole evidence she possessed that confirmed it had really happened. Like a warrior's prize, she held it up, challenging him, reproaching him.

"Look what I have, Marcus." She wiggled her fingers. "It's your ring. I can't explain why I have it. Can you? Are you cringing? Are you presuming I stole it? I haven't been back to your residence in London, yet the accursed bauble materialized here at mine. How will you respond? Will you call for the law to come fetch me?"

He held up his own hand, the cuff of his jacket pulling away, and she saw a piece of green ribbon tied around his wrist. "This is yours. Do you recognize it?"

"I had one like it. I lost it when I was in London."

"You didn't *lose* it. It surfaced in my bedchamber after I swallowed that blasted love potion."

She blanched. "You knew about that?"

He advanced on her. "And after you were released from Newgate, after you left for Doncaster without speaking to me or saying farewell, after you indicated that you wanted nothing to do with me, I threw it away a dozen times. But it kept reappearing on my dresser." He halted in front of her, the toes of his boots slipping under the hem of her skirt. "I went to the apothecary."

"You didn't."

"I did. He maintains that the reason I can't be shed of it is because we're meant to be together."

"He's mad. *You* are mad."

"Am I?" From inside his jacket, he retrieved a vial, and balanced it in his palm. "I bought some more."

"It isn't genuine."

"Isn't it?" He tugged at the cork, and the musty smell of the red liquid permeated the air. "I think it is. Will you drink it for me, Kate?"

"Are you insane?"

"I'll try anything, so long as I can make you love me again." Like the snake, tempting Eve in the Garden, he dangled it, offering it to her, daring her. "My house is so quiet without you, and I am so lonely."

"Whose fault is that?"

"My own. I've no one to blame but myself. I've ruined every relationship that ever mattered to me, but I'm weary of being so alone. You showed me a different way."

Her head began to throb, and to ease the ache, she rubbed her temples. He was confounding her, mystifying her with his frank and blunt confessions. "What do you want from me?"

"I'm begging you to give me another chance." He linked their fingers and squeezed tight. "You used to insist that I was worth loving, that I was worth having. I can be the man you supposed me to be. Let me try. Let me prove to you that I can do better. Please."

She scrutinized him, caught up in the blue of his eyes. The stark depth of his pronouncement had stunned her. Such bald emotion was foreign to him, fervent remarks being alien to his character, and she couldn't conceive of why he'd humble himself with the gallant articulation.

Unless he really loves me?

The gripping prospect washed over her. Could he be serious? He certainly seemed earnest and sincere. What if he was?

The likelihood that he might acknowledge his feelings had never occurred to her. She hadn't imagined she'd ever see him again, hadn't imagined that they'd have a subsequent opportunity to talk, so she'd never tortured herself with striving to envision how a make-believe conversation might progress.

But he was here, and reaching out to her, uttering declarations that she'd never dreamed she'd hear from him. He was beseeching her, for her forgiveness, for her absolution and empathy. He was proud and vain, yet he'd lowered himself to implore that her affection be restored, and she couldn't disregard such a startling gesture.

What did she want? Did she want him? Could she return to being the person who'd been so dreadfully

smitten? Was that woman still lurking somewhere inside? Could she risk so much again? Could she bear the
agonizing, fabulous spiral of lust and ardor he so read-
ily induced?

The questions made her heart pound.

Over her weeks of reflection and recovery, she'd
condemned him for what had transpired, but deep
down, she grasped that he wasn't responsible. Regina
had manipulated them all, had coerced and bullied and
connived. Who had been immune? Even the lawyers
had been duped by her schemes.

From discussions with Selena, Kate was aware that
Marcus had struggled, behind the scenes, to rectify the
damage Regina had wrought. He'd had her punished in
the fashion that would most torment her, recouped Selena's monies, fixed the problems with Kate's father's
will so that she wasn't a poverty-stricken servant but a
woman of consequence.

He'd acted privately, discreetly, being not the sort of
man who would want others to learn of his good deeds,
one who wouldn't want to be complimented or praised
for his efforts.

Though she'd yearned to hate him, she couldn't.
She'd worked to persuade herself that her fondness
for him had been an aberration, a blunder brought on
by their odd circumstances, but as she gazed into his
dear face, she realized that she'd been fooling herself.
He meant the world to her, and she was eager to revert
to those bliss-filled days when she'd been consumed
by him, when she'd been obsessed, addicted, devoted.
It was the sole time she'd ever felt truly alive, truly
content.

Had she ever ceased loving him?

"I don't need any potion." She clasped the vial, tossing it to the ground. "I love you. I never stopped."

Desperate to be in his arms, she took the first step. In their separate isolations, they were both wretched. Perhaps together, they could build something durable and worthwhile.

He drew her to him, holding her so tightly that she couldn't breathe.

"I'm a mess without you, Kate. Marry me. Come to London. Be my wife. Be my friend. You are my sun, my moon, my very existence. Without you, I'm nothing at all."

He was shaking, his sentiments as ragged as her own, and she nestled herself closer, melded so that her pulse beat in a rhythm with his own. "I'm so afraid to say yes. Convince me that it's the right thing to do."

"Oh, Kate," he murmured, "of course it's the *right* thing. Do you have any idea how miserable I've been?"

He dipped down and kissed her, his lips falling lightly on hers, but quickly, the embrace intensified, becoming profound and overwhelming. She clutched at his jacket, relishing the ferocity of their joining. Memories had been too painful, so she'd forced herself to forget the taste of him, the feel of him, but she was like a starved animal that had finally been fed, a lost, wandering nomad who'd finally stumbled upon an oasis.

Their lips parted, and he nervously studied her. She could tell that he was scared he'd miscalculated, terrified that a mere kiss would be ineffectual and that he'd failed in his quest to sway her. But he couldn't know the joy that was singing inside her. After all that had happened, it seemed a miracle that they could bond with such elation and ecstasy.

How could she have had any doubts?

She smiled. "I'd have to visit Doncaster occasionally. To see my sister."

"Absolutely. She'd have my head if you didn't."

"And you'll have to buy a new bed, one that's been used just by us."

At the request, he chuckled. "I already have."

"I expect you to be a real husband to me. That you'll be at home, and not off gallivanting, where I'm worried about you and wondering where you are."

"I wouldn't want to be anywhere but by your side."

"You'll have to give me many, many children, and be around to help me raise them."

"I can't wait."

"There can be no other women. Only me from now on."

"Only you, Kate. Only you, forevermore."

"Then, yes, I'll marry you."

He nodded solemnly. "Are you sure?"

"Yes, I'm sure."

"I'm so glad."

"So am I."

"I'm not much of a catch."

"I think you are."

"But I swear that I will always love you. Till my dying day and beyond. I will always make you happy."

"I know you will."

The sun dropped below the horizon, and they lingered in the grass, listening to the sounds as night fell around them. The sky faded to indigo, and the stars began to twinkle. There were so many things that needed to be said, so many issues that had to be addressed, but they could be postponed till later. It was so marvelous simply to be together. No words could make the moment any more special.

"Are you going to invite me in?" he ultimately asked.

"I'm tired of eating supper alone, so yes, I guess I am."

Without warning, he scooped her up into his arms, one hand behind her back, and the other under her knees.

She giggled and swatted at his shoulder. "What are you doing?"

"I'm claiming you."

"As your what?"

"As my prize."

"Put me down."

"No. I want your servants to have something about which to gossip."

This was the Marcus she remembered. He could be imperious, he could be bossy, he could be impossibly arrogant, but he was hers, and he loved her beyond imagining. How lucky she was!

She hugged him, as he marched across the grass, entered her house, and kicked the door shut behind them.

"I'm here to stay," he announced—loudly—for anyone lingering nearby, and she grinned, thrilled to know that he meant it.